IMPROPER

Gripping noir crime mystery fiction

RAY CLARK

THE BOOK FOLKS

Published by The Book Folks

London, 2024

This book is a work of fiction. Names, characters, businesses, organizations, places and events are either the product of the author's imagination or are used fictitiously. Any resemblance to actual persons, living or dead, events or locales is entirely coincidental.

ISBN 978-1-80462-264-3

www.thebookfolks.com

IMPROPER is the twelfth book in a series of mysteries by Ray Clark featuring DI Stewart Gardener. The full list of books is as follows:

1. IMPURITY

2. IMPERFECTION

3. IMPLANT

4. IMPRESSION

5. IMPOSITION

6. IMPOSTURE

7. IMPASSIVE

8. IMPIOUS

9. IMPLICATION

10. IMPUNITY

11. IMPALED

12. IMPROPER

Improper: 1. *Indecorous and not in accordance with accepted standards, especially of morality or decency.* **2.** *Lacking in honesty or probity.* **3.** *Against a law or moral code.*

It is wrong and immoral to seek to escape
the consequences of one's acts.

Mahatma Ghandi (1869 – 1948)

Chapter One

Standing in a plush, luxury apartment building on the side of the River Aire, Detective Inspector Stewart Gardener was staring at the dead body of twenty-eight-year-old Sonia Markham. Though difficult to tell because she was still in an armchair, she was probably around five feet five in height, a brunette with shoulder length hair, an oblong face, a square jaw, and brown eyes. She was currently dressed in a pair of *Winnie-the-Pooh* pyjamas, with one slipper on her foot and the other on the floor – no dressing gown.

The room was deathly silent, suggesting she had not been listening to the radio, or watching television at the point of her demise; but considering the view of Leeds she had, he couldn't blame her. Next to the chair was a small table, on which were Sonia's mobile, the remains of a cold bowl of soup, and a napkin – unused. The clean spoon next to the bowl suggested she had either not started before she had died, or had taken no real interest in eating it. Wearing gloves, Gardener lifted a near-empty cup and took a sniff, it was tea.

From what he knew, she died two days ago. As he knelt down to inspect the body further, his scene suit rustled. Her blood had pooled to her lower extremities under gravity, leaving her very pale. He could not discern any noticeable decomposition, most likely because of the moderate temperature in the room.

He reached out and touched her face, which felt quite cold. He knew the body stopped producing heat at the time of death. Rigor mortis had come and gone. The skin appeared drawn tight around her skull – typical of a cadaver. Her head was drooping down in front of her, touching her chest. Her arms were balanced in her lap. The stale smell was redolent but not overpowering.

Gardener heard a rustling behind him as his partner, Detective Sergeant Sean Reilly began searching for any evidence that would suggest what had happened.

Gardener stood. Reaching over, he picked up Sonia Markham's mobile, pressing one of the buttons to make the screen come to life. The battery was very low, almost out of power, but it did light up, revealing lots of text messages and missed calls notifications, all of which had remained unread. In another corner of the room, he noticed a landline, with a rapid blinking light, suggesting further missed calls. The voice messages may well prove important.

Gardener reflected on how he came to be here. The initial call had been made sometime around four-fifteen in the afternoon – Tuesday afternoon. She was discovered by her friend and flatmate, Jodie Thomson, at a little after four o'clock. Jodie had neither seen nor heard anything from Sonia since their night out three days previously on Saturday – despite trying to make contact.

A wooden top had initially turned up to have a poke around. Not too happy with what he'd seen, he secured the scene before calling in DI James Stott. *He* hadn't liked what *he'd* found either, so he referred it to MIT. The case now belonged to Gardener, who was still awaiting the arrival of the Home Office pathologist.

Gardener and Stott had spoken at length. The latter had been in the force a long time and he'd seen a lot of things. He told Gardener that there was something not right about Sonia Markham's demise but he couldn't put his finger on it. Given that he had a full case load already, he felt it best to pass it over to someone else.

Stott had spoken briefly to Jodie Thomson, who had told him where and when she had last seen Sonia Markham on the Saturday – a night club. They did not see each other on Sunday because Jodie had stayed overnight with a friend who lived very close to the station in Leeds. They were both leaving for London to attend a course on the Monday.

Gardener turned to his partner. "Found anything?"

"Not yet," said Reilly. "Nothing at all. Looks like she lived a very ordered life, nothing much out of place."

Gardener glanced around the apartment. "Certainly nothing to indicate what's happened?"

"No," offered Reilly. "Doesn't look like a struggle's taken place."

Gardener observed the place was high end – very high – billed as a luxury city centre apartment with two spacious double bedrooms and two bathrooms, solid wooden floors, a secure parking space and riverside balcony. His partner was now positioned in front of the living room window, which offered a cracking view of the River Aire, and the apartments at the other side, most of which at one time would have been old warehouses. It was amazing what developers had done with the redundant buildings.

The Quays apartment block was off Concordia Street, close to a popular restaurant called Mal Maison, only a few minutes stroll from The Calls. They were also quite close to the railway station, affording stunning river views from the heart of Leeds, with all the convenience that brings.

He suddenly thought about the railway station being close by, and wondered why Jodie Thomson had stayed with a work colleague before their trip to London. Even if the other apartment was closer, it still wouldn't have saved much time.

The scene before him was like that you might see in a luxury lifestyle magazine; possibly a perfect place to live. Though God alone knew what the rent was, or what you'd have to do to be able to afford one. He imagined most – if not all – the clients living here would make good neighbours, if only for the fact that you probably never saw them – except when sitting on your balcony with a glass of wine.

Gardener turned and studied the dead girl once again. He could see nothing whatsoever to indicate the cause of death; nothing at all to suggest why – or how – she had died. If her eyes hadn't been open, he would have said she'd been asleep. There were no cuts, no grazes and no puncture marks of any description. She had not been stabbed or strangled or suffocated, neither had she been shot.

He reached for his phone – time to call his team.

Chapter Two

"It's going to be interesting," said Reilly, still staring at the panoramic view of the river.

"I really can't see anything to go on," replied Gardener, leaning further in towards her body. "At least until we speak a little more to her friend, Jodie Thomson."

Gardener lifted the dead girl's head slightly, staring into her eyes, but they gave nothing away.

Reilly glanced at his watch. "It's Tuesday, early evening. Jodie said they spoke briefly on Sunday morning."

"When Sonia Markham claimed she didn't feel well," said Gardener, standing back up again to face his partner. "She mentioned a sore throat. Could have been a cold coming on."

"Could have been a hangover," offered Reilly. "Particularly if they'd spent Saturday night in a club."

"I wonder what time she arrived home," said Gardener, "and in what state?"

Reilly glanced at the corpse before speaking. "My guess is, she wakes up, feels crap, maybe rolls over and goes back to sleep."

"Judging by the table," said Gardener, "she's risen at some point, made tea and managed to keep it down."

"But not the soup," said Reilly.

"I don't think she's touched that, Sean," said Gardener. "So maybe she was still alive at lunchtime, when she may have felt a bit better and decided to try making something."

"Which is as far as she got by the looks of things," said Reilly. "Maybe she actually *died* before eating it. So that's not a likely cause."

"Unless it was something she ate the night before," said Gardener. "But we've seen no evidence of that. No takeaway cartons. Judging by how clean the kitchen is, it doesn't look like she came home and made anything before going to bed. There are no pots in the sink."

"Or any evidence in the bin," offered his partner. "And it's unlikely she made something and left the pots and cleaned up Sunday morning. These girls don't seem that type – everything is pretty ship-shape."

Gardener suddenly heard a patio door sliding open from the next apartment, followed by a scraping of chairs and voices.

Ignoring the sounds, he bent down and carefully checked Sonia's eyes again. "Drugs?"

"Possible," said Reilly. "Whatever it is, it doesn't appear to have caused her too many problems. There's no sign of a struggle, no stress. It looks like she's come home, gone to bed, got up the next day and eventually died in that chair."

"But what of?"

"I think we'd all like to know the answer to that question."

A knock on the door interrupted their conversation. Gardener turned. "Sounds like the man who may have some answers has arrived."

"Here we go," said Reilly.

Gardener crossed the wooden floor. He opened the door to a man who bore a passing resemblance to a Victorian doctor but was in fact the Home Office pathologist, otherwise known as Fitz.

Dr George Fitzgerald was tall, with a lean frame. His wrinkled complexion suggested an age of around mid-sixties, and his trademark half-lens glasses were perched lower down his nose than they should be, on the verge of falling off. He, too, was wearing a scene suit, but Gardener could see his trademark black suit and cape underneath, and the top hat, which he removed before edging forward.

Gardener opened the door further and let him in. The PC in the corridor advised the SIO that his team had also arrived.

"Thank you," said Gardener. "Can you pop down and let them know that we're still with the scene and I'll talk to them later?"

The PC nodded and set off but Gardener called him back. "Where is Ms Thomson?"

"Having a cup of tea in the concierge's private office, sir," he replied. The young man was around eighteen years of age, tall and thin and still sporting a face full of teenage acne.

"Okay," said Gardener. "Perhaps you can also mention to her that we'll come and interview her as soon as we're finished here."

The PC nodded and left, as if he had no wish to actually enter the apartment, even had he been allowed.

Fitz glanced at his watch. "Are you two feeling well?"

"What do you mean?" asked Gardener, leading him toward the body in the chair.

"It's not even teatime. The pair of you normally make a habit of calling me out after midnight."

"Well," said Reilly. "You're getting a bit long in the tooth, so you are, for too many midnight sessions, Fitz, my old son. We don't want Mrs Fitz on the warpath, do we?"

Fitz smiled but chose not to reply, instead asking Gardener what they had found. When the SIO had finished explaining, the pathologist said he would make an initial examination to see if that might tell him anything; otherwise, it was straight down to the mortuary, where no doubt a session under the knife definitely would.

Gardener left him to it and with the help of his trusted sergeant, made a study of the rest of the rooms.

Both girls had separate bedrooms and it appeared that the first one they searched belonged to Jodie Thomson. The room was impeccably tidy. The clothes in the walk-in wardrobes – all trendy and very smart – were neatly pressed and stored. The bedside table had a light and a docking station. Gardener glanced through the playlist; most of the music was modern, with artists he had actually heard of.

The en-suite bathroom was equally as neat. Face masks, perfume, talc and a whole range of beauty treatments were neatly lined up.

Sonia Markham's room was almost identical. She had a range of CDs from the likes of Lewis Capaldi and Harry Stiles, as well as many other modern-day entertainers. She also had a bookshelf full of autobiographies and a number of keep-fit publications, suggesting that she may work out. She had a portable TV, with a number of DVDs that were mostly rom-coms and feel-good films: no crime or horror. Her en-suite bathroom was equally as tidy as Jodie Thomson's and many of the products were the same.

Something that really interested Gardener were a number of signed photos of people from the world of television, including the local soap, *Emmerdale*, which was filmed in the area.

"Looks like she's met quite a number of famous people," said Reilly.

Gardener nodded. "I wonder what she did for a living."

Placing the photos back on the top of a dresser, he noticed several trinkets also linked to TV. He recognized ornaments from *Heartbeat* and *Last of the Summer Wine*, both Yorkshire-based TV programs.

The pair of them left the bedroom and slipped into the kitchen, which was almost as sterile as an operating theatre, with bright strip lighting under cupboards and steel-top counters and cupboard doors.

"Christ," said Reilly. "It's like being in a hospital."

"It's definitely not your traditional farm kitchen with a heated range, is it?"

"I doubt it gets used anywhere near as much, either."

Gardener opened some cupboards, which contained everything from cleaning products to utensils and cutlery. On the counter, next to a window that also had a river view, was a microwave, a toaster, a kettle and a cafetière.

Gardener checked another cupboard and found bottles of spirits, one of which was Tia Maria. He was interested in the food contents, so he continued opening doors. In another cupboard he found pasta, rice, a number of different sauces, and a range of food supplements designed to keep the weight down. The fridge revealed mostly salads. All of the food in there was fresh.

"I can't even begin to think what's happened here, Sean," said Gardener. "They appear to have lived a very ordered life. A very quiet one. One of those people who gets up every day and simply gets on with things, earning a reasonable living, eating the right foods, exercising and living cleanly, as far as I can tell. There's nothing here other than food supplements that would suggest otherwise. So what the hell's happened?"

"Something clearly has," said Reilly. "Perhaps we should go and see what Dr Death can tell us."

Gardener smiled and the pair of them returned to the living room. "Have you found anything, Fitz?"

As the elderly man closed his medical bag, he turned to stare at them. "I'm afraid not."

"Nothing?" questioned Gardener, struggling to believe that.

"No," said Fitz. "According to what you were telling me, she was out on Saturday night, returned home, well enough to continue normally until some time on Sunday. The condition of the body bears out what's been said. She was alive and well on Sunday, but at some point, somewhere between forty-eight and sixty hours, she died."

"And you don't know why?" asked Reilly.

"I'm afraid not, gentlemen," said Fitz. "I'd like to remove the body now, where hopefully, a post-mortem will tell us a lot more."

Fitz collected his bag and bade them a good evening before leaving.

After Reilly had seen him out, he returned to the large bay window and his partner.

"What do you reckon, boss?"

"I've no idea, Sean," replied Gardener. "Let's see what the post-mortem tells us. In the meantime, let's do what we always do, and ask some questions."

Chapter Three

After securing and leaving the apartment, Gardener and Reilly took the lift to the ground floor and the reception area where they saw the concierge sitting at his desk, with a rather grim expression.

As soon as they approached, he stood up to greet them. He tipped and removed his cap and offered his name. "Harold Faulkner, sir."

Faulkner was a tall man of around six feet with short cropped grey hair and glasses. Gardener estimated his age to be around sixty and thought he carried his weight very well. He was dressed in a grey uniform of jacket and trousers with a white shirt and grey tie. He spoke with a clipped accent and from what Gardener observed, he took his job seriously.

Gardener asked about Jodie Thomson. Faulkner nodded and pointed, then asked them to follow him.

He had an office of sorts behind the reception desk, which was a similar size to an average living room, decorated with Regency striped wallpaper. Apart from a dark oak desk, Gardener saw a bunch of computer monitors, which obviously allowed Faulkner to keep track of the comings and goings of people should he *not* be at the front desk.

A cupboard in the corner had the doors open and Gardener noticed the concierge had everything he needed for making himself snacks and drinks, one of which the girl he took to be Jodie was sipping on.

He indicated they were going to speak to her and asked for two more chairs to be brought in and for the concierge to leave them. He informed Faulkner that two of his officers would be coming to see him as soon as he had spoken to his team about what had happened.

Faulkner nodded and left without the need for any further conversation, leaving Gardener to wonder if the man was ex-military.

Once they were seated, Gardener tipped his own hat and addressed Jodie Thomson. "How are you, Miss Thomson?"

"I've been better," she replied. "I never want to see anything like that again."

He introduced himself and Reilly and they both flashed their warrant cards. "I fully understand. Must have been a real shock for you."

Jodie's eyes widened and she shifted uncomfortably in the armchair. "You can say that again."

Gardener suspected by her posture that she wasn't very tall, perhaps five feet, possibly a couple of inches more – maybe a little overweight for her height. She had long blonde hair and wide framed glasses. Her voice was thick and she talked with a strong Yorkshire accent. She was dressed in a two-piece navy trouser suit with a white blouse, and wearing only a minimum of make-up.

"I realize this is very difficult for you, Miss Thomson, but I would like to ask you some questions about yourself and Miss Markham and see if we can build up a picture of what happened."

"I'll do my best," she said, sipping her tea, close to tears.

"If you're sure."

She nodded.

"How old are you?"

"Thirty," she replied. "Thirty-one in a couple of months… what a birthday that's going to be!"

There wasn't really much he could say to that, so he continued with his questions.

"What was your relationship with Miss Markham?"

At the mention of past tense, Jodie immediately burst into tears and reached into her handbag for a tissue. When she had finally calmed somewhat, she answered him.

"We were best friends and flatmates."

"How long have you known her?" asked Reilly.

"We met at school," said Jodie. "Got on really well, from day one."

"You've pretty much grown up together," said Gardener, which caused a few more tears.

She nodded by way of an answer.

"Where do you work, Miss Thomson?" Gardener thought it might be better to divert her away from her best friend to see if he could help her a little.

"I'm an assistant manager at Lloyds Bank on Briggate, but I also spend a lot of time at other branches."

"In Leeds?" asked Gardener.

She nodded. "Harehills and Crossgates."

"The DI you spoke to earlier mentioned you'd been on a course in London for a couple of days."

She smiled, displaying a top and bottom row of very white teeth. "The course was only one day, but we went for a couple of days. It was the run-up to a promotion, which will eventually land me a branch of my own."

"Good for you," said Reilly. "You must be pleased about that."

"It's something to look forward to – or was."

Gardener asked her about the apartment itself. He was very curious about the cost of living in something so grand.

To begin with, she explained pretty much what Gardener had read in the brochure.

"I imagine the rent is quite high," said Gardener.

"You're not kidding. Twelve hundred pounds per calendar month. But, you know what," said Jodie, "we figured we were worth it. We both worked hard and we earned the money, so why not have a slice of luxury? Life is short, after all. And look where it's bloody well got us."

Her voice had climbed almost an octave on the last sentence and she reached for the tissue again.

"I imagine you need references," said Reilly.

"Oh God, yes," said Jodie, regaining her composure. "Everybody is required to pass stringent background checks."

Gardener asked for the landlord's details, which Jodie supplied.

At least he now had her talking without too much upset, but he was going to have to really push home the reason they were here.

"Can you tell us about Sonia, please, Miss Thomson?"

She finished her drink, placed her cup on the floor and composed herself. Gardener could see from her facial expressions that talking was going to be hard but he appreciated the effort she was putting in.

Chapter Four

"I'm really going to miss her," said Jodie. "She was great, and we both got on so well. We were a bit chalk and cheese on some things."

"Take your time, Jodie, love," said Reilly.

Jodie smiled and then laughed. "She was really conscious of her weight. She tended to eat mostly salads, and used food supplements to keep the weight down."

Gardener had wondered about those but said nothing, instead choosing to make a mental note to have Fitz check them out.

"She liked a glass of wine and the odd Tia Maria, she loved that stuff. But she could take a drink or leave it – made no difference. Sonia went to the local gym twice a week. Maybe she was a little obsessed with keeping her weight down and how she looked. Regularly had her hair cut and her nails manicured. She usually rattled on about having to look your best and taking care of yourself."

"Can you let us have the details of the local gym and the hairdresser?" asked Gardener.

"I can," said Jodie, reaching into her handbag and pulling out two cards. She passed them over to Gardener. "She kept asking me to go, I could do with losing a few pounds, but all that huffing and puffing and sweating… not really for me."

Gardener put the cards in his jacket pocket. "What about relationships?"

"There was no one special. She had one or two men that she went out with but she saw them as friends rather than romantic prospects. In fact, I can't remember the last time she went out with a man. She seemed happy with things as they were."

Jodie broke down at that one. She suddenly stared at Gardener. "What's happened to her? Why?"

Gardener couldn't answer that one, because he had no idea. He waited for Jodie to calm down and then asked.

"Any illnesses?"

"She had asthma. To be honest it was really mild, very rarely did she need to use an inhaler."

Gardener noticed Reilly writing that one down, another point for Fitz.

"So, she was never really very ill with it?" asked Gardener. "I'm assuming that if she went to the gym, it didn't bother her too much."

"No, not at all," said Jodie. "Can't remember the last time she had an attack. Probably when she last went out with one of her men friends."

They all raised a smile.

"Where did she work?" asked Gardener.

"She was an actress, managed by a local company called The Casting Couch."

That would explain the signed photos, thought Gardener.

"The work was really varied," continued Jodie. "She could earn a grand a week, easily."

Gardener was impressed. "That's good money. What exactly did she do?"

"All sorts. She had lead roles, supporting roles, speaking roles. Sometimes she worked as an extra, appearing in training films and adverts; she worked on *Emmerdale* quite a lot."

"Can we have the contact details for the company as well, please?" asked Gardener.

Jodie quickly reached for her phone and scanned through her contacts. She gave them the address and phone number.

"Does she have any family?" asked Gardener. "And do they live locally?"

"Oh God," replied Jodie. "Her mum and dad, they'll have to be told." Tears rolling, she managed to give him the information. "Her parents live in Alwoodley, and she has a younger sister called Polly, who's still at home with their parents. I can't imagine how she's going to take this. Sonia spent a lot of time on the phone with Polly, and saw her at least once a week."

She gave Gardener Polly's contact details. He was very impressed with how organized Jodie Thomson was, particularly under the kind of shock she must have been suffering.

"What about friends?" asked Reilly. "I imagine she was quite a popular girl."

"You can say that again. Twice a week at the gym, as I mentioned. But then once a week she joined some other friends in a group known as Reelfriends."

"Real friends?" asked Gardener.

It must have been the way he said it, because Jodie picked up instantly. "No, reel, as in film reel. Every week they would go to a local cinema, watch a film, and then go for a meal afterwards to dissect the film and mark it."

"I like that idea," said Reilly. "Great way to spend your time."

Gardener once again asked for contact details although he suspected his next question might cause some upset.

"I'd like to go over Saturday night itself – what can you remember?"

Jodie reached down for her cup before realizing she had finished her tea. Reilly didn't need asking twice. He jumped up and put the kettle on, making tea for each of them, while Jodie continued.

"We finally got the night started around eight, we went to the Caracas Grill on York Place, it's a Spanish tapas bar – we only wanted a light snack. We left there at nine-thirty and then dropped into the Queen's Hotel, near the railway station for another drink. Finally, we moved on to the Pryzm nightclub in the Merrion Centre at ten, or just after."

"Did you stay there?" asked Gardener.

"No, we had one drink and then shifted to another Merrion Centre club called The Key. That must have suited us because we did stay there. But we split up shortly after entering the place. Not usual practice but we both saw people we knew, which sometimes happens."

"What time was that?" asked Gardener.

"Not late, about ten forty-five."

"How did she seem?"

"She was in a great mood." Jodie's gaze was far away, perhaps reliving the last time she saw her friend, but at least it seemed a happy time. "She'd really enjoyed the night."

"And you didn't see her on Sunday at all?" asked Reilly.

"I didn't *actually* see her. I was with Masie Stringer from work, which is where I stayed. We caught a really early train. I did call Sonia on Sunday morning. She was complaining about the hangover from hell, and said she felt shocking. She also had a sore throat, and thought she may have been coming down with a cold. She said that work could be a problem, especially as she had a training film lined up for Tuesday. Although she cracked on about looking after herself and didn't drink a great deal, she had been known to let herself down on the odd night out. That must have been one of them." Jodie sniffed hard, possibly in an effort to hold it together.

"Did you try calling her from London?"

"Yes, more than once."

"And no answer, I take it."

"No," said Jodie. "Just went to voicemail."

"Take me through what happened when you returned from London."

"Well, by Tuesday I was worried sick. I'd heard nothing despite God knows how many texts and phone calls. I also called The Casting Couch, and her parents, but they're on holiday. No one had seen her. I got home, to the apartment, this afternoon, sometime around quarter to four."

She suddenly stopped talking.

Gardener allowed her a minute.

"I was totally shocked. Honest to God, I never really thought anything had happened to her. I just thought she was busy and hadn't had time to call me back."

"Is that normally how she operates?" asked Reilly, placing everyone's teas in front of them.

"Not really, no," replied Jodie. "But all sorts of things change in your life, don't they? I never thought I'd come home and find her dead in her armchair. I had no idea why. I couldn't see any reason for it. Colds don't kill you, do they?"

"Not very often," said Reilly.

Gardener held his question for a minute, but then asked, "Let me come back to Saturday night itself. When was the last point you can remember seeing Sonia on that night?"

Jodie thought long and hard. "I have no idea what time, but the last thing I remember seeing was Sonia kissing some guy."

"Did you talk to her after she'd been kissing the man?"

"Yes. We were in the toilets together. I asked her who he was but she had no idea, or what he did for a living, because they never really had the chance to talk about it. She seemed really happy, said he was good looking – lean, fit. Had dark hair. They'd been talking for a while; then she said it started getting a little heavier. At that point, he was at the bar buying drinks. That wasn't really like her. She never just picked up some random guy and started kissing him. I told her to be careful, but I think she'd had one drink too many."

Gardener was on red alert. It was important for him to find out as much as he could about the man.

"Did you see her leave the club?"

Jodie's eyes teared up. "No. I was with Masie, and we were talking about the following morning, and not drinking too much and not being late. I remember, at one point, getting up to leave myself, with Masie, and wanting to say goodbye to Sonia, but I couldn't see her anywhere."

"Did *you* actually see the man she was with?" asked Reilly.

"Yes, but only very briefly, not enough to give you a better description than what I've already said."

"Did you recognize him?"

"No," said Jodie. "No idea who he was."

"Did she give you a name?"

"She said he was called Alan. No surname."

"Do you think that was genuine?"

Jodie stared at Gardener with imploring eyes. "I've no idea. I wish I did."

Chapter Five

Gardener needed as much information as Jodie could give, but it didn't sound like she knew much more.

"You've done really well, Miss Thomson, but can you try and think extra hard about Alan? Is there anything at all that stood out?"

She didn't answer immediately, but when she did, she was still rather vague. "No, like I said, dark hair and slim.

He was wearing black jeans and a white shirt from what I can remember."

"Do you know if Sonia and Alan made plans to see each other again?" asked Gardener.

She shook her head. "I don't, because I didn't see her again after that."

"And she never mentioned anything on Sunday morning?" asked Reilly.

"No, she was feeling really rough by the sound of it."

"Do you go to the club often?" asked Gardener.

"Every couple of months, maybe."

"Had either of you seen Alan in the club before?"

"Speaking for myself, I'd say no," said Jodie. "I don't know about Sonia."

"Have you ever seen him anywhere else, Jodie, love?" asked Reilly. "In the town centre, maybe, or shopping in the area?"

"Not that I recall," said Jodie. "But like I said, I never really got a good look at him. It was a club. Too many flashing lights, too much going on. Unless you're interested you don't get too close."

"I take it you didn't talk to the man yourself," asked Gardener, "to detect an accent?"

"No."

"Did any of your friends see the man, or do they know him?"

Jodie thought again. "Masie said she didn't see him. We were with a couple of other friends but I haven't spoken to them."

Gardener asked for names and addresses.

"Do you have a photo of the man on your phone, by any chance?"

Jodie checked, but after a couple of minutes of skipping through, she said she hadn't.

"You don't have any live footage from the night, do you?" asked Reilly.

"I have two or three bits," replied Jodie. "Let's have a look."

The footage of all three segments only lasted a total of two minutes but she said that Alan was not in any of it, nor was Sonia for that matter.

"So, we don't know if they left together – Sonia and Alan?" asked Gardener.

"I definitely don't."

"Not to worry, love," said Reilly. "We *will* be visiting the club so we'll ask for their CCTV."

Gardener glanced up at the CCTV monitors in the concierge's room and made a note for the officers interviewing Faulkner to obtain the footage to see if Sonia arrived home alone, or with the man in question – or any other man for that matter.

"You've done really well, Ms Thomson," said Gardener. "I think we have everything we need to be going on with, but just one more question. Can you think of anything else that might help us?"

Jodie hesitated, which was gold dust to Gardener. There appeared to be something she hadn't told him.

He pushed the point. "Your expression tells me there is."

"There is one thing," she said. "But I have no proof at all about what I'm going to say."

"Anything you tell us will be treated in the strictest confidence, Miss Thomson," said Gardener. "Even if you can't prove anything, it could help us to secure a conviction eventually. So, please, if you think you know something, tell us."

"The local kingpin of the drug circuit was in the club that night."

Gardener let the silence hold, before Reilly asked her to go on.

"He's scum," said Jodie, rather venomously. "I don't trust him at all."

"What's his name?" asked Gardener. "Do you know?"

"I only know his first name," she replied. "In fact, to be honest, I don't know anyone who knows his surname. He's called Viktor. He's usually somewhere around on a Saturday night in the clubs around here, and he was there on the night we were there."

"What makes you think he might have had anything to do with Miss Markham's death?" asked Gardener.

"I did notice Sonia talking to him at one point. But I never saw any exchanges between them, and I'd be really surprised if drugs were the reason for her death."

Gardener thought she had finished, but she finally added, "But I can't see what else it could be."

"Can you tell me anything about him – anything at all?" asked Gardener, figuring the information was unreliable.

"Not really," she replied. "I know his name is Viktor, mainly because no one else knows his surname either, or if they do, they can't pronounce it."

"He's foreign?" asked Reilly.

"Yes. I've no idea where he's from. If you ask around, you're bound to find him. In fact, I'm pretty sure he'll be known to you lot. And he's always with his fat creepy friend, Arthur, though I don't suspect Arthur of anything untoward – unless if eating was made illegal, he'd be banged up for life."

"Viktor and Arthur," repeated Gardener. "No surnames."

"Shouldn't take a lot of finding," said Reilly.

"Like I said, I have no idea if he has anything to do with it, but it wouldn't surprise me, and you did ask."

"Don't worry, Jodie, love," said Reilly. "You've done the right thing."

"I really appreciate everything you've given us," said Gardener, "especially as it must have been so difficult for you."

"I just want whoever did this caught." Jodie burst into tears again.

"We'll do our best," said Gardener. "And you *have* helped immensely."

"When will I be able to go back into the apartment?" asked Jodie, before adding, "Not that I want to right now, but I will have to at some point."

"At the moment it's a crime scene," said Gardener. "It'll be that way for a few days, until we've made a thorough search. Is there somewhere else you can stay for the time being?"

Jodie nodded. "My parents." She reached down for her handbag. "Though I'm not looking forward to telling them."

Chapter Six

Detective Sergeant Bob Anderson had been joined by his colleague Detective Sergeant Frank Thornton, and both were now sitting in the office behind the reception desk in the apartment block with Harry Faulkner; Jodie Thomson having already left.

They had met with Gardener and Reilly in the reception area with the rest of the team, where the SIO had briefly outlined the crime scene and what they had discovered.

As it was late, Gardener did not go into too much detail other than who the deceased was. He informed them that he and Reilly had interviewed her flatmate before suggesting that, as it was an apartment block, the team should split up and do a flat-to-flat search, and should they discover anything of use, to arrange a follow up call. He didn't think they would gain too much information, particularly from other floors, but it was worth a try whilst everything was fresh in people's minds. He had then asked Thornton and Anderson to speak to the concierge, Harry Faulkner.

Gardener then explained that he and Reilly were going to the crime scene again to advise the SOCOs to go through the place with a fine-tooth comb, before going to see Sonia Markham's parents to break the sad news. Then they'd retreat to the station to set up an incident room, where everything would be covered in much more detail.

* * *

Harry Faulkner had made both Anderson and Thornton tea, and to his own he had added a drop of brandy; after what he'd heard, he probably needed it.

As he sat and took a sip, he said, "What a terrible business. We've never had anything like this happen before."

"It's a sad business, Mr Faulkner," said Anderson, with his pen and pad at the ready.

"Not a nice job you have."

"Someone has to do it," replied Thornton.

Eager to move things on, Anderson asked Faulkner his age.

"Sixty-four, sir," replied Faulkner.

"How long have you been here?"

Faulkner stared at the ceiling, mentally calculating. "About ten years, I think."

"A fair while, then," said Anderson. "Where were you before that?"

"In the British Army, sir. Made it to the rank of Lieutenant."

"You must have seen some action, then," said Thornton.

"I suppose I have." He smiled, before adding, "Nothing I'd like to talk about."

"Are you married?"

"Not any more," replied Faulkner. "My wife died a few years back. I do this job because it keeps me occupied."

"Sorry to hear that," said Anderson, quickly wondering what would happen to him if *his* wife died. He supposed the family would rally round and take care of him, it was big enough, but he certainly didn't want to put it to the test.

"Where do you live, Harold?" asked Thornton.

"Here, in the building. I'm in a place no bigger than a shoe cupboard." He then gave both detectives a wry smile. "Something to do with a miscalculation by the builder; the developer couldn't really rent the place out. But we're close friends, so he allowed me to live here on a bit of a skeleton rent in return for the job and a smaller salary – it's enough for me."

"You could say it's worked out well," said Thornton.

"I can't grumble."

Following a suggestion from Gardener, Anderson asked if they had any problem with drugs.

Faulkner shook his head. "It's not that sort of a place, and it certainly wouldn't be allowed on my watch."

"I didn't think it would be," replied Anderson, judging by what he'd seen of the place.

"All the people living here," said Faulkner, "are professionals of the highest standards: bank managers, hedge fund operators, developers, even a footballer or two."

They'd have to be to afford the rent, thought Anderson.

"Can you give us a brief description of what you do?" asked Anderson.

"Not a great deal, really," replied Faulkner. "I receive guests. Run the odd errands for people. Sometimes they leave me notes to sort things out for them: making restaurant reservations, booking hotels, arranging for spa services, recommending night-life hot spots, booking transportation such as taxis, limousines, airplanes, boats. I sometimes coordinate porter service when luggage assistance is requested. I get tickets to special events, assist with various travel arrangements and tours of local attractions. I also assist with sending and receiving parcels."

"I thought you said you didn't do much," said Anderson.

"It's not that bad."

Having judged how helpful the man might be, Anderson asked, "Can we take you back to Saturday, Mr Faulkner? We'd like to know what you remember about the day, and how much you saw of the lady who died, Sonia Markham."

"I'm not sure I can tell you much."

"You'd be surprised," said Thornton.

Faulkner finished his tea and said, "Let me have a think. I saw her mostly between three and eight on Saturday. Not all the time, of course."

"Where was she when you saw her at three o'clock?" asked Anderson.

"Arriving home. It was a little *after* three."

"Had you any idea where she'd been?" asked Thornton.

"Shopping, I assume. She had two carrier bags with her, one of which was Primark. That really surprised me."

"Did you speak at all?"

"Only for a couple of minutes, mostly about the night ahead. She was quite excited. Said she'd not been out for a while. Been working hard. Deserved a night out. I told her she was right. Life was too short. We laughed about that and she went to her apartment."

"Did you see Miss Thomson at all?"

"Yes, about fifteen minutes previous; she had said pretty much the same thing, although her forthcoming training trip was on her mind, but she wasn't about to miss celebrating their friend's birthday, whose name, if I can remember correctly, was Masie Stringer. Lives in Yeadon."

"So, Jodie Thomson was already in the apartment when Sonia Markham arrived?"

"Yes, sir."

"When did you next see them?" asked Thornton.

"When they were leaving for their night on the town."

"What time?"

"About six o'clock."

"And how were they?"

"Excited, and looking absolutely stunning," he replied. "I wish I'd been forty years younger."

They all laughed. "They didn't happen to say where they were going first, did they?" asked Anderson.

"Not to me."

Anderson didn't really think there was much more he could ask. At least he had a little more information, but whatever happened to Sonia Markham had done so much later in the evening, and probably not here.

"Were you on duty when she arrived home?"

"No, sir. Well past my bedtime," said Faulkner. "But I still might be able to help with that."

"The CCTV, you mean?" asked Thornton.

"Yes. Everything that happens in the building – as far as people coming and going is concerned – is recorded. Would you like to see it?"

"We would," said Anderson. "We'd also like to take a copy with us."

"I'm not sure I can help you there," said Faulkner. "I'm not very good with technology."

"Don't worry about that," said Thornton. "We have two officers on the team who are genius at this stuff, and they're still somewhere on the premises."

Before calling Gates and Longstaff, the pair of them watched Faulkner go through the painful process of trying to find it.

But he did.

However, the CCTV within The Quays showed that Sonia Markham entered the building at two o'clock in the morning, alone, and she went to her apartment alone.

Chapter Seven

Approximately eight hours after Sonia Markham had been discovered dead in her apartment, Martin Short was wandering around Lazers nightclub, outside Batley, hoping to make a quick killing – though not in the literal sense of the word.

Recently, things had not been going well for him. He had split from his girlfriend; no great loss, he'd had trouble remembering her name from day one. Women tended not to like that, especially in the throws of passion.

His car had failed its MOT the month before. He'd continued driving it even after the garage had advised him not to. An engine oil leak had reached the point of a fresh gallon every week – until yesterday, when it suddenly went bang.

The landlord had given him notice on his flat. They could be like that, especially if you hadn't paid them for three months. Martin had managed to avoid his landlord quite skilfully until yesterday, when he'd been served with a Section 21. The bastard must have been stalking him.

The form had almost been shoved down his throat as soon as Martin had opened his front door. He'd been forced back upstairs for his belongings, marched back down again, and thrown out onto the street whilst the locks were changed in front of him. Martin had told him he couldn't do that, but thought better of causing a fuss when he saw the landlord's expression.

Glancing around, he realized what a fruitless task he had ahead of him. There were little more than fifty people in the place, the lighting was low – the music soft and the atmosphere was more akin to a funeral parlour than a club. How the hell did they make money?

More to the point, how was he going to? Dealing in here would be a problem. He would be seen all too easily, no matter where he went. Even the toilets would be closely monitored. Martin needed money, and he had a load of gear that he'd managed to water down so to speak. Plenty of white sachets full of ground paracetamol mixed with self-raising flour to make it go further, and only a little of the hard stuff.

Wouldn't exactly be a problem. Once he'd shifted it all – hopefully sooner rather than later – made enough money, he'd be out of here. Pick up another cheap car and make his way to somewhere fresh. Start again.

Martin strolled to the bar as the DJ put something livelier on, which was probably a step too far. The lights started flashing, the smoke machine near the stage belched out the white mist, and the brash music was more akin to Benidorm rather than Batley.

He ordered a soft drink, which the barman served with an expression of disgust. Something was muttered but Martin couldn't hear it, nor did he care. It was possible that the DJ had done him a favour by changing the mood. Now he might be able to circulate.

He collected his drink and turned around, finding his view completely blocked by a fatberg.

Martin was about to tell him to sling his hook when he realized it was Arthur Pierrepoint. That meant one thing. If Arthur was here, so was Viktor – though Martin couldn't see him. But then few people ever did, unless he requested your presence.

"Viktor would like a word with you," said Arthur. "He'd like to make you an offer you can't refuse."

Arthur was a square-headed, jovial-faced monster of a man, weighing in at around thirty – or more – stone. He had a thatch of grey hair, with a neatly trimmed beard and moustache, with tortoiseshell glasses. Arthur's dress sense left a lot to be desired, outdated check suits that were way past their sell-by date, but no one said a word because he was part of Viktor's inner sanctum. Martin had heard that Arthur was as bent as any solicitor on planet Earth. No one knew his exact relationship with Viktor or how the pair met, but right now, it seemed irrelevant.

Martin glanced around, his mouth suddenly very dry. No amount of drink would cure that problem. The whole club appeared to have shrunk, with the music becoming a muffled distraction, as if the DJ had reduced the volume so the whole fucking club could hear the conversation.

As he studied Arthur, he realized there was no way around the situation. He might well be able to dodge the fat man, but he'd never outrun Viktor's henchmen. Although he couldn't see them, he knew they wouldn't be far away.

"Well?" said Arthur.

"Well what?" asked Martin, playing for time.

"What are you waiting for?"

There were a hundred reasons he could give Arthur for not wanting to go with him, but he valued his face too much. Not that that would make much difference right now. He owed Viktor, big time. Apart from managing to dodge his landlord, Martin had been reasonably successful at keeping out of Viktor's way as well.

His luck appeared to have run out on all accounts.

Arthur reached over and removed the glass from Martin's hand. He placed the drink back on the bar. The barman nodded, removing the glass. Martin wouldn't be needing that anymore tonight.

With little chance to resist, Arthur grabbed Martin by the arm and dragged him toward the toilet block in the far corner. If you wanted to do business without being seen, it was as good a place as any.

As they reached the door, a tall, thin man of student age and dress sense grabbed the door handle and tried to make his way into the toilets.

"It's out of order, young man," said Arthur.

"But I'm dying for a piss," replied the man, almost squaring up to Arthur.

"Really," replied the big man. He leaned a little closer to the student, whilst still grasping Martin's arm tight enough to stop the circulation. "Well, that's better than just dying, isn't it?"

Chapter Eight

Gardener had called an incident room meeting early the next morning. There were things he wanted to say, and information he needed to gather, all of which would lead to actions being instigated. The whole team had assembled, including DCI Briggs, who had taken his usual place at the back of the room. Whiteboards had been put into position, with photos of Sonia Markham, and the scene. An overhead projector had also been set up.

Gardener described the scene in detail to his team: what time the call came in, the route it had taken to reach him, what he and Reilly had discovered on arrival, and the fact that Fitz could tell them nothing at that time.

"Fitz had no idea?" asked WPC Julie Longstaff.

"I know," said Gardener. "Shocked us as well."

"No inclinations whatsoever?" asked Detective Sergeant Sarah Gates.

"Nothing," said Gardener. "What does bother me is that Sean and I could find no evidence of foul play within the apartment. It's as if the girl had come home, locked the door, sat in her chair and fallen asleep."

"So, what are we treating it as?" asked Briggs.

"Suspicious," replied Gardener, "at least until we see the post-mortem results." He went on to explain that they had interviewed her flatmate, Jodie Thomson, so they had an idea of Sonia Markham's final movements up until late evening the day before she died. He relayed how the girls had both left the apartment block at six o'clock, and the last that Jodie had seen of Sonia was sometime around eleven in the club.

Gardener then asked what Thornton and Anderson had learned from the concierge.

"Well," said Anderson. "We have her movements from three o'clock on the Saturday afternoon. That's when she got back to her apartment after a shopping spree. Jodie Thomson was already at home and the pair of them didn't surface again until six."

"Okay," said Gardener, updating the whiteboard.

He then turned and explained to his team the movements the girls had made after six o'clock, starting with the tapas bar for a light snack, before dropping in at the Queens, and finally the club.

"Any idea what time she arrived back home on Saturday night, or Sunday morning?" asked Sharp.

"A little after two o'clock," said Anderson. "The CCTV in The Quays showed her walking through the entrance alone, and going to her apartment alone."

"Do we know how she got home?"

"I'm guessing taxi at that time in the morning," said Anderson, "but we couldn't see that from the CCTV."

"So there's an action for someone," said Gardener, "when we finally get around to sorting them out. I take it the concierge wasn't still on duty at that time?"

"No, boss," said Thornton. "But at least we know she arrived home safe enough. Just don't know what the bloody hell happened after that."

"Did anyone else show up on the CCTV, arriving at The Quays after Sonia Markham got home?" asked Reilly.

"There is someone," said Gates. "We have been looking a bit further into the CCTV since the lads brought it back with them."

"Another couple appeared about an hour later," said Longstaff. "They were Keith and Gloria Whiteley. They had suitcases with them."

"Yes," said Gates. "Returning home on a late flight from Tenerife. All checks out."

Gardener nodded, disappointed. "Has anyone learned anything from last night's flat-to-flat calls?" he asked.

The answer was negative. No one had seen anything.

"Not many people actually know them," said Longstaff.

"Doesn't surprise me," said Gardener.

"The next-door neighbours, the Harrisons, said Sonia was very quiet," replied Gates. "She was very polite, sometimes had a few minutes to stand and talk, but because they all had unusual jobs, it didn't happen very often. The Harrisons are event managers, so they didn't have a lot of free time to meet up."

"Jodie and Sonia were both well-liked," added Longstaff. "But like everyone nowadays, they kept to themselves. They weren't rowdy neighbours – no wild parties, no playing music too loud too late. The Harrisons had been over for a meal once, which went down well."

"But that's about it," said Gates. "So, this lady – or to be more precise – her death, is still a conundrum."

Gardener updated the whiteboard again before turning to the team. "Okay, actions. One thing we will need is a more in-depth flat-to-flat check, especially people we did not see last night, and I'm sure there must have been a few."

"There was," said Rawson. "We intend to go back today."

"Okay," said Gardener. "Moving on, I'd like someone checking out the landlord, see what kind of tenants they were. I imagine they were good ones. They'd been there a while and it strikes me as the kind of place that if you didn't pay your way you wouldn't last very long.

"We also have the details of a number of friends that we can talk to. Jodie and Sonia were at the club with at least one friend – Masie Stringer. Now, we know Masie was with Jodie Thomson in London, which gives her a pretty good alibi. She may, however, know something about Sonia Markham that Jodie Thomson doesn't, so it's worth a try."

"And then we have a number of friends that formed a group she was part of, called Reelfriends," said Reilly, explaining what that was all about. Gates and Longstaff thought that sounded brilliant and indicated they'd like to join.

"She also frequented the gym a couple of times a week, and she went regularly to the same hairdresser," said Gardener. "We have all the details."

"She sounds like a very clean-living, active lady," said Briggs. "Which begs the question, should it turn out to be anything other than natural, who the hell wanted to kill her?"

"That's what we'd like to know," said Reilly.

"And how they did it," said Gardener. "At the moment, it doesn't look like someone has. It appears as if she went home and simply died."

"Drugs?" asked Briggs.

"Not likely," said Gardener. "Neither girl seems that type, but Fitz is going to pay that some particular attention."

"That said," added Reilly, "her mate, Jodie, reckoned she saw Sonia Markham talking to a known drug dealer in the club."

"Who?" asked Rawson.

"We only know his first name," said Reilly. "Viktor."

Blank expressions were all that came back to Gardener, as if no one had heard of Viktor.

"So someone needs to have a brief look at him," said Gardener. "At the moment, I'm not too concerned that he has anything to do with it, so we need to be cautious until we find out otherwise."

"Why are you not sure about this link?" asked Briggs.

"Because Jodie Thomson was simply throwing it out there. When I asked if she knew anything else at all, his name came up."

"Came up how?" asked Briggs.

"Like we said," offered Reilly. "She'd seen them talking."

"And that was all?" asked Longstaff.

"Pretty much," said Gardener. "She indicated that she wasn't sure if he had anything to do with Sonia's death, but we did ask, and that's what she felt."

"Any history, do you think?" asked Briggs.

"No idea, sir," replied Gardener. "But worth bearing in mind, which is why I want someone to take a brief look at it – and while we're at it, have a quick look into Jodie Thomson's background. Who knows, there might be some history."

"Point noted," said Briggs. "I'll have a word with narcotics, see what they know."

Gardener glanced at Gates and Longstaff. "Can you two ladies go through the rest of the CCTV from the apartment block, see if you can find out anything more?"

Gates nodded.

"We also have Sonia Markham's electronic devices so I'd like you to check out her footprint: social media sites, laptop, phone, etc. And we also have the landline number to the apartment for you to check out as well."

Longstaff indicated that it was right up their street and started making notes.

"I believe you spoke to her parents," Briggs said to Gardener. "How are they taking all this?"

"They're devastated," said Gardener. "They live in Alwoodley. They first got wind of the problem on Tuesday morning when Jodie Thomson called them. She had been trying to call Sonia since Sunday, without success. The parents were on a family holiday in the Lakes with Sonia's sister, Polly. As soon as they discovered something was wrong, they tried calling Sonia themselves. They cut the holiday short and drove straight back to Leeds, trying her mobile and her landline all the way home."

"They pretty much arrived home at the same time as we pulled up outside their house," said Reilly.

"Oh, Christ," said Anderson. "If they hadn't suspected by that point, their hearts must have been in their mouths when they saw you."

"That's one way of putting it," said Gardener.

"The mother had already guessed," said Reilly. "We didn't actually need to tell her. She asked if we were absolutely sure. We told her Jodie had identified the body, that it was her who'd found Sonia."

"They asked how Jodie was holding up," said Gardener. "That's the kind of family they appear to be. Their daughter had died, and because the flatmate had found her, they were equally as concerned for her welfare."

"Poor buggers," said Briggs. "We certainly owe it to them to pull out all the stops on this."

Gardener nodded. "Bearing that in mind, we need someone at the two clubs Jodie mentioned they were in. Both are in the Merrion Centre. One is called Pryzm, and the other is The Key Club."

"I know 'em both," said Rawson.

"In that case, Dave," said Gardener. "Take Colin with you, and some photos, and ask questions: Does anyone remember seeing her? What time did she leave the Pryzm? In the case of The Key Club, do they know how she left and at what time, and check on any available CCTV."

"But most importantly," added Reilly. "We really need to try and find out about this mystery man called Alan. Do they know anyone called Alan?" Reilly gave them the description that Jodie Thomson had given them.

"Not much to go on there, boss," said Rawson. "There were probably twenty blokes in the place, either called Alan, or using that name, and half of them will have looked similar."

"I realize that, Dave," said Gardener. "But it's all we have, and we have to start somewhere."

"We'll give it a go," said Sharp. "You never know, we might turn something up."

Gardener nodded. He turned his attention to Briggs, hoping to try and wind up the meeting so everyone could make an early start in the morning.

"Can you arrange a press release, sir?"

Briggs nodded. "Leave that with me, Stewart. So, what are you guys going to be doing?"

"We'll need to speak to Fitz," said Gardener. "With a bit of luck, he might have found something. Sonia Markham seemed a bit of a health freak. She liked going to the gym, she ate very healthily and she used food supplements. We have those with us so we're going to leave them with Fitz to see if anything in them, combined with any possible underlying health problems, may have caused her death."

"Did she have any?" asked Sharp.

"Only a very mild case of asthma," said Gardener, realizing he had forgotten to mention it. He filled them in on what Jodie Thomson had said, adding it seemed very unlikely that asthma would have been the cause. "And we also need to call on her place of employment, a company called The Casting Couch."

Chapter Nine

Helen Grace had done everything possible to take her mind off what she was about to go through today. She'd read the brochure three times, which still hadn't helped.

Parkinson & Son were an independent family business based in Skipton, established in 1923 by Frank Parkinson as a joiners and funeral directors in a small parish church with extensive grounds on Otley Road. The church building was sold off by the diocese in 1921, and after two years of renovation, Frank turned the place into a funeral parlour.

A stone cottage had been built in the grounds, close to the gated entrance for Frank's aged parents, which had subsequently been handed down through the generations. Frank's son, Rodney, had lived in the cottage before he had taken over the business. Rodney's son, Alec, now lived there. The grounds were populated with spruce and poplar trees, a large number of ornaments, and a variety of carved bushes.

The company was currently run by Rodney and Alec, evolving into a funeral directors and memorial business. They employed six staff, two front of house, two in the offices, a gardener, and a cleaner. Parkinson & Son were also members of the National Society of Allied and Independent Funeral Directors (SAIF), a recognized governing body for funeral directors. From its humble beginnings it had grown over the years and was one of the most modern and well-equipped funeral services in Skipton. The present suite of buildings included a mortuary and chapel of rest, both added by Rodney Parkinson in 1995.

Helen placed the brochure back on the smoked-glass-topped table, located perfectly in the middle of the large room between two three-seater sofas. Her daughter, Erica, was sitting on one of them. There were also a number of independently placed, wing-back leather chairs, which Helen and her husband, Ross, had chosen to sit on. Along the opposite wall was an open fireplace with a large log burner, currently not in use, which pleased Helen. She was warm enough as it was. The music in the background was a pan pipe rendition of something classical.

"Are you okay?" asked Ross.

Helen glanced at her husband. "Not really." He meant well. Ross was on the short side, stocky, and carried more weight around the middle than he should. He was balding, wore glasses and often dressed in a drab grey suit, which summed him up because he was a banker in the city. But for all that, she loved him.

He reached out and touched her hand. "Give it time."

"I keep trying," she replied, "but it's not helping."

Helen glanced at Erica, who was managing to hide her grief well by constantly scanning and scrolling through her phone.

Helen was about to say more when the door opened and Rodney Parkinson walked in. He was every inch the funeral director: tall, thin, with a long angular face, and deep, penetrating black eyes that matched his jet-black hair. He reminded her of an old horror film actor but she couldn't for the life of her think which one.

He smiled as he crossed the room, carrying a manila folder under one arm. He let the folder slide into his left hand and held out his right to greet them.

"Mrs Grace." He then shook hands with Ross and Erica. "How nice of you to come and see us."

He asked if they would like drinks. At that point, his son Alec entered. Ross and Helen said they would like tea. Erica wanted a Coke. Alec left again to prepare them.

"I'm so sorry for your loss," said Parkinson, to all of them.

"Thank you," replied Helen.

The music in the background changed but it was still pan pipes. She recognized the song as *Bridge Over Troubled Water*, her late mother's favourite. It was going to be a tough session.

"How are you bearing up?" Parkinson asked Helen.

She reached for a tissue. "I'm not."

"A very difficult time for you, dear lady," said Parkinson. "But rest assured, we will do everything we can to make this journey as easy as possible for you."

Helen Grace knew it was his job to put her at ease but he was *too* nice. She really didn't think she would reach the end of the session unscathed.

"I believe your parents were not very old," he said.

Alec opened the door and wheeled in a tea trolley and distributed the drinks. He then took a seat next to Erica.

Helen noticed that Erica's phone disappeared as soon as she saw Alec. He was about the only thing that had broken her daughter's concentration from her mobile in weeks. He was tall and lean like his father, also with jet black hair, a trimmed beard and moustache, and the whitest teeth Helen had ever seen.

Helen turned and spoke to Rodney. "No, they were only late fifties."

"Oh, dear. Was it sudden?"

"Yes," said Helen, wiping her eyes. "Car accident. They were returning from the Alhambra theatre in Bradford, three weeks ago now. They'd been to see a show."

Everyone took a moment, sipped their drinks and, in an effort to perhaps deflect the pain, Helen Grace asked what would happen now, and what personal details he would like to know.

Parkinson opened the manila folder, and Alec opened a notepad and held his pen in anticipation. The senior of the two explained the undertaker's tasks and responsibilities in great detail and asked a number of questions about Helen's parents in order to obtain as much information as necessary, in an effort to make the service a more pleasant experience – if that were possible.

Helen was quite surprised that nearly two hours had passed incredibly quickly.

As he was about to close the meeting, Parkinson smiled and said, "I think we have everything we need, Mr and Mrs Grace. Thank you for being so open in what must be a very difficult time.

"The chapel of rest will be open for you, to come and visit your parents whenever you want, day or night. Please don't concern yourself about that. We will be here to serve and look after your needs."

Helen wept. "I'm not sure if I could face them, in the coffins, you know."

"You've no need to worry. A lot of people feel the same about viewing the deceased. But sometimes, it's very soothing, and I know a lot of people who have said afterwards that they found an inner strength from such a simple act, seeing their loved ones at peace.

"There's nothing to worry about, seeing them. My son is a dedicated professional." Old man Parkinson glanced at Alec when he said it. "He's a perfectionist. He has been known to work all through the night into the next day to make sure your loved ones are looked after properly."

Alec smiled, as if he was a little embarrassed by the praise.

Chapter Ten

The Casting Couch was located in a two storey, light blue brick building on Kirkstall Road, roughly a mile or so from the Yorkshire TV studios. The building had an arched front doorway with arched wooden windows, a grey slate roof and a round porthole window in one corner. Someone had painted a mural from a film set in the bottom right-hand corner, featuring performers and cameras and a boom microphone.

There was nothing next door, only a large piece of land that was closed off by fencing. An open gate on the right of The Casting Couch building allowed access. Four high-end cars were parked against the wall. Reilly slipped the pool car into the only place available.

The pair of them jumped out and Gardener glanced around. "Let's go and see what we can find out, Sean."

Reilly locked the car and they approached the building. The sky was blue and cloudless but there was a nip in the air. The city of Leeds was going about its business as normal and a host of trucks, buses and taxis passed them as they entered the premises.

The outside of the building was pretty standard, and Gardener wasn't sure what to expect on the inside but it was clean and smelled fresh. The front door opened into a carpeted corridor with a number of doors leading off, and a large room at the end. Gardener noticed the flash of a lightbulb and he could also hear distant voices.

"Can I help you?"

Gardener glanced to his right. He hadn't noticed a hole in the wall with a plastic screen leading into an office, where a Hollywood blonde sat at the desk.

Both officers displayed warrant cards and Gardener introduced them. The blonde indicated they should open the door into her office.

"We don't often get visits from the police," she said, standing. She was sensibly dressed in a two-tone blue trouser suit and introduced herself as Janice Lawson. "How can we help?"

"We'd like to talk to you about a lady called Sonia Markham," said Gardener. "We believe she worked for you."

"She does," said Janice, her hand covering her mouth. "Do you know where she is? We've been trying to contact her for days. She was supposed to be working with us today. Nothing's happened, has it?"

Gardener was relieved when Janice sat back down. "Miss Lawson, do you work here, or are you management?"

"I just work here."

"Okay, can we speak to someone in management, please?" asked Gardener. "It is a matter for management."

"Oh my God," said Janice. "She hasn't got herself into trouble, has she? That would be so unlike her."

Gardener didn't actually reply because Janice then said, "Please, take a seat, both of you. I'll be straight back."

To her word, she came back rapidly. The man accompanying her was middle-aged with silver grey hair, moustache and beard, dressed in jeans and a check shirt.

"Can I help you gentlemen?"

Gardener showed his warrant card. "And you are?"

"James Haughton, one of the directors." He held out a hand for Gardener to shake.

"Is there somewhere private we can talk, Mr Haughton?"

"Yes, of course." Haughton didn't seem to know what to do with himself. He turned one way and then the other and then asked the detectives to follow him. He also asked Janice if she could take care of all the calls until the police had left.

Haughton led them both into a rather plush office with two large sofas and two leather chairs, along with a variety of office equipment.

"Grab a seat. What's happened? Is Sonia okay?"

"I'm afraid not, Mr Haughton." Gardener went on to explain the circumstances in which Jodie Thomson had found her friend.

"Oh my God," said Haughton, putting his head in his hands. "That's awful. How is Jodie?"

"Bearing up," said Reilly.

Haughton jumped to his feet. "Would you wait here for a minute, please?"

Without waiting for a reply, he left the office. On his return he had three more people with him, all of which had serious expressions. As Gardener and Reilly were in the chairs, they each settled down on the sofas.

"Let me introduce you to the other partners," said Haughton. As he said their names, he pointed to the individuals: Adam Baxter, Sylvia Perkins and Cleo Lansford.

"This is awful news," said Baxter. He was around thirty years of age with thinning black hair and a smooth complexion. His attire was jeans and a T-shirt. "What actually happened?"

"I'm afraid we don't know at the moment, Mr Baxter. But we'd like to ask you some questions about Sonia, see if we can build up a character profile and possibly her last movements."

They each nodded. Gardener asked Haughton about the company.

He coughed before he started talking and at that point, Janice wheeled in a trolley with drinks and some biscuits on a plate. Gardener didn't give much for the chances of the others where the biscuits were concerned once his partner had clocked them.

"The Casting Couch," said Haughton, "is run collectively by the four of us."

"What do you do?" asked Gardener.

It was Sylvia Perkins who spoke up. She was quite large, with her dark hair tied up in a bun and dressed all in lemon.

"We work primarily with directors, producers, film-makers and TV companies."

Cleo Lansford suddenly took over. She was probably the youngest and didn't appear to Gardener to be long out of school. She was slim with shoulder length black hair, blue eyes, and was wearing a tight black leather skirt and a white blouse.

"We supply actors, supporting artists and models as well."

"How long have you been in business?" asked Reilly.

"Around thirty years," said Haughton.

"And the business is varied," said Baxter.

"Soaps, commercials, TV, short films," said Perkins.

"Feature films, catalogue promotion shoots," added Lansford.

"And promotions and voice-overs," said Haughton. "We pretty much do it all."

Cleo Lansford suddenly put her hands to her mouth. "Oh God, I can't believe this. Sonia dead." She glanced around at her colleagues. "We're not going to see her anymore."

Sylvia Perkins put her arms around Cleo's shoulders. "Don't upset yourself, love. I know it's awful, but sometimes these things happen."

"Yes," said Cleo, "but to other people, not one of my friends."

When the atmosphere had calmed a little, Gardener asked when each of them had seen Sonia Markham last.

"I haven't seen her for a while," said Baxter, "but I spoke to her one the phone about a month ago."

"I saw her," said Sylvia. "Her contract had her working four of the five days. She popped into the office on Monday."

"Which days was she working?" asked Reilly.

James Haughton tapped his keyboard and quickly came up with an answer. "Monday to Thursday."

"No one saw her on Friday?" asked Gardener.

Each of them shook their heads to indicate they hadn't.

Reilly made notes before Gardener asked what she had been doing on those days.

Haughton checked his screen again. "On Monday and Tuesday, she appeared as an extra in *Emmerdale*."

"That's right," said Sylvia. "Most of the work she did on Monday was exterior scenes on location in the village."

"And then she had two studio scenes on Tuesday," said Cleo. "She enjoyed the studio scenes because they were just down the road there." She pointed, as if he could actually see through the wall.

"Do you know what she was doing in these scenes?" asked Gardener.

"One in the hairdresser's chair," said Baxter. "She was only really staring into the mirror. The main character, Mandy, was doing all the talking. Sonia was just nodding and smiling."

"What was the other scene?" asked Reilly.

"She was in the pub, sitting at a table at the back, chatting to another extra," said Haughton.

"Is that something we can see?" asked Gardener.

"I'm afraid not," replied Haughton. "The film crew and the editors will have those because it won't have been aired yet, but I can send an email and request them to get in touch with you."

Gardener nodded and said he would appreciate it.

"How long was she on set that day?" asked Reilly.

"They're usually there all day," said Baxter. "Although the directors have a good idea when they're going to shoot, they like them there all day."

"Yes," said Cleo. "Sometimes they get extra scenes to do, so it's handy if they're still around."

"And how was she on those days?" asked Gardener.

"From what everyone saw of her she was fine," said Sylvia Perkins.

"She was very upbeat," said Cleo. "Very easy to work with."

"All the directors liked working with her," said Haughton, "because they usually only asked her to do something once and it was done."

"Almost always first time," added Baxter.

"What about the other two days?" asked Reilly.

"Wednesday and Thursday saw her on location in the middle of Leeds shooting a training safety film," said Haughton.

"Both days she was in Roundhay Park," said Baxter.

Gardener asked for all contact details to carry out follow up interviews.

"So how was she on those days?" asked Reilly.

"The people who worked with her on Wednesday and Thursday said she was fine," replied Sylvia Perkins.

"But she always was," said Cleo. "A real professional and a pleasure to work with. Everybody loved her."

"That's true," said Baxter. "I can't imagine anyone wanting to hurt Sonia."

"She was so professional," said Haughton. "She turned up on time, every time, and did everything that was asked of her. She was a sheer delight to be around."

"Did any of you see her on Thursday before she finished for the day?" asked Reilly.

"I saw her after she'd finished," said Cleo. "We met for a quick coffee in The Coffee Room, the place on the railway station."

"And she was okay – nothing bothering her?" asked Gardener.

"She was fine," replied Cleo. "Looking forward to the weekend. She said they were going to be shop-till-you-drop days."

"Did she mention anything else about the weekend?"

Cleo nodded. "Yes. On Saturday she was meeting a friend called Jayne Preston for lunch at a vegan café in the Crescent called Oranaise Cafe. I only remember that because I love eating there myself, and I recommended it."

"Oh, I know that place," said Sylvia Perkins. "It's North African cuisine. I love it. They specialize in Moroccan and Algerian dishes. And they have vegan pizzas and meat-free chicken."

"Was she a vegan?" asked Gardener, thinking about what had been in her fridge and the supplements.

"No," said Cleo. "But her friend, Jayne, was, so she was happy to go along with that."

Gardener asked for contact details for Jayne Preston but The Casting Couch didn't know where she lived nor had a phone number. That didn't matter because he was sure he would find it easily enough with everything they had on Sonia Markham.

He really didn't think there was anything more he could ask that would push the investigation on. They now had pretty much all Sonia Markham's movements from the previous Monday until the early hours of Sunday morning.

He needed any information he could glean from the nightclubs if he was going to find any answer as to what actually happened to Sonia Markham.

And he hoped there *would* be something, because he sure as hell had nothing at the moment.

Chapter Eleven

Another two days passed before Gardener and Reilly managed to catch up with Fitz at the mortuary. As always, his desk was impeccably clean and tidy, and as usual, an opera played at low volume, adding some background noise to an otherwise clinically silent room.

As they entered, Gardener was the first to notice that coffees had been poured and a small tray containing a variety of biscuits had already been laid out.

As both officers took their seats, Gardener placed a small bag on the floor and Reilly eyed the tray suspiciously. "Is there something wrong with those?"

"Why should there be something wrong with them?" asked Fitz.

"Because they're usually hidden, you normally make me work for them."

"You don't work for them, you steal them. Hiding them clearly doesn't work."

Gardener enjoyed the banter. He took his coffee and a biscuit and hoped the lightened mood would lead to good news.

"Have you anything to tell us about Sonia Markham?" he asked.

"I'm afraid it's not straightforward."

"When is it ever?" asked Reilly.

That deflated Gardener a little. "Go on."

"I have found evidence of encephalitis," said Fitz.

Reilly glanced at his partner. "He never speaks English, does he?"

"That's rich coming from him," said Fitz to Gardener, nodding at the Irishman.

The elderly pathologist laughed. "Anyway, just for you, it's an uncommon but serious condition in which the brain becomes inflamed, or should I say swollen. It *can* be life threatening – as in this case, I believe it was – and requires urgent treatment in hospital. Which of course couldn't have happened with this young lady because she was on her own. Anyone can be affected, but it's usually the very young and the very old that are most at risk."

The phone rang but Fitz rejected the call and continued. "It sometimes starts off with flu-like symptoms, such as a high temperature and headache. Some of the more serious symptoms develop over hours, days or weeks."

"She did mention something about a sore throat to Jodie Thomson," said Reilly. "But she put that down to a cold."

"Or a hangover," added Gardener.

"I suppose the symptoms would be very similar," said Fitz. "Other symptoms of encephalitis might include confusion or disorientation, seizures or fits. She could have had changes in personality and behaviour, possible difficulty in speaking. She might have had weakness or loss of movement in some parts of the body, and even loss of consciousness. This is where it gets difficult. Not many of the latter symptoms are associated with colds, and the fact that no one was around to tell us, doesn't help."

"As we've already mentioned," said Reilly, "colds don't normally kill you."

"Not normally, no," agreed Fitz.

"Wouldn't you be able to tell if she had a cold?" asked Gardener.

"In most cases yes, and I would say that in this case, she didn't," replied Fitz. "I'm more concerned with the swelling of the brain, of which there are a variety of derangements.

"The most common is vasogenic, resulting from a disruption of the blood-brain barrier. Fluid is forced into the cerebral parenchyma – the supporting tissue."

Fitz clicked a few keys on the keyboard and checked his notes. "A cerebral oedema quite often stems from a tumour, but I haven't been able to find anything there. It's always possible that she could have suffered some type of trauma but it doesn't look like she has. I did check for hypoxia, which is a lack of oxygen – but once again there is no evidence.

"Infections are often the cause of such problems, but there was nothing to suggest she had one – yet."

"What do you mean by yet?" asked Gardener.

"I'll come to that," said Fitz. "I started to look for metabolic derangements, whether acute or severe, they will really affect brain function. With that you would see a real decline in the level of consciousness; she'd become unresponsive to most situations, less receptive, and perhaps suffer loss of memory. But as far as I could tell, the brain was in reasonable health, apart from being swollen.

"I decided to weigh and measure the brain, and then cut it open. I thought the inside of the brain was quite intriguing but it still hasn't given me the cause of the encephalitis. There were signs of small haemorrhages, the white matter was increased more than normal, and some of the structures were asymmetrical, or deformed.

"Another thought to cross my mind was acute hypertension; a hypertensive crisis is often quite sudden, and you would see a severe increase in blood pressure, which can lead to a medical emergency. It can also lead to a heart attack, stroke or other life-threatening health problems; so far, none of my medical investigations has indicated anything in that direction."

"So, you know the brain has swollen, but you have no idea why," said Gardener. "You know it's caused her death but there is no clear indication as to what actually caused the swelling?"

"I'm afraid not, gentlemen. At least not yet. I will go so far as to suggest that whatever happened did so between Saturday night and Sunday lunchtime."

"Can you be more precise?" asked Gardener.

Fitz shook his head. "The best I can tell you is sometime between ten o'clock Sunday morning and two o'clock in the afternoon."

"It looks like whatever has caused this, has come on so fast that she didn't even have time to call for help."

"Even if she had, would the help have arrived in time?" asked Reilly.

"It's not likely," said Fitz. "I'm afraid this poor girl has succumbed to something quite lethal."

"But what?" asked Gardener, a little frustrated.

"For what it's worth, it's either an unknown virus…" replied Fitz.

There was a short silence, in which Reilly said. "Or?"

"I'm inclined to think that maybe she suffered a seizure; they interfere with the brain cells, causing abnormalities in muscle tone or movements, for example: stiffness, twitching or limpness. They are not all alike. A seizure can be a single event due to an acute cause, such as medication."

"But we've found nothing in her life – or her cupboards – to suggest she was on anything," said Gardener.

"That's a point, boss," said Reilly. "We should ask Jodie Thomson if Sonia Markham had a GP, see if we can find out for definite."

Gardener nodded.

"If she had been having seizures constantly," said Fitz, "then the likelihood is, she would have had epilepsy."

"Again, something we need to check with her doctor," said Gardener.

"If she'd had epilepsy, I'm sure Jodie Thomson would have known," said Reilly. "She didn't mention anything, apart from mild asthma."

"Would she have had cold symptoms in the build up to a seizure?" asked Gardener.

"Hard to say," said Fitz. "Symptoms of seizures can vary. There could be partial or full loss of consciousness. They can cause involuntary twitching, or a stiffness in the body, sometimes quite severe stiffening. Or you might experience shaking of the limbs and a loss of consciousness – a convulsion in other words."

"She didn't really look as if she'd had a convulsion," said Reilly. "We found her in the chair as if she'd fallen asleep. Surely if she'd had a convulsion, there would have been some evidence, such as the small table overturned."

"Maybe not," said Fitz, "especially if she was in the chair and it came on suddenly. There are two major classes or groups of seizures: focal onset and generalized onset. A focal onset seizure starts in one area of the brain, causing mild or severe symptoms, depending on how the electrical discharges spread.

"A generalized seizure can start as a focal seizure that spreads to both sides of the brain. But in my experience, generalized onset seizures are usually first identified during childhood and are similar to a thermostat surge or a light flash. Abnormal electrical regulation between parts of the brain can cause the seizures. If you're speaking to her GP, you may want to investigate this one a little more."

Gardener realized they were still no further on. "So, where do we go from here?"

"I have sent a variety of tissue samples off for toxicology tests," said Fitz. "I'm hoping they will tell us something more."

"Can a blood test detect the cause of a seizure?" asked Reilly.

"Possibly," replied Fitz. "Analysing blood might be of some help when identifying the cause of the symptomatic seizures."

Gardener leaned forward and reached down to the small evidence bag on the floor, placing it on the desk. "Could these supplements have caused it?"

Fitz picked up the bag and briefly browsed the contents. "I really wouldn't think so, but I will do some research. It's possible she could have been allergic to something in these. But if that's the case, she can't have been taking them for long."

"According to Jodie Thomson, she used them a lot."

"Then maybe she had recently changed to a different brand, so that's something else you may be able to look at."

"No drugs in her system?" asked Reilly.

Fitz shook his head. "None that I can find. If there had been, it's somehow left no trace of itself."

That one sentence took Gardener back a little. He was suddenly reminded of a case a few years back, in which someone was killing department store Santas in the middle of Leeds. A compound that left no trace of itself had been used on those victims. It hadn't left very much of the body either.

Fitz's expression suddenly grew grave. "That said, there is something new hitting the streets. I came across it recently. Something that has very similar symptoms to what Sonia Markham might have suffered."

Gardener sat forward, suddenly thinking of the foreign drug dealer, Viktor. "What would that be?"

Fitz returned to his screen and started tapping keys. "I'm not sure. Hold on a minute. Ah, here it is. This new stuff is pretty lethal. They call it Devil Dust."

"Jesus," said Reilly. "Where do they think of these names?"

"What are these similar symptoms?" asked Gardener.

"Fever, headache, cough, sore throat. The people who have taken this sometimes have difficulty breathing.

Vomiting is a popular one. Not severe enough to cause death but it does put you in bed for a few days.

"However," continued Fitz, "symptoms are more severe for victims who have other underlying health problems. Disorientation, drowsiness, or confusion. I've seen two cases where this lethal powder has caused a seizure, and even put one person in a coma."

Fitz stopped staring at his screen and glanced at Gardener. "There is one more thing we've come across that you're going to find interesting."

"Go on," said Gardener.

"In one very rare case, the victim's brain swelled, encephalitis occurred, which led to his death."

"Any idea where this stuff originated?" asked Gardener.

"We don't," said Fitz. "Have a word with narcotics, they should be able to tell you more."

"But correct me if I'm wrong," persisted Gardener. "The autopsies you've done on these victims, you've found traces of this Devil Dust, yes?"

Fitz nodded. "Yes."

"So why is there no trace with Sonia Markham?"

"Only one reason I can think of," replied Fitz.

"That is?" asked Reilly.

"It might be some kind of third generation hybrid – maybe it's been mixed with something new that is not leaving any trace."

As the detectives left, a dozen or more thoughts ran through Gardener's mind; uppermost was an inconclusive post-mortem – nobody liked those, it meant more work.

Chapter Twelve

Disappointed after leaving Fitz, Gardener immediately phoned Briggs and told him what he and Reilly had discovered. He said they would both be back as soon as they could. He felt there was enough of a connection for Briggs to try and pick up something on Viktor, and possibly the new drug on the street – even though no trace had yet been found in Sonia Markham's body.

Gardener entered the station with a feeling of trepidation. Cases were sometimes difficult, but Sonia Markham's death was proving almost impossible to work through. Information had been plentiful, but nothing that would point them in the right direction to solving the mystery.

Once the team had assembled, and drinks and snacks had been distributed, Gardener asked Sharp and Rawson if they had discovered anything.

"In a word, no," said Rawson.

"We covered another floor at The Quays," said Sharp. "Admittedly, it was a different floor to the one they lived on but all we got was the same old story. Few people knew them, and those that did had nothing bad to say about them."

"They appeared to be model tenants," said Rawson, "who kept to themselves. Not work shy, and lived life how they should. One or two recognized Sonia Markham from the TV and referred to her as the girl on *Emmerdale*, though she wasn't a big name."

"And no one was around at the time she was on the Saturday, either leaving or arriving?" asked Gardener.

"No," said Sharp.

Gardener grew frustrated. He turned to Thornton and Anderson, asking what – if anything – they had come up with.

"We tracked down the landlord, Neil Finn," replied Anderson. "Decent enough bloke. Lives in a big posh place in Roundhay."

"He said the same as everyone else," said Thornton. "He'd had no problems with them – either of them. Always paid and never caused him any grief."

"Did he say how long they'd been there?" asked Reilly.

"A little under two years," said Anderson. "They'd ticked all the boxes where renting was concerned. He'd only ever had a couple of callouts for minor problems."

"The usual thing with the ladies," said Thornton. "Shower blocked due to a build up of hair. Nothing that caused any real issues."

"He said he'd be very sorry to lose them," offered Anderson.

"Bit premature, isn't it?" said Reilly. "Technically speaking, Jodie Thomson still lives there."

"But for how long?" asked Anderson. "It's not likely she can afford the rent on her own."

Gardener let that one slide. It wasn't for him to comment on. "I take it we've checked out everything with the utility companies?" he asked. "I'm assuming all bills were up to date?"

Gates and Longstaff nodded and said they had already been through that one. Nothing was outstanding.

Gardener glanced back at Thornton and Anderson and asked about the gym.

"Confirmed she visited twice a week – Tuesday and Friday. The time she spent there depended on what she was doing but the days rarely varied," said Anderson. "She was very dedicated."

"We spoke to other people that used the place," said Thornton. "She sometimes had a drink afterwards with them. But she tended to keep her distance."

"Meaning what?" asked Gardener.

"As in no personal relationships."

Gardener nodded. "She doesn't seem to have entertained personal relationships. Jodie Thomson said there were no special men in her life. She'd had one or two dates but nothing special."

"To Sonia, maybe," said Briggs. "Perhaps we should press Jodie Thomson on these blokes and check them out. Maybe one of them saw it as personal and she didn't. And it didn't sit well with him."

Gardener nodded his approval. He asked someone to check that lead out, before turning his attention to Gates and Longstaff.

"We spoke to the group known as Reelfriends, who were totally devastated," said Gates.

"How many of them were there?" asked Gardener.

"Four including her," said Longstaff. "Met at least once a week, time permitting. She was a great member of the team, knew Christ knows how much about films and TV and actors."

"Even got them all a tour of *Emmerdale* once, and a chance meeting with a number of the stars," added Gates.

"Bet they loved that," said Gardener. "When did they last see her?"

Gates checked her notes. "That would have been last Wednesday night. Sonia had finished her training film early. Went home, got ready, and met them all at The Cottage Road Cinema in Headingley."

"They went to see the new Bill Nighy film, *Living*," said Longstaff. "Then literally all walked around the corner to a Greek Mediterranean restaurant called *Acropolis*."

"I really hate to ask this question," said Gardener, "because I feel like I already know the answer, but how did she seem?"

"Full of the joys, apparently," said Gates. "She'd been working in Roundhay Park that day on some kind of medical safety training film and she was really enjoying it."

"No health problems at all?" asked Gardener.

"Certainly not that they could tell," said Gates. "They said she was glowing, looked radiantly healthy."

"One of them even asked if she was pregnant," said Longstaff.

"She just laughed," said Gates.

Gardener knew she wouldn't have been because Fitz would have said something.

"We also managed to speak with the hairdresser," said Longstaff. "She last saw Sonia two weeks previous. She didn't know her that well, but they got along great – no problems."

"She never complained about anything in the hairdressers chair?" asked Gardener. "That's where it usually all comes out."

"No," said Gates. "Hairdresser never mentioned anything."

"As if there would be," said Gardener. "This is getting ridiculous. What about social media?"

"It pretty much bears out what everyone else has said," offered Longstaff. "There was nothing on Facebook, Twitter or Instagram that related to any problems, or anything that would give us any leads worth following."

"She really didn't have many friends on any of them," said Gates. "Which would suggest they were genuine friends. In fact, we didn't find many people at all outside all of those we've interviewed."

"There were always lots of good photos from a day's shoot," said Longstaff. "But we couldn't find anything that would suggest an argument or a feud of any kind. And to be honest her posts were limited – as in, not many."

"Phones?" asked Gardener, as if he was simply going through the motions.

An eventual check of Sonia's phone and landline numbers revealed everything they'd expected. They'd lost count how many times they had recorded Jodie Thomson's number; there were quite a number of calls from her parents, more from her sister, Polly; and a number of calls on Monday and Tuesday afternoon that turned out to be The Casting Couch, two of which had messages. In the first they were asking where she was; in the second they sounded a little more worried because she had never let them down before.

"We're not really getting anywhere, are we?" asked Gardener, turning to Sharp and Rawson to ask about their visit to the clubs. "Surely you must have something."

"Well, we know she wasn't in Pryzm for very long," said Sharp. "Barman recognized both girls, served them one drink and they left around eleven as far as he could tell. He couldn't say for definite because he was busy, but he never saw them after that time."

"What about The Key Club?"

"There is a bit more from that one," said Rawson. "We have a witness who said she left the club alone at one-thirty in the morning."

"Alone?" asked Gardener, hoping for more, particularly where the mystery man, Alan was concerned.

"And the CCTV backs that up," said Sharp. "The lady we spoke to was called Rachel Stephens. She was outside having a smoke."

"Rachel thought Sonia had had a drink but was not the worse for wear," said Rawson. "She jumped into a taxi." He checked his notes. "Ace Cars, and was taken home."

"Home?" questioned Gardener. "I take it you've spoken to the driver."

Sharp nodded. "He said he dropped her off at The Quays at two o'clock. She seemed quite chatty, paid him and tipped him well and walked in a straight line to the apartment building. He could not see a concierge on duty but he did drive off quickly for another fare."

"So, if she left at one-thirty, and arrived home at two," said Gardener, "that leaves little or no time for a deviation. Everything that's been said and done bears out. Which really leads us back into thinking about the club – did something happen *inside* the club?"

"Something that either involves our mystery man, Alan," said Reilly, "or our drug-dealing friend, Viktor."

Gardener glanced at Sharp and Rawson. "Anything on Alan?"

"Yes and no," said Sharp.

"They did recognize someone from the vague description we had, but it was very little to go on," said Rawson. "Like I said, there could have been twenty blokes in the place who all looked similar, and might have had a similar name. Let's face it, when it's a Saturday night and you're knee deep at the bar, you don't pay attention to faces."

"A photo would help," said Sharp.

"Did any of the bar staff see Sonia Markham with our mystery man?"

"If they did," said Rawson, "they haven't said."

"Did you ask about Viktor?"

"We did," said Sharp. "This is where it gets interesting. Most of the bar staff either claim not to know him, or they clammed up and said they knew very little about him."

"And whatever they knew," said Rawson, "they weren't keen on sharing."

"So, no one saw her talking to Viktor – apart from Jodie Thomson?"

"If they did," answered Rawson, "they're not saying."

Gardener glanced at Briggs. "Have you found anything on this man?"

"Enough to warrant a closer examination."

Chapter Thirteen

"Really?" said Gardener.

"They're a strange pair of characters," said Briggs.

"Aren't they all," said Gardener.

"You must be talking about Arthur too," said Reilly. "Jodie Thomson mentioned him."

Briggs referred to some notes he had with him. "No one really knows where Viktor is from or how long he's been here."

"That's pretty much what Jodie said," offered Reilly.

"Some say Latvia, and five years," said Briggs, rifling through the notes. "Others say Lithuania and ten years. Others claim Russia, but still have no idea how long."

"And the drugs team don't know?" questioned Gardener, a little surprised.

Briggs shook his head. "Apparently, he's never spent a day on remand or in prison, and despite having been arrested, he's never been charged."

"Does he have a surname?" asked Rawson.

"He does," said Briggs, "but we're not sure if it's genuine. We've got Borishenko down."

"Is this new street drug down to him?" asked Gardener. "This stuff they call Devil Dust."

"We don't know for certain," said Briggs. "All narcotics have managed so far is a trail. They believe the drug originates somewhere in Russia, and by the time it reaches these shores it appears to have travelled through a number of Eastern European countries where it's been modified into the stuff that finally comes into Britain."

"And can they connect him to it?" asked Sharp.

"No," said Briggs. "Like I said, he's never spent a day inside. He's like an eel. But everyone knows that's down to Arthur Pierrepoint, his unscrupulous lawyer, who's as bent as they come."

"What do we know about *him*?" asked Gardener.

"He was jailed for four years for money laundering offences, but he has since been readmitted to the roll after the SDT, the Solicitors Disciplinary Tribunal, found he'd been totally rehabilitated."

"Are you serious?" asked Reilly. "People like him are never rehabilitated."

"There might be something in what you say," said Briggs. "Seems the move was opposed by the SRA, the Solicitors Regulation Authority. They reckoned that limited evidence of recent rehabilitation had to be balanced against Pierrepoint's conviction for serious offences involving money laundering in relation to drug dealing."

"Does that surprise anyone?" asked Anderson, glancing around.

"What did he do?" asked Gardener, wondering which of the two was the more dangerous. According to Jodie Thomson, Viktor never went anywhere without Arthur, so who was really running the show?

"He was apparently involved in assisting a drug dealer to launder the proceeds of crime through various conveyancing transactions," said Briggs. "The trial judge said that Pierrepoint failed to report glaringly obvious suspicious transactions, and also criticized him for not giving evidence."

"I don't know why they do that," said Gates. "It never helps their case, does it?"

"Where did all this happen?" asked Gardener.

"He was convicted at Leeds Crown Court in 2009," said Briggs, "on one count of money laundering, and two counts of failing to disclose knowledge or suspicion of money laundering."

"And he was struck off when?" asked Gardener.

"2012, by the SDT, after he was found to have acted with a lack of integrity, but not dishonesty."

"Not dishonesty?" shouted Reilly. "Who makes this stuff up? How can you be money laundering and failing to disclose knowledge of it and not be considered dishonest?"

"That's why we're in the state we're in," said Rawson.

"The SDT reckoned that he had utilized his time well while he was in prison, by helping to teach fellow inmates English and maths."

"I'll bet he did," said Reilly. "They all probably came out with degrees so they knew how to do it again and not get caught."

"The SDT claimed the tribunal was satisfied that this was one of that narrow category of cases where there *was* a route back into the profession for those who had made demonstrable, credible and real steps to rehabilitate themselves as the applicant had done. But don't shoot the messenger, I'm only reading what's here."

"When did he get back into it?" asked Anderson.

"He first applied in 2017, but the SDT rejected the application, partly because it was made only six years after the strike-off."

"Oh, they had something about them, then," said Reilly.

"Maybe," said Gardener. "But they must have let him back in at some point."

"Pretty much when he actually did give evidence, before the last tribunal panel. Pierrepoint said he had been mentored by his barrister Sergei Kominsky, who had acted for him since 2012, and helped him realize that he had excused and minimized his role in the crimes."

"Sergei Kominsky," repeated Longstaff. "That says it all. Who was that, Viktor?"

"He really laid it on thick," said Briggs. "Pierrepoint agreed that, at the time of his first application, he had not accepted the basis of the conviction, but now does so without question."

"How much money were we talking?" asked Gardener.

"Something in the region of £425,000," replied Briggs. "Pierrepoint said he had reacquired integrity he had lost over a decade ago.

"The SDT imposed conditions on his practicing certificate, preventing him from being a sole practitioner, a partner or manager of a law firm, a COLP or COFA or holding client money. It appears that Arthur is still practicing but Viktor is his only customer. He's slippery."

"You'd have to be," said Gardener, "to be able to get away with stuff like that, particularly with such large sums of money."

"Where did the money go?" asked Reilly.

"It wasn't recovered to my knowledge," said Briggs.

"It wouldn't take a genius to work out where it is," said Anderson.

"Let's go back to the elusive Viktor," said Gardener. "Do we have an address?"

"We do," said Briggs. "He's obviously not short of a bob or two. His registered address is Ambler Mansion, Park Avenue, Roundhay."

"Roundhay?" repeated Gardener. "That's interesting. Sonia Markham was seen talking to Viktor in the club and she had a two day shoot last week in Roundhay, and that's where he lives."

"It's tenuous," said Briggs. "But I'll grant you, it is a link."

"Even so," offered Reilly. "Her flatmate doesn't buy the drugs thing. She reckoned Sonia Markham really looked after herself and wouldn't touch the stuff."

"With the greatest of respect," said Gates. "Even if you're close family, you wouldn't know everything."

"Maybe Sonia Markham wasn't taking drugs," offered Longstaff. "But that doesn't mean she wasn't selling them.

She might have crossed Viktor, maybe that's what they were talking about in the club."

Gardener accepted what was being said. "Even so, her lifestyle doesn't appear to allow her much time for selling drugs – although it could have been done covertly. On top of that, we've interviewed a lot of people, no one has even accused her of the slightest wrongdoing."

"What did Fitz have to say?" asked Briggs. "Surely he must have tested for drugs."

"He doesn't have anything to report," said Gardener. "He's found absolutely nothing other than her brain having been swollen. He's not sure what's caused that, so the best thing he could do was send tissue samples away for toxicology."

"He might find something there," said Briggs. "What about where she works?"

"The Casting Couch," said Gardener. "Same story. Everybody loved her, said she was a delight to work with. From what we've heard, I can't really believe she would have anything to do with drugs, or this Viktor character."

"Certainly doesn't sound like it," said Briggs.

Silence descended on the room; the kind that suggested evidence was thin on the ground.

"Are we looking for something that isn't there?" said Sharp, eventually.

"What do you mean?" asked Gardener.

"Has she even been killed?" asked Sharp.

Gardener could not actually answer that question. "I can see where you're coming from. Maybe she did simply go home and die of natural causes."

After another short silence, Briggs said, "But?"

Gardener glanced at him. "I keep thinking about DI Stott. He said that something about the situation was not right."

"Copper's instinct," said Reilly.

"It's not something you can ignore," said Briggs. "What's your take on it?" he asked Gardener.

After a pause, the SIO said, "I'm inclined to agree with him. I have enough reasons to keep going for a while longer: a dead girl, an inconclusive PM, a drug dealer, and a mystery man. I think there is more to the situation, and we're going to have to look under a lot of rocks, but my gut feeling is, it will pay off."

"So where do you want to go now?" asked Briggs.

"We can't give up," said Gardener. "At least not until Fitz comes back with the results. And she *was* seen talking to Viktor in the club, so we really need to know what that was about."

Gardener turned and updated the whiteboard, before facing his team. "With that in mind, I would like the ladies to visit *Emmerdale* and the people involved in the Roundhay training film. We have all the contact details, go and find out what you can about her week's filming."

"Oh no, sir, we can't be having any of that," said Rawson.

"What are you on about, meathead?" said Gates.

"You two are IT specialists. We can't have you going off to film sets. That needs to be a more experienced officer." Rawson was smirking.

"Like you, you mean," said Longstaff. "No woman on that set will be safe if we let you loose."

"I don't know what that's supposed to mean." Rawson faced Gardener. "Tell 'em, boss."

Gardener smiled. "Nothing to do with me, Dave. Office politics and all that." He glanced at Sharp. "Colin, do me a favour, please. Will you phone Jodie Thomson and get the details of Sonia Markham's doctor, and ask if she can remember anything else regarding our mystery man, Alan?"

Sharp left the room and returned within a few minutes with a possible glimmer of hope. He had the doctor's details.

"Anything on the mystery man?" asked Gardener.

"Not much," replied Sharp. "Jodie still can't really remember what he looked like, but one thing that has come to mind is a shirt he was wearing. It was white with some kind of red V-shaped pattern running down the front."

"That's something," said Gardener. "Not much but someone else might remember it." He turned to DCI Briggs. "Did anything come of the press release?"

"Nothing so far."

Gardener asked if he would run another. The one scrap of information about the shirt might make a difference.

He turned back to Anderson and Thornton. "Bob, Frank, can you go and speak to Sonia Markham's doctor, see if he or she can tell us anything that might help with what we're investigating?"

He turned his attention to Rawson and Sharp. "Likewise, can you pop back to the clubs with that extra information? The shirt might ring a bell, it is the kind of thing that might stand out, get noticed."

"What about you and Sean?" asked Briggs.

"I think it's high time we paid Viktor a visit," said Gardener. "I realize we can't question him about drugs, but he *was* in the club the night Sonia Markham died, and he *was* seen talking to her. That's good enough for me.

"Meanwhile," continued Gardener. "When you all have the time, let's keep looking at Viktor. See what else we can find out about him."

Chapter Fourteen

"Something's bothering you," said Vanessa Chambers. "You're not yourself. Is it the case?"

She passed Gardener a cup of tea and then sat down with her own.

"It's a real puzzle."

"Try me."

Gardener and his new girlfriend were sitting opposite each other over the breakfast bar in her kitchen which was a mixture of old and new. Pine shelves with old fashioned jars, an Aga, utensils hanging from beams, with pans on hooks, hanging down the walls. The modern side of the room included a DAB radio, LED lighting and a number of labour-saving devices positioned all over the place. Walls were tiled and the floor was wood. He liked it.

"I'm not supposed to talk about it," he replied, without conviction.

"I know," replied Vanessa. "But don't you just love breaking rules?"

He laughed. "You're a bad influence on me."

"About time someone was. I've been dying to see the devil in you for ages."

Gardener smiled and explained in detail the events of the past few days and the real mystery it had created.

"And you're quite sure she hasn't died of some natural cause?" asked Vanessa.

"I'm not convinced."

"Has Fitz said anything?" As she asked the question she reached up to a shelf and pulled down a large jar full of oatmeal biscuits. After removing the lid, she helped herself and pushed the jar towards Gardener.

"Not yet. He's sent off samples." Gardener reached in. He couldn't resist an oatmeal biscuit.

"Fitz is puzzled?" said Vanessa, her expression of disbelief. "That's really unusual."

"Tell me about it."

"But you're not happy about it being classed as a natural death, are you? I can tell."

"No." He shook his head, and grabbed another biscuit. He rolled off all the reasons he had given Briggs. "Something's nagging me about this. Something that James Stott said keeps rolling round my head."

"What did he say?"

"Not a great deal, other than the fact that something seemed wrong. Stott had what we call a copper's instinct."

"And that's something you don't go against?"

"You learn not to. You can't use it in a court of law and it's very hard to argue your point if that's all you have. But we all understand the feeling, so we won't discard it."

"I get it," said Vanessa. "We botanists pretty much run by the same rules. Once you've been in the game a long time, instinct is a pretty strong feeling. I'm sure you'll sort it. Anyway, how are your dad and Chris?"

A good diversion tactic, thought Gardener.

"Chris is fine," he replied. "He called me last night. He's still in London, still studying to be a solicitor, and loving it."

"You must be a proud dad."

"I am. He could so easily have gone the other way after what happened with Sarah."

Vanessa leaned over the breakfast bar and covered his hand with hers. "Be thankful it didn't, and live for the moment."

He smiled with his eyes. "My dad, however, is lost."

"I get that as well. How long has he lived with you?"

"A few years now. I remember him being lost when my mum died all those years ago, but he had me to look after, which focused him. What with his job and me he had little or no time to worry about the future."

"He did a good job."

"Then eventually, I left home and did all the usual stuff: job, married, then Chris came along. It was after Sarah died that he came to live with us. He'd retired by then and he was fed up of rattling around in *that* house, as he put it. Now he's back to square one – on his own in *my* house."

"He's bound to be feeling it. *You* can't control when you're home and neither can Chris. So, he's back to rattling."

"I know," replied Gardener. "And it bothers me."

"We should take him out more," said Vanessa, excited. "Make a fuss of him, treat him, make him feel special… because he is. Look what he's done for you and Chris. And I know how much you appreciate him, and how it must be getting to you that you can't spend more time with him. So that's what we're going to do, we're going to make him feel wanted in his twilight years."

Gardener didn't know what to say, until eventually, he found the right words. "You're a wonderful woman, Vanessa Chambers."

"I know." She smiled. "Even though I *am* a bad influence."

"Modest with it."

"Which is why I've found myself a wonderful man."

Gardener flushed. He didn't deal with compliments very well. "So, where shall we take him, and when? Strike while the iron is hot. Job permitting."

"Okay," she said. "Well, we know he likes gardens. What else is he interested in?"

"Films. He never stops watching films. What he doesn't know about them isn't worth knowing. If he hadn't been a landscape gardener, I'm sure he'd have been an actor."

"Okay, so we can take him to the cinema and the theatre. But maybe he'd be interested in somewhere else, perhaps somewhere I've wanted to go for ages."

"Where's that?"

"A place called Tropical World."

"I don't think I've heard of that," he said. "Where is it?"

"Tropical World?" she repeated. "It sounds amazing. It's a butterfly house and an animal attraction. It's a licensed zoo as well, with an amazing collection of tropical plants. It's over in Roundhay."

The mention of Roundhay struck a chord with Gardener. "What else is there?"

She grabbed another biscuit and reached over to switch the kettle on for more tea. "It's got a great history to it. Started in 1911 as a conservatory building named the Coronation House. It was built in the Canal Gardens of Roundhay Park.

"It's a major attraction, with several climate-controlled glass houses, each replicating a tropical environment from around the world. The houses have tropical plants and live animals, including some which roam freely, such as butterflies and turtles.

"And all sorts of amazing things. Terrapins and koi in various ponds, Morelet's crocodiles, both freshwater and marine species, including poison dart frogs, and red-bellied piranhas."

"Are you sure it's open to the public with all that stuff?" joked Gardener, knowing if anything was going to happen it would be to him.

"Of course it is," she replied, "and safe as houses. They have a tumbling waterfall, tropical fish, and reptile displays, including snakes, lizards and iguanas."

"Sounds amazing," said Gardener, not too sure about his statement.

"The big thing is the rainforest canopy, with free-flying birds; a desert house with a mob of meerkats. And a nocturnal house with armadillos, rats, and bats.

"But don't worry, they also have a cafe overlooking the Canal Gardens and a gift shop at the entrance."

"Are you sure you haven't been to this place?" asked Gardener. "I think you're right, though. This is just what my dad needs, a family day out. He'll love it."

"And I'm hoping you can persuade Reilly and his wife, Laura, to go. I'd love to get to know them better."

Gardener laughed. That was a first. "That would depend."

"On what?"

"How well-stocked on food they are."

Chapter Fifteen

Jodie Thomson was sitting with Sonia Markham's parents in the lounge of their house in Lakeland Crescent, Alwoodley. She could remember the room having been freshly decorated only a few weeks previous, and it still had that new smell, particularly of leather, as the Markhams had decided to treat themselves to two large sofas.

The carpet was pale green, the new wallpaper a shade darker. They had also splashed out on a log burner, which was currently crackling away. Gone, however, was the atmosphere of a month previous. The large, flatscreen TV on the wall was switched off, and there was no soothing music in the background.

Jodie sipped tea from a mug before placing it back on one of the two pine coffee tables. "I can't believe what's happened. I'm so sorry."

"Thank you, love," replied Sonia's mother. Angela Markham was forty-eight years old with straight, shoulder-length blonde hair, blue eyes and a lined complexion.

"Please let me know if there is anything I can do, Mrs Markham."

"Oh, Jodie, love, how long have you known us?" asked Angela. "You shouldn't be calling me Mrs Markham. It's Angela, and always should be."

Jodie allowed the tears to fall. "I just feel responsible. I should have been at home, not on some stupid course."

"Don't you go blaming yourself, love," said Will. "I'll not have that." His skin was ashen because he had taken

Sonia's death very badly. Of the two, Angela appeared to be coping much better, perhaps because of her devout religious upbringing, and the belief that the Lord would take care of everything.

"How are *you* coping?" asked Angela.

"Badly," replied Jodie. "I can't eat, I can't sleep. I haven't been to work since it happened. It's as if I'm blaming work, for being on the course when I should have been at home."

"Why?" asked Angela. "It wouldn't have mattered. You couldn't have done anything. All of these things are pre-ordained."

"No," said Jodie. "If I'd been at home, it might have made a difference."

"How?" asked Will, finishing his tea.

A sudden image of Sonia came to Jodie's mind. She was so happy on the Saturday night before going out. The pair of them had dressed to the nines. They were laughing and joking over an early drink, giddy. They were making arrangements to have a holiday later in the year. They *could* afford it, having saved enough. And very early plans for Christmas.

And bang, it had all ended in an instant. What did they have now?

"I would have spotted some signs," argued Jodie. "Called an ambulance, stayed with her, helped her when she most needed it. Instead, she died on her own. Oh my God, if only I'd been there."

Will reached forward and pressed on Jodie's hand. "You mustn't blame yourself, love. There might have been absolutely nothing you could do. She might have died before the ambulance got there anyway. You know what waiting times are like these days."

Jodie glanced at Will, full of sorrow and heartache. "But she wouldn't have died alone, would she, Will?"

No one had an answer to that one. It took quite a few moments of recollection before Angela spoke out.

"The coroner will find out what happened."

"Yes," said Will. "They're very good at this sort of stuff nowadays. All that DNA technology. They'll find an explanation."

Angela leaned forward. "You should concentrate on yourself. Have you thought about what you'll do now?"

"How do you mean?" asked Jodie.

"How will you cope in the apartment on your own?"

Jodie hadn't thought about that. It was a beautiful place but it was so expensive. "I might have to give it up."

"That would be such a shame," said Angela, close to tears herself. "You and our Sonia loved that place. You both worked bloody hard for a slice of luxury and you bloody well deserved it. We were so proud of the pair of you when you managed to rent it. You'd set your hearts on the place."

"I know." Jodie reached for a tissue to wipe away the tears. "But even if I could afford it, do I really want to be there, after what I've seen?"

"I can understand that," said Angela. "But you mustn't do anything rash. You might feel differently in a month or so."

"Oh, I don't know," replied Jodie.

"I'm sure our Sonia would want you to keep it. Maybe when we've had the funeral and we've had some closure…"

Angela could not finish that sentence. She broke down in floods of tears herself. Will reached over and put his arm around her shoulder. "Come on, love. We'll get through this."

Angela didn't reply, but her expression said she was trying to believe her husband.

He stood up and collected the mugs and offered to make more tea, as if that was the answer.

By the time he returned, Angela had recomposed herself.

"Can I ask you a question, Jodie, love?" said Will.

"Of course," she replied.

"Is there is anything you can think of that happened on the night, anything that might have caused her death?"

Jodie paused, wondering how much of her personal opinions she should actually divulge, but then said, "Not that I can think of."

"Are you sure?" asked Will. "You seemed to hesitate, as if there might be something."

Jodie stared at him, agonizingly, eventually realizing that it would all come out anyway. "I did see her talking to someone."

"What do you mean?" asked Angela. "Talking to who? Someone who might have had something to do with this?"

"I wouldn't say directly responsible," replied Jodie, "but he has quite a reputation."

"Who is it?" asked Will, his expression having darkened.

Jodie mentioned Viktor's name.

"And who is Viktor?" asked Angela, staring at Will, as if he might know.

Jodie told them what she knew about Viktor, and what he was up to.

Sonia's parents were momentarily stunned.

"Do you mean our Sonia was taking drugs?" asked Angela.

"No," said Jodie. "Nothing like that. I just saw them talking."

"Talking how?" asked Will. "Calmly, or was there a problem? Why do you think this Viktor could be involved, especially if she wasn't taking drugs?"

"Oh, I can't believe this," said Angela. "I know my daughter, there is no way she would have been taking drugs."

"She wasn't," said Jodie. "I would have known."

"But yet you still have a reason to mention it," said Will. "Why?"

Jodie hesitated. Trouble was, it was out now, and she was going to have to finish what she started.

"You remember Pippa, my sister."

"We do, love," said Angela. "And what happened to her was just awful. We were so sorry for you."

"Pippa died two years ago, and there isn't a day goes by when I don't think of her."

"Wait a minute," said Will. "Was this Viktor responsible for Pippa's death?"

Again, Jodie hesitated.

Will sat up ramrod straight. "You have to tell us, Jodie."

Jodie had to relive the moment. "The last person to see Pippa was me. It was Christmas Day, sometime after lunch. I was really worried that she hadn't returned any of my texts or phone calls. I had to use my own spare key to get in to her place."

Jodie stopped speaking, staring into space.

Eventually, Will said, "And?"

"I found Pippa face down on the bathroom floor in her own vomit. I called for an ambulance straight away, but it was way too late. Pippa had already died."

Angela came and sat beside Jodie and held her hand. Sonia's mother couldn't have known about it because it was the first time Jodie had spoken about it, to anyone.

"The coroner's report was awful," continued Jodie. "He was concerned that Pippa's death had been linked to a designer drug. A number of Leeds based newspapers had been reporting the serious issues connected to the dangers linked to these designer drugs. The popular belief was that they had been created in labs to mimic the effects of a number of established drugs."

"Like what?" asked Angela.

"Cannabis, amphetamines, cocaine, and maybe heroin," replied Jodie.

"You must feel cursed," said Will. "First your sister, and now our Sonia."

"And you blame this Viktor chap?" asked Angela.

Jodie turned and stared at Angela. "I was completely devastated by it. But I was also confused. I knew Pippa would never touch drugs. At least, that's what I believed."

Jodie stopped talking, her tears rolled. "But the post-mortem said otherwise. So, did I really know my sister as well as I thought? I just couldn't understand how they ended up in her system."

"So, what happened then?" asked Will.

Jodie noticed his fists clenching and unclenching.

"I couldn't accept the verdict of accidental death. After Pippa's funeral, I started my own investigation. Some time after the event, I spoke to someone called Eve, who said she had seen Pippa outside the club with a few other girls, ten minutes before her taxi arrived."

Jodie had stopped talking again, so Will egged her on.

"Eve said they were talking to a foreign man, and money was seen changing hands for packets of white powder. She couldn't say whether or not Pippa had bought drugs, because she didn't stick around. What she did know was that the dealer had a nasty reputation and she had no desire to cross him for fear of ending up dead.

"She gave me a description, but then she clammed up as though she'd said too much already at that point. She was not prepared to give his name. But a member of staff in the club, who was not so frightened, did. He only knew the man was called Viktor."

"The bastard," said Will. "What is wrong with these people?"

"Did you tell the police?" asked Angela.

"Yes."

"And?"

"I've no idea. Viktor was questioned, but he walked, which was obviously down to Arthur, his smarmy lawyer."

Will Markham left the room without comment.

Chapter Sixteen

The large, double gates to Ambler Mansion were open, so Reilly took the pool car down a tree-lined drive to the house, which had to be at least half a mile from the road. A fountain stood in the middle of a circular parking area in front of the building. The house was three storeys high with a grey slate roof, covered with solar panels. The width of the house appeared to be at least that of three normal houses, with turrets dividing each section, making four altogether.

Gardener and Reilly left the car and the first thing they noticed were two stone lions sitting on supporting columns either side of the steps leading to the front door. Standing to the side of those were two human Rottweilers, both at least six feet five inches tall and wider than the stone columns supporting the lions.

Gardener had already done his homework, and knew exactly how big the house was and how much it was worth. Ambler Mansion on Park Avenue in Roundhay, was an eight-bedroom house on multiple levels, with three kitchens, five bathrooms, a swimming pool, a gymnasium, a terraced patio, two double garages and extensive grounds, with under-floor central heating. Outside one of the garages was what appeared to be a brand-new Bentley with a private registration; inside, also on a private registration, was a Maserati of some description.

Gardener displayed his warrant card, and introduced them both. Without speaking, the guards turned and walked up to the front door. Once through the entrance, they were led through a marbled hall, and then into a huge lounge with a large-screen TV fixed to the wall, two sofas facing each other, with tables in between. An open fire maintained a nice heat in the room. The décor was minimal with pastel-coloured walls and carpet, and more examples of fine art than Gardener had ever seen in a private home.

"Viktor will be with you shortly. Please take a seat."

That said, both men left.

"How much do you think all this is worth?" Reilly asked his boss.

"How it's been paid for would be the more interesting question," replied Gardener.

"I think we both know the answer to that."

"You can never really prove it, though, can you, Sean," said Gardener. "And the thing is, we can't really question him on that."

"You wouldn't get a straight answer anyway."

Before the conversation went any further, Viktor walked in, dressed in only a large towel, wrapped tightly around his frame, which was six feet three inches of solid muscle. He had jet-black hair, cut short. His complexion resembled a large piece of granite, chiselled from marble. His face was lined, weatherbeaten. Gardener immediately noticed a scar, running from his right ear, closing in towards his eye and down his cheek to his mouth.

"Gentlemen, please, take seat, allow me to change."

Reilly went straight in. "That's a nasty looking scar you have there, my friend."

Viktor smiled. "You should see the other guy. Please take seat, I'll be back."

Without warning, a gargantuan man, who Gardener took to be Arthur, rushed into the room in chef whites, carrying a large silver tray with, judging by the smell, a freshly made quiche.

"Viktor, I've cracked it."

"Cracked what?"

"Oh, I'm so sorry," said Arthur, spotting the other people. "I didn't realize we had visitors."

"The police," said Viktor.

Arthur's mood changed instantly. Without saying another word, he backed out of the room, taking the quiche with him. Viktor followed, leaving Gardener and Reilly to their own devices.

"Whatever the hell he'd cracked smelled nice," said Reilly.

"What's going on there, then?" asked Gardener. "That looked to me like the infamous Arthur Pierrepoint. I thought he was a lawyer."

"Unless he has a twin brother," offered Reilly.

"That would be some shopping bill."

"Don't think the cost-of-living crisis will bother this lot, do you?" asked Reilly.

Both men returned reasonably quickly. Arthur was dressed in a pale blue business suit with white shirt and blue tie, and was carrying a briefcase. Viktor was dressed in a grey suit of the finest cut with a black shirt and grey tie and very expensive shoes.

The transformation was unbelievable, thought Gardener, signifying to him that the pair of them really were taking the visit seriously.

Before they were all seated, another staff member popped in with drinks and some of the infamous quiche that Reilly had been so disappointed to see leave with Arthur.

"Gentlemen," said Arthur. "Please, help yourselves to drinks, and do sample a piece of that lovely quiche I made this morning."

"Have you been having problems with it, Arthur, old son?" said Viktor.

"I have with this one," said Arthur. "Couldn't get it to set properly. Now, how can we be of assistance to you?"

Arthur had quickly changed the course of the meeting. He opened his briefcase, which was full of all sorts of paraphernalia.

Gardener explained in detail the reason for the visit. He also explained that, with their permission, he would like to ask a few questions about the night in question.

Arthur had him repeat everything twice, whilst he wrote it all down. Gardener knew very well that the man was not incompetent, he was simply trying to wind them up. Gardener was not biting.

So far, other than his first appearance, Viktor had yet to speak. Gardener was going to change all that as he addressed him personally.

"Viktor Borishenko is your full name?"

Viktor nodded.

"And this is your current address."

Viktor nodded again. Arthur said nothing but watched them both like a hawk, as if he'd figured out that Reilly may well eat more of the quiche than he could.

"How long have you lived here, Mr Borishenko?"

"Ten years." Nothing more was said.

"Why here?" asked Gardener.

"I like it."

"Wouldn't you?" asked Arthur. "It's beautiful, very conducive to our lifestyle. Viktor likes to get away from the rat race, relax a little."

"That doesn't sound good," said Reilly. "How does he earn his living?" He faced Arthur with the question, which Gardener found amusing.

Arthur answered Gardener, as if Reilly didn't matter, or he was snubbing him because he was currently on his second piece of quiche.

"He doesn't need to earn a living. He has family money, and the family look after him very well."

"Where are the family based?" asked Gardener.

"Moscow," replied Viktor.

If it was true, that might have answered a question that no one else seemed to know, but Gardener somehow doubted it. "So how *do* you pass your time?"

"Look around you, Mr Gardener," said Arthur. "Viktor has a very extensive art collection. Which earns him a very good living – should he actually need to make additional money – which passes his time nicely."

Gardener went in for the kill. "Going back to the night in question, and the reason we're here, can you tell us where you were?"

"Visiting clubs," said Viktor.

"Which ones?" asked Reilly.

Viktor glanced at Arthur, who made a show of consulting a list and then mentioned them all. There were in total, six, two of which were Pryzm and The Key Club in Leeds.

"That's a lot of places for one night," said Reilly. "Why so many?"

"Viktor is very popular," said Arthur. "He has a lot of friends and they all like to see him. He buys them drinks and they appreciate it."

"How do they appreciate it?" asked Reilly.

"I think we're straying from the point, gentlemen," said Arthur, with a tone forceful enough to suggest that no more would be forthcoming on that subject.

Gardener passed over a photo. "Do either of you know the girl in the photo?"

Both replied they didn't.

"You've not seen her before?" Gardener asked Viktor.

"Apart from newspaper," said Viktor. "The dead girl."

"But you don't know her, and you've not seen her before?" pressed Gardener.

"No."

"We have a witness who says they saw you talking to her, in The Key Club. Do you remember now?"

"Mr Gardener," said Arthur, "Viktor talks to a lot of people–"

Gardener shut him down. "I'm talking to Viktor, not you."

He faced the Russian. "Do you remember speaking to her?"

"Not particularly. As my lawyer say, I talk to many people."

Gardener thought he might try and catch him out. "What did you talk about?"

Viktor was too sharp. "How do I know, if I can't remember her? Six clubs, all busy, lots of people. No one stood out. I do not know the girl."

Gardener realized he would need CCTV of them talking if he was to take it any further.

"What time did you leave The Key Club?"

"About midnight," replied Arthur.

Gardener made a mental note to try and check the CCTV and press for witnesses.

"Where did you go when you left the club?"

"Here," replied Arthur.

"Where were you on the following days: the Sunday, Monday, and the Tuesday?"

"Home," replied Viktor. He turned to Arthur. "Go get the CCTV, so the policemen can watch."

Arthur left the room. Viktor remained completely silent, as if unwilling to be drawn into anything without the presence of the big man.

Gardener knew he had nothing on which to hold him, or anything to take the case into another direction.

Arthur returned with a USB stick. "It's all on there."

He suddenly reached into the briefcase and pulled out a box that resembled something medical. He extracted and pulled on a pair of gloves. He then towered over Viktor. "Open your mouth."

Viktor obliged. Arthur ran a swab around the inside, placed it in a sealed container and passed it to Gardener.

"What are you doing?" asked Gardener.

"That, gentlemen, is a sample of Viktor's DNA."

Arthur then made a show of taking Viktor's prints and passed them over as well.

"You'll be needing these to prove my client's innocence. He does not know the girl, he cannot remember talking to her, but if he did, that is not a crime. And once you've lifted all the prints from the scene of the crime, I think you'll find my client's are not present."

Gardener immediately noticed the use of the word "client". The interview had changed again.

"Now, gentlemen," said Arthur. "If there is nothing else, I'm afraid we need to be somewhere."

They were quickly ushered outside.

Gardener and Reilly approached their own vehicle.

"What do you make of that?" Reilly asked Gardener.

He faced his sergeant before opening the passenger door of the vehicle. "The point is, Sean, that Viktor didn't *need* to be in the apartment if he had sold drugs to Sonia Markham, which may have caused an allergic reaction."

"And that's the problem," said Reilly. "Fitz hasn't yet found anything. And if the Godfather in there did sell drugs to Sonia Markham, we still need to prove it."

"I know," said Gardener. "And all we have left will be the results of the toxicology tissues. Everything is going to hinge on what Fitz tells us."

"And if that's nothing, then what?"

Gardener didn't have an answer.

Chapter Seventeen

A couple of hours after the police had left, Viktor summoned everyone into the office for a meeting. His mood was volcanic and things needed sorting out. He left the kitchen, crossed the marble hall, walked through the lounge and into his study, where he opened another door to what appeared to be another room.

It wasn't. It was a lift.

Viktor hit the "B" button and the lift took him two floors down. The door opened onto a tiled corridor and he quietly and purposefully strolled its length to the door at the end, passing more doors along the way.

Once inside the room he had chosen for the meeting, he noticed everyone had gathered. It would have been foolish not to. The two human Rottweilers were standing at the back of room and, Arthur, having returned to his chef whites, was munching on home-made cookies. Viktor closed the door. He crossed the room and sat in a leather chair behind the dark oak desk, with more expensive works of art adorning the walls.

"We have work," he said. "Anyone know what about?"

They each remained silent, but Viktor knew that they'd know why he had summoned them.

"I want to know who has been talking. Why are police coming here about this dead girl? It was nothing to do with me."

"They were here because you were seen talking to her, Viktor," replied Arthur. "Standard operating procedure. *Can* you remember the girl, and what you talked about?"

Viktor shrugged and raised his hands. "Yes, she's in TV or something."

"Anything else?" asked Arthur.

"Snooty bitch told me to do one."

"She said that?"

"No," replied Viktor. "Not like that, but obvious she did not want to speak to me."

Apart from the people in the room it was deathly quiet and rather cold, chilled almost.

"Why?" asked Arthur. "Did you try and sell her drugs?"

"No. She was with someone else. She didn't want to be seen talking to me."

"And you accepted that?"

Viktor reared up from the desk, as if he had personally been insulted. "I am not a fucking monster. If they don't want to talk, they don't want to talk. There are plenty of other girls. I don't need the attention."

Viktor returned to his seat. "But now I have attention, from the wrong people." He jumped up again and started pacing, staring at his henchmen, Ygor and Boris. "Where did we go? Clubs, clubs, I want names. Come on, where did we go?"

"After Dark and Reflex in Wakefield," said Boris, the larger of the two, though it was difficult to tell.

"Time?" demanded Viktor.

"Around nine."

"Around nine?" repeated Viktor. "Be more precise. The police want to nail me."

"Okay, okay," said Ygor. "It was nine."

"Too early," said Viktor. "We're okay, nothing happened there. What time we leave?"

"9:45."

"Good. Where else we go?"

"Into Keighley," said Arthur.

"Where to?" Viktor sat back down.

"Bar 61 and K2," said Ygor, still unsettled, judging by the slight movements he was making. Good, it was how Viktor wanted them – unsettled. *He* was fucking unsettled.

"What time we leave?"

"10:45."

"Then we were in Leeds, at Pryzm and Key? What happened in the Key?" Viktor stared at the Rottweilers. "Either of you know the girl who is dead?"

Both shook their heads in unison.

"Either of you see the girl who is dead?"

Both agreed they had at some point.

"Some point? Some point?" scolded Viktor. "No good to me. When?"

"About eleven," replied Boris.

"Who was she with?"

"She was talking to you."

Viktor stepped back and glared over the top of Arthur, which was no mean feat. "You want a smack in the fucking mouth? I know she talked to me. Idiot. Who else?"

The pair of them thought about it. "She was with another girl, for some time."

"Who?" Viktor demanded.

"We don't know," replied Ygor.

"Find out."

"How?" asked Boris, moving forward.

Viktor scowled at him and he immediately stepped back. "You think that is my problem? What do I pay you for? Was she with anyone else?"

"Yes," said Ygor. "That idiot in the white shirt with the red stripe."

"Who is he?"

"We don't know," replied Boris. "We have seen him before but we don't know him."

"Where you see him?" Viktor asked.

"Most of the nightclubs we go in," replied Ygor.

"Good. Find him," said Viktor. "Should be easy. I want his name, where he lives, where he works, what he had for fucking breakfast the next morning."

"Do we have any pictures of these people you want finding?" asked Boris.

"Who do you think I am?" shouted Viktor, throwing his arms in the air. "Lord fucking Snowden? What do you think, I take pictures of everyone I speak to? Go back to clubs every night from now on, until for fucking ever if you have to. Work day and night. Speak to everyone. Find out who talked to the police. I want to know, and when you do, I want them here, day or night. No one does this to Viktor and gets away with it. I want them here. We'll interrogate them, and find out what they told the police."

Quite some time passed in silence before Ygor spoke. "What if we don't find them, boss?"

Viktor stared daggers. "Then find yourself a new country to live in, because wherever you are in this one, I *will* find you. And when I do…"

The sentence remained unfinished but everyone knew how it ended. Boris and Ygor left the room, leaving Viktor alone with Arthur, who was currently inspecting his nails.

"Can you believe this?" Viktor said to Arthur.

"I wouldn't worry about it, Viktor. They have nothing on you. It's a fishing expedition."

Viktor took his seat behind the desk again, leaning forward, staring at Arthur and speaking quietly. "When they start fishing, they drag up other crap in the net, and they find things out, and then they stick their noses into my business."

"Which is why we cooperated," said Arthur, labouring the point. "They didn't expect us to supply them with your DNA – which they no doubt already have – and your fingerprints, but they got them. They won't find anything, because we didn't do anything. That's why they will leave you alone."

Arthur stood up.

"I'm going back to the kitchen." He walked to the door, but suddenly turned. "Three pieces of quiche that copper shovelled down his throat. Three! Did you notice?"

Viktor stood up, agitated. "You think I'm blind? Of course, I noticed. Why worry? You have more."

"Not the point," muttered Arthur, quietly, like a sullen child.

Chapter Eighteen

Gardener and Reilly entered the pathology lab and walked straight through to the office. Fitz had phoned them earlier in the day to let them know he had something for them, which Gardener thought may possibly be the one shining light so far, the helping hand they needed.

The office was quiet. Richard, Fitz's lanky assistant, was cleaning up the lab on the promise of an early finish.

They each took a seat and the elderly pathologist removed his half-lens spectacles, rubbed his eyes, ran his hands down his face and put the glasses back on.

"How's your day been?" he asked Gardener.

Reilly was back on his feet, helping himself to coffee, and anything else he could find.

"About as good as yours by the look of it," replied Gardener.

"The case isn't progressing?" asked Fitz.

"Not the way we'd like it to," replied Reilly, dishing out coffees for all of them, but holding on to a chocolate bar for himself.

"Everywhere we go is a dead end," said Gardener. "Everyone we speak to has nothing but good to say about Sonia Markham. Everything we have investigated connected to their night out stacks up: the time she left the club, the time she arrived back home, the journey in between. There are no contradictions, or anything that we can pursue."

"How is Briggs taking it?" asked Fitz.

"I've persuaded him that we have enough loose ends to keep it going," replied Gardener. "Depending on what *you've* found. Are we looking at death by natural causes?"

"I wouldn't quite say that," said Fitz.

"You've found something?" asked Reilly, hopefully.

"I wouldn't say that either," said Fitz. "At least, not something you're going to want to hear."

"That's all we need," said Gardener.

"If it's that bad, I'm going for another chocolate bar," offered Reilly.

"What do you have, then?" asked Gardener.

"I've studied this at some length," said Fitz. "All the early indications suggest a virus."

"A virus?" repeated Reilly.

"I'm afraid so," said Fitz.

"In other words," said Gardener. "Natural causes."

"Maybe not," said Fitz. "It looks like the virus she has picked up is extremely rare. That would leave us with one question, where exactly has it come from?"

"What is it?" asked Reilly.

"The nearest thing we have been able to liken it to is something called the Nipah virus."

"What the hell is that?" asked Reilly.

Fitz smiled. "I told you it was rare."

"I've never heard of it," said Gardener.

"It's an infection," said Fitz. "Well, to be honest, the Nipah virus is a zoonotic illness, which is usually transmitted between animals and humans. There are other ways in which it can be transferred. Contaminated food is one way. Directly from person-to-person is another. People infected with it tend to have a range of illnesses, one of which is an acute respiratory disorder. In extreme cases however, we could see fatal encephalitis – inflammation of the brain – which is of course, what I noticed in Sonia Markham.

"Having said that," continued Fitz, "although the Nipah virus does infect a wide range of animals, and can cause severe disease and death in people, the only few known outbreaks have been in Asia."

"Asia?" said Gardener.

Fitz nodded. "I had to do a lot of research into this. The first recognized outbreak was discovered in 1999. The disease struck mainly in pigs in Malaysia and Singapore. That resulted in nearly three hundred human cases and more than one hundred deaths. It caused substantial economic impact as more than one million pigs were killed to help control the outbreak."

"So, it was a pandemic?" asked Reilly.

"I don't think it was quite on that scale," said Fitz. "It seems that most human infections resulted from direct contact with sick pigs, or their contaminated tissues. Transmission is thought to have occurred via unprotected exposure to secretions from the pigs, or unprotected contact with the tissue of a sick animal."

Gardener was at a loss. "From what we've seen, Sonia Markham did not appear to have done anything that would bring her into contact with sick or diseased animals."

"Nor did she live in Asia," said Reilly.

"Unless she's been there recently," offered Fitz.

Gardener realized that that was a question he would have to ask Jodie Thomson.

"There are other ways you can catch it," said Fitz. "In further outbreaks in Bangladesh and India, the eating of fruit products such as raw date, or the drinking of palm juice believed to be contaminated with urine or saliva from infected fruit bats appeared to be one of the most likely sources of infection."

"Fruit bats, for Christ's sake," said Reilly. "This is getting worse."

"You'd better tell us everything you know, Fitz," said Gardener.

"Human-to-human transmission of the Nipah virus in those countries had also been reported among family and carers of infected patients."

"Have there been any other outbreaks anywhere else?" asked Gardener.

"None that we know of in Malaysia and Singapore since 1999," said Fitz. "They have however, recorded it somewhere almost annually in certain parts of Asia since then – primarily in Bangladesh and India."

"Was that from animals, or person to person?" asked Gardener.

"In the ones they know about it was mainly person-to-person, raising concerns about the potential for NiV to cause – as you mentioned earlier – a global pandemic."

"NiV?" questioned Reilly. "They have a name for it. How the hell does all this shit happen? We never had this kind of thing years ago."

"We probably did," said Fitz. "It's just that we didn't know enough about it, and we never had the technology to deal with it.

"For what it's worth," continued Fitz. "NiV is a member of the family Paramyxoviridae, genus Henipavirus. It is mainly a zoonotic virus, meaning that it initially spreads between animals and people. The animal host reservoir for NiV is almost always the fruit bat – genus Pteropus, also known as the flying fox. People to people is rare but not unknown. And on occasion, as discussed earlier, pigs can also be infected."

Gardener was beginning to wish James Stott had kept the case, and never called him in.

Reilly glanced at Gardener. "She was an extra in *Emmerdale*. You don't think…"

"Hardly Asia, is it," said Gardener. "There are no reports of it in Yorkshire, are there?" he asked Fitz.

"None that we know about," said Fitz. "And I'm sure we would know about it. How often have you heard reports in the news recently about the re-emergence of bird flu? You don't have to drive far to see the quarantine posters on telegraph poles."

Gardener made a note of what Fitz had said.

"What kind of symptoms would these people suffer? What should we be looking for?" asked Gardener, before adding, "Just in case."

"They range from mild to severe symptoms," said Fitz, "which may initially include one or several different things – fever, headache, cough, sore throat."

"All of which Sonia Markham apparently had," said Gardener.

"It would have become worse," said Fitz. "She'd have had difficulty breathing. People do tend to vomit, but that didn't happen with her. Your crime scene was quite clean. The symptoms do become more severe – disorientation, drowsiness, confusion. And then seizures, which is what I initially thought she'd had. Eventually a coma, and definitely encephalitis, swelling of the brain."

Fitz searched around the top of his desk and finally located what he wanted. "Some of the figures I have here suggest death occurring in 40-70% of those infected in documented outbreaks between 1998 and 2018."

"Sonia Markham certainly had some of the symptoms," said Gardener. "What about the incubation period?"

"From the information I have, it varies," said Fitz. "It depends how healthy a person is, whether or not they have underlying problems."

"Just like Covid," said Reilly.

"Yes," agreed Fitz. "Generally, most symptoms can typically appear in four to fourteen days following exposure to the virus. The illness initially presents as three to fourteen days of fever and headache, and everything Sonia Markham reported. A phase of brain swelling can follow, which in this case, it did. That can rapidly progress to coma within twenty-four to forty-eight hours. It's not very pleasant."

Whatever Gardener had expected Fitz to tell him, he was not prepared for the Nipah virus. Where in God's name could she have contracted that?

"We really need to have another chat with Jodie Thomson," said Gardener. "We need to find out if they had recently returned from holiday, and if so, where from?"

"Some people have been known to suffer long-term side effects," said Fitz. "Including persistent convulsions and personality changes. Infections that lead to death much later after exposure are known as dormant or latent infections, which have also been reported months and even years after exposure."

"Just like Covid," said Reilly, again. "Are you sure this isn't Covid?"

"Definitely," said Fitz.

Gardener was mystified. "How the hell did she get it?" He'd said it more to himself.

"I have no idea," replied Fitz. "That will be something for you to find out."

"But from what you've said, she'd have to have been in Asia – and she hasn't as far as we know."

"I don't suppose she *has* to have been over there," said Fitz. "But she appears to have caught a virus from somewhere, and we definitely know nothing about an outbreak over here."

"Until now," said Reilly. "Do you have to report this?"

"We have one or two more tests to do," said Fitz. "Once it's confirmed, everyone and his brother needs to know."

"Oh, Christ," said Reilly. "We're not heading for another lockdown, are we?"

"Hard to say," said Fitz. "But to be fair, not everyone dies from this. It can be very unpleasant, but most people will get over it."

"Just–" said Reilly.

"Don't," said Gardener. "I think we get the message now. What about Jodie Thomson? She hasn't complained of any symptoms. Surely, she must have come into contact with it."

"Not necessarily," said Fitz. "It is possible someone could be a carrier and not know it."

"In which case we will definitely need to speak to her," said Gardener.

"Unless Sonia Markham had any underlying problems that we don't know about," said Fitz. "I certainly didn't see anything in the post-mortem. I have contacted her doctor, and I'm waiting for a call back. I'm not hopeful. There is still one other possibility."

"Which is?" asked Gardener.

"It could still be something to do with drugs."

"*Have* you found any trace of drugs?" asked Reilly.

"Not yet," replied Fitz. "But there is always the chance."

Chapter Nineteen

The whole team had gathered for the early evening briefing, and spirits were high. Gardener hoped the signs were positive, because although he had something to tell them, it may not send the investigation into a new direction, or in fact, even save it.

He nodded to Gates and Longstaff, asking first if they had anything to report from their visits to *Emmerdale* and Roundhay.

"I'm afraid not, boss," said Gates.

"Everything checked out," said Longstaff. "She turned up on time, did everything they asked of her, and she was in a good mood all day."

"She didn't come across as a girl who had any problems?" asked Gardener. "Particularly drug related."

"Nothing at all," said Gates. "They have a very strict policy when it comes to alcohol and drugs. If there's any sign at all that you're under the influence of anything, you're off set, and very likely for good."

"Even though they have real beer in the Woolpack," added Gates.

Reilly's ears pricked up. "Now that sounds okay, so it does. I think I might have a word with that there Casting Couch, see if they need any extras."

The comment raised a smile but under the intense pressure to find something, that was all it did.

"And I take it she was healthy on all days?" asked Gardener. "Not suffering from anything else?"

"Not that anyone could tell," said Gates.

The SIO turned his attention to Thornton and Anderson who had managed to track down Sonia Markham's doctor. Despite patient confidentiality he was happy to speak to them to confirm she very rarely suffered with anything, and her asthma was mild.

"Had he seen her recently?" asked Gardener.

"No," said Anderson. "The last time he saw her was last year, just before Christmas. It was a routine check up and blood test, and everything was fine."

That was the last thing Gardener wanted to hear, but it was what it was. He would have to find another angle, so he turned his attention to Sharp and Rawson.

"Mystery man, Alan. Anything at all?"

"He has been seen in the clubs regularly," said Rawson. "But he's one of those people who comes across as a bit of a loner – never caused any trouble."

"They don't know his name," added Sharp. "Having said that, one of the barmaids thought he was called Adam, not Alan."

That caught Gardener's attention. "Adam?"

"That's what *she* thought he was called," replied Sharp, referring to his notes. "Her name is Yolanda and she works in Pryzm."

"We asked if she was sure," said Rawson. "It's an easy mistake to make. You're in a nightclub, there's no shortage of noise so if someone shouted your name, any bar staff might hear it wrong."

"I'll grant you that," said Gardener. "Perhaps I'm clutching at straws."

"Why?" asked Briggs. "What are you thinking?"

"That we've come across the name Adam before."

"Where?" asked Briggs.

"The Casting Couch," replied Reilly. "His name is Adam Baxter, he's one of the shareholders."

"Alan, Adam," said Briggs. "Both common enough names."

"You're probably right," said Gardener, "but the descriptions of both people are not a million miles apart. According to Jodie Thomson, Alan had dark hair, possibly black, and he was slim. We've seen Adam Baxter, who has black hair, quite a smooth complexion, and also rather thin."

"You interviewed them," said Briggs. "Did you pick up on anything?"

"To be honest," said Gardener. "No. He seemed fine, didn't look like a man under pressure."

"Could be hiding it," offered Briggs.

"He could be," agreed Gardener. "Having said that, I'm sure that if Adam Baxter and Sonia Markham had history, one of the team working there might have said something, even privately."

"If they didn't, I'm sure Jodie Thomson would have done," added Reilly.

"As I've said," offered Gardener. "Maybe I'm clutching at straws but it is something we should consider. See if we can find out more about Adam Baxter. Check his bank accounts, his card spends and where he was on the night in question."

"We did get all the CCTV we could from The Key Club," said Rawson. "Maybe Sarah and Julie can check it out. They might see something."

"We can certainly check to see if we can spot a man in a white shirt with a red stripe," said Gates.

"Could be awkward," said Longstaff, "depending on the lighting, but we can give it a go."

"We can also lift a photo of Adam Baxter from The Casting Couch's website," said Gates. "See if he's the man in the shirt."

"Good idea," said Gardener. "At least it's something for you ladies to concentrate on. Check out all the CCTV in the club, and the material we obtained from Viktor. See if everything he told us checks out."

Gardener then went on to tell the team about the meeting with the suspected drug dealer, informing them it was very doubtful that he had anything to do with Sonia Markham's death, especially in the light of offering them both DNA and prints, and personal CCTV from the home.

"He gave you all that?" said Briggs, astounded.

"Takes some believing," said Gardener. "But he cooperated without question."

"Not the sign of a guilty man," said Briggs. "If he'd had anything to do with her death, or he'd been in her flat, we'd know."

"The chances of him being in the flat are nil," said Gardener. "We have all the CCTV from The Quays; he's not seen anywhere on it. All of which still leads us back to the mystery man in the white shirt with the red stripe. Who is he, and what part – if any – is he playing in all of this?"

Gardener glanced at Briggs. "Is there anything from the latest press release?"

Briggs shook his head. "Not so far. We haven't had a dickie bird. And I must say, Stewart, none of this is looking good for us. What about Fitz? What – if anything – has he come up with?"

"He's found something to go on," said Gardener. "But there are more tests he needs to do before he confirms anything."

"Really?" questioned Briggs. "Go on, then, tell us what he said. God knows we need something."

Gardener explained the pathologist's findings. He could tell from the blank expressions that none of them had ever heard of the Nipah virus, if that's what it was.

"What do you mean?" asked Briggs. "If that's what it was? It either is, or it isn't. I mean this stuff sounds pretty weird, not your everyday virus. Did she have it, or not?"

Gardener could see what Briggs was edging at. If Sonia Markham had picked up the virus, then it was pretty much game over for the team. End of investigation. Time to call the World Health Organization.

"He also mentioned something else quite interesting."

"What?" asked Briggs.

"There could be someone out there who goes to the clubs on a regular basis who might be a carrier. Maybe he even knows he's a carrier."

"Well, if he knew he was a carrier and he was deliberately going out and infecting people, and killing them," said Gates, "then surely that is a crime."

"It probably is," said Briggs. "Not quite sure what crime."

Gardener, however, couldn't remove the matter of Devil Dust from his mind. It simply couldn't be eliminated. Although, he also realized, that if it was the drug, he could lose the investigation to narcotics.

"There is also the slight possibility that she may have been given something that imitates the Nipah virus – particularly where the symptoms are concerned."

"From what you've told me," added Briggs, "that isn't how Fitz is thinking."

"Not yet," said Gardener. "Fitz has not found any traces of Devil Dust in her system, but there are more tests for him to do. At the moment, it looks more likely the virus has done the damage."

"If that's what it is," said Anderson. "How has she caught it?"

"At the moment, I have no answer," said Gardener. "On the way here, I phoned Jodie Thomson. She said that they had not been on a proper holiday for about eighteen months, and when they did, they spent a week in a place called Argassi in Zante, one of the Greek islands. Since then, they have had odd weekends away across the UK. They have certainly been nowhere near Asia."

"Jodie Thomson," repeated Briggs, "She claimed Sonia was talking to the drug dealer in the club. He claimed he wasn't; no one else says he was. How reliable is Jodie Thomson? Perhaps we need to question her again, see if there's anything personal going on."

Briggs had made a good point. If there was a key element missing for the case to continue along the lines of a murder investigation, Jodie Thomson might provide it if he pushed her hard enough.

If not…

"I'm inclined to accept what you're saying, sir, about Sonia Markham. From what we've so far seen, there is no evidence of an attack *in* her home. We have the CCTV footage from the second she left the club, to the second she entered the apartment. Nothing happened to her in between, and the distance travelled and the time taken all tally up. Nothing external appears to have happened in her apartment."

"So, we're back to the club," said Reilly. "Has something happened earlier, *in* the club?"

"That's the only thing left," retorted Gardener. "We have to go back, and press the matter further. We really need to try and find out what – if anything – happened inside that club. Who did she speak to? Did she go anywhere with anyone? Did Viktor sell her any of this new drug called Devil Dust?"

"But we've done all this," said Briggs. "And we've launched two press appeals and we still have nothing. If Viktor had sold her the drug, surely we would know by now. Fitz would have found something."

"As yet," said Gardener, "she doesn't appear to have drugs in her system. But when we first spoke to him, he mentioned the possibility of a hybrid drug, something that had been manufactured and leaves no trace of itself."

"That could take weeks," said Briggs. "Maybe months. What you're uncovering here, leads me to think that it's not murder."

"You might want to hang on with that," said Gardener.

"Why?" challenged Briggs. "Even if he's sold her the drug, he hasn't forced her to take it, so technically, it's not murder."

"Unless it was slipped into her drink," said Gates.

"From what we've seen," said Reilly. "That's not Viktor's style, what would he get out of that?"

"Maybe it's not Viktor," said Rawson. "Could be someone else doing all of this."

"And maybe that someone else has done it before," said Anderson. "Maybe this isn't the first time."

"Okay," said Briggs. "Let's just assume it is a lethal drug, why haven't we come across more dead girls?"

"What if she's the only one that's died who's been found?" said Longstaff.

"Meaning?" asked Gardener.

"What if other girls have gone missing, and have never *been* found," continued Longstaff. "They're still out there, somewhere, somehow connected to all of this?"

"Or dead," added Gates.

Gardener's mind went into overdrive. "Mispers? That's a very good point. It's quite rare for someone to be murdered, with no body recovered."

"And there not be a missing persons report," said Reilly.

"Let's just assume that some girls *have* gone missing, from the club," said Gardener. "It would be a reasonably simple search on the misper reports."

"Maybe," said Sharp, "but where do we start with this, where do we go with the dates? What are we looking for?"

"When do we start and finish?" asked Rawson.

"Put in the locations," said Gardener, "and leave the reported dates open-ended. Admittedly, we would end up with every report ever made since records began, in that area."

The team grew silent, obviously considering the ramifications.

"Could be quite a long list," said Gardener. "We can narrow it if we pull out only females within a certain age range. It might get us a good start."

"Might work," said Briggs. "If we could reference mystery man's appearance – or someone else – at the club on a few occasions, and a misper report, we might have more than enough to bring him in, question him."

"In the absence of absolutely nothing else we can do," said Gardener, driving the point as hard as he could, in order to keep the investigation open. "I'd like to request that the whole team study mispers."

He glanced at DCI Briggs who eventually nodded his approval.

"Let's give it one last shot to see if we can come up with something," said Gardener. "If anything looks odd, and you believe you have found a girl fitting the requirements, dig deeper. Let's have the last movements of them all – see if there is a pattern of sorts that we can investigate."

Gardener also threw out a parting shot. "Having said all of that, we cannot rule out this so-called Devil Dust that is hitting the market hard, we still need to run as many checks on Viktor as we can, until I am satisfied that he has nothing whatsoever to do with Sonia Markham's death."

Chapter Twenty

The telephone on Gardener's desk suddenly rang. Reilly stood up quickly, beat him to it.

"When?" he heard his sergeant question.

"Where?" asked Reilly.

"Do we know why?"

Gardener wondered what the hell was going on. He suspected it was *something* to do with the case.

"That was Dave Williams on the front desk," said Reilly, after replacing the receiver. "Will Markham is in Great George Street."

"Leeds General?" questioned Gardener, leaning forward. "Will Markham? Why?"

Reilly didn't bother to sit back down. "Seems he got himself into some trouble last night."

"What sort of trouble?"

"The sort that lands you in hospital."

Gardener stood up. "Where was he when it happened?"

"Pryzm, in Leeds."

"Pryzm?" repeated Gardener. "What was he doing in Pryzm? Hardly the kind of place I'd expect to find him."

"I could think of one good reason," said Reilly.

"Viktor," replied Gardener.

"Just can't think how or why he might have got wind of anything," said Reilly.

"Someone's obviously stuck a bee in his bonnet," said Gardener. "We'll have to go and see how bad this is, and find out what he was up to."

Gardener grabbed his jacket from the back of his chair, and picked up his hat from the desk. They left the office.

With Reilly driving, and midmorning traffic having thinned out since the rush hour, they made it to the hospital in a little over twenty minutes. Once inside, Gardener showed his warrant card at the reception desk and asked about Will Markham. They were directed to a small side room. When they arrived, Gardener was not surprised to see Will's wife, Angela.

"Thank goodness you're here," said Angela, appearing every year of her age and more. She was dressed in jeans and a T-shirt. Her straight, shoulder-length blonde hair was listless and appeared unwashed. Her eyes were tired. She had obviously had a sleepless night.

Gardener glanced at Will Markham. He was in a bed in a side ward and had obviously come off far worse in whatever disagreement he had been involved in. His head was bandaged turban style, with bruises covering his face. One eye was closed and, above his eyebrow, he had a line of stitches. One arm was in a sling, and he was propped up by three pillows. The expression on his face and his laboured breathing said he was in a lot of pain.

Gardener noticed a number of chairs but before taking one he asked Angela how she was.

"Worried sick, with this one." She stared at her husband.

"Would you like a drink, Mrs Markham?"

"I'd love one."

"Something to eat?"

"No, I don't think I could."

Gardener asked Reilly if he would do the honours. The sergeant returned quite quickly, by which time Gardener and Angela were seated. He passed over the drinks, placed one for Will on his bedside table before taking a seat himself.

"Would you like to tell us what happened, Mr Markham?" asked Gardener.

"I walked into a door."

"Was it still attached to the bank vault?" asked Reilly. "I've never seen a door big enough to do that kind of damage."

"What were you doing in Pryzm in the first place?" asked Gardener.

"That's what I want to know," said Angela. "You told me you were going out for a drink with the lads."

"I did," said Will.

"Not in a bloody nightclub, surely?" challenged Angela.

"Wasn't my idea," retorted Will.

"I bet it wasn't," said Angela. "I know bloody well what happened. You lot had had one drink too many and you decided to go looking for the man you *think* killed our daughter."

"Is that right?" asked Reilly.

"Can't remember," said Will, wincing as he tried to lift his drink to his lips.

Angela stood up and helped him. When he'd finished, she placed the cup back on the table and returned to her seat.

"For God's sake, Will, what are you playing at?" asked Angela. "You're well out of your league with this one. You're too old for a start."

"Oh, thanks," said Will.

"Don't thank me for telling the truth," she retorted. "You were out of your depth."

"Sounds as if she's right on the ball, Will, old son," said Reilly. "You thought you'd take the law into your own hands and got yourself a beating into the bargain."

Will remained silent.

"Who were you looking for, Mr Markham?" Gardener asked.

Will stared out of the window, refusing to answer.

Gardener suspected he knew exactly who Will had been after. Trouble was, he couldn't prove anything without the man's say so.

"Come on, Mr Markham," said Gardener. "You're not doing yourself any favours. Or us, for that matter."

"You're not getting anywhere, are you?"

"Did you?" asked Reilly. "Doesn't look like it from where I'm sitting."

Will Markham leaned forward, pulling a face that Phil Cool would have been proud of, as the pain appeared to hit new heights. He immediately retreated to his pillows but the damage had been done, and his breathing worsened. Gardener suspected a broken rib, maybe more than one.

Eventually, Will said, "That bastard drug dealer."

"We're talking about Viktor, are we?" said Gardener.

"Who else?"

"How did you know he had anything to do with it?"

"Never you mind," he replied. "But he's still walking the streets, isn't he? He's not behind bars."

"Nor will he be," said Gardener. "Until we find some concrete evidence that he is involved, or is guilty of the death of your daughter."

"Did Viktor do this to you?" asked Reilly.

"I've already told you, I walked into a door."

"Come on," said Reilly. "Tell us how you found out that Viktor might be in the frame."

"I keep my ear to the ground."

"We can go and speak to the people at the club," said Gardener, although he didn't hold out much hope of a confession. They would clam up if Viktor was involved.

"Yes, that's right," said Will Markham, venomously. "Go and do your job for a change."

"Will!" admonished Angela. "You should take that back. I'm sure these two *are* doing their job, but maybe it isn't as simple as you want it to be. Maybe they have no evidence against this drug dealer."

"How much evidence do you want?"

"Some would be nice, Mr Markham," retorted Gardener. "We've been investigating this for a while now. There's been no let up, we haven't had a break. But I have to be honest with you, so far we have drawn a complete blank."

"Nothing at all?" asked Angela, her wide-eyed expression one of shock. "You have no idea who or what killed our daughter, even after all this time?"

"We *were* coming to speak to you today," said Gardener.

"What about?" asked Angela.

"That we, too, know about Viktor the drug dealer. We have interviewed him at length, and as far as we can tell, he had absolutely nothing to do with Sonia's death."

"You would say that," offered Will Markham.

Gardener ignored him and continued speaking to his wife. "The pathologist has found absolutely no trace of drugs in Sonia's system."

"None," replied Angela, weakly. She placed her coffee on the table, next to Will's. "I didn't think you would, detective. She isn't that type of girl. She was brought up properly in a house occupied by the good Lord."

Gardener did not want to start on a religious path, but to be fair, on the occasions he had met Angela Markham, although he knew her thoughts on the matter, she was not one for ramming it down your throat.

"So how did she die?" asked Angela.

"She appears to have succumbed to a virus of sorts, which somehow shut down her respiratory system."

"A virus?" shouted Will Markham.

Angela's complexion paled a little, as if that was possible. "Was it Covid?"

"No," said Gardener. "Have you heard of something called the Nipah virus?"

"Are you making that up?" asked Will.

Gardener went on to explain what he knew.

Angela Markham broke down and wept. "It must have been awful, and my baby had to suffer that on her own."

She stared at her husband. "She died alone, Will. Alone. There was no one there to help her. We were on holiday."

"It wasn't our fault," said Will, obviously affected more than he was letting on, as tears came to his eyes. "We weren't to know this was going to happen."

"No one could have known," said Reilly.

"Where did she get it?" asked Angela.

"We don't know," said Gardener.

"It could have been anywhere, at any time," she replied. "Should we go and get ourselves tested?"

Gardener explained the symptoms. "Are you feeling ill at all?"

"No," they both replied in unison.

There was a break from talking, a point where very little else could be added.

Gardener then turned his attention to Will Markham. "I'm really sorry for your loss. We are doing everything possible, but I must warn you about taking the law into your own hands."

Will Markham glanced at Gardener, his expression of sorrow also had traces of embarrassment, as if he knew he had done the wrong thing.

Perhaps the drink *had* been responsible, thought Gardener.

"Please leave any investigating to the professionals – namely us," said Gardener.

"Next time, Will," added Reilly. "You may not be so lucky."

"*Your* job is to be by your wife's side," said Gardener. "This is a tough time for all of you. She has already lost a daughter, I'm sure she doesn't want to lose a husband as well."

Chapter Twenty-one

Sunday lunchtime in the Parkinson household was much like most other houses in the UK – a ritual. People rose, had breakfast, read papers, did the odd job, and it was very likely the lady of the house who would prepare a Sunday roast so she could gather her family around her for a catch up.

And Della obviously needed one, thought Rodney, studying the fractious atmosphere, especially with the pots and the cutlery clanging around. The radio on the windowsill in the kitchen was turned to Greatest Hits, providing a small amount of respite. The kettle boiled. Della grabbed it as if she was going to throttle it, poured the water into the pot and dropped it back on its base.

Rodney – sitting at the kitchen table – lowered the paper a little, taking everything in, wondering who was to blame for what was coming.

With the tea made and the beef joint in the oven, Della sat at the table. *Lowering* the paper wasn't an option now. Setting fire to it might help.

"What's wrong with our Alec?"

Straight in for the kill, thought Rodney, placing his newspaper on the table and adjusting his glasses. A vase of flowers blocked his view slightly, so she moved it.

He couldn't fault Della. She had been a good mother, a fine wife, and an astute business partner. When he married her, he had done himself proud. If only she wasn't so fiery.

"Why should there be anything wrong?"

"I'm his mother," she replied, tersely. "Credit me with some sense. Mothers know when there is something wrong with their children."

And wives seem to know everything else, thought Rodney.

"He seems to have been in a strange mood of late. Have you noticed anything, Rodders?"

Rodney cringed. He hated the use of his nickname. Made him sound like a spiv.

"No," he replied. "You should leave the boy alone and let him live his life. What have you noticed that you think is so wrong?"

"He's very quiet."

"Is that a problem?"

"It must be, for him," replied Della.

"He's hardly the life and soul of the party as it is," said Rodney. "Probably comes with the territory. He *is* an undertaker. He's never been noisy."

Della took a sip of her tea, reaching for a Marks & Spencer biscuit barrel. She removed the lid and grabbed a chocolate digestive. After eating it, she glanced around the room.

"It's more than that. We don't see as much of him as we should these days, or even as much as we used to. And when we do, he's a bit withdrawn, as if he has something on his mind."

Rodney couldn't say he'd noticed, and they worked quite closely together.

"Has he said anything to you?" asked Della.

"He's not likely to, is he?" said Rodney. "He's a grown man and I'm his father. The only possible problems he might have are to do with girls, and should that be the case, he's hardly likely to talk to either of us."

Rodney rather foolishly hoped that might be the end of the matter, so that he could return to his newspaper, or anticipate his Sunday lunch, especially now he could hear the joint crackling in the oven. And the smell!

"Where was he last night?" asked Della. "Do you know?"

Rodney was buggered if he knew. "No."

"Precisely."

"But I don't keep tabs on him," he argued. "And I wouldn't have appreciated *my* father keeping tabs on *me*, or poking his nose into my business."

"Time was," pressed Della, "he would tell us where he was going."

Rodney was tiring of the conversation. When Della had a bee in her bonnet she was like a bulldog; she wouldn't let go.

"As I keep saying, my love," said Rodney, with a cheesy smile. "He's an adult. There are things he will want to keep to himself."

"Maybe it *is* a girl. It's about time he found himself a nice one and settled down."

As if that was the answer to everything, thought Rodney. "Why do you have to have a girl to be considered settled? Why can't he just be settled and not want or have one? Define settled for me."

Della appeared slightly stuck for words, which was a first, thought Rodney. She took a sip of tea, perhaps giving herself more time to load up her ammunition.

Rodney jumped in quick. "I'll tell you what settled is, shall I? How about a nice place to live? He certainly has that. There's nothing wrong with his little cottage in the grounds. It's well built, nicely furnished. It doesn't cost him anything. He has money in his pocket, a nice car, and the freedom to come and go as he pleases. I wish I'd had that at his age. So, before you go looking for a problem where there isn't one, perhaps you should think of what he does have. And maybe you'll see that as settled."

After a slight silence, Della muttered, "It's not normal. A man needs a good woman."

Rodney rolled his eyes, doubting there was such a thing.

"I sometimes wonder if you're the man I married."

Here we go, thought Rodney, Della was losing the argument, so she'd change the subject – to him.

"Well, I wouldn't be, would I?" he countered. "You've spent years changing me."

"Never mind changing the subject," said Della.

"I didn't, my love," countered Rodney, with another cheesy smile, hoping he could reunite himself with the Sunday paper.

"We're talking about Alec."

"Then why did you bring me into it?"

Della stood up. "You men, you're all the same. Thick as thieves. When that boy comes over for his Sunday lunch, I'm going to have a few choice words."

God help him, thought Rodney.

Chapter Twenty-two

It was approaching eleven o'clock in the evening when Viktor and Arthur stepped through the door of The Key Club, along with the two human Rottweilers. The lighting and the music were low, and he wasn't surprised to see that the possible audience was also small in number.

He was disappointed. But most were working class, unlike him; most would have work in the morning, unlike him. The usual rats lurking in the corners trying to sell drugs suddenly bolted upright and scurried for the entrance at the sight of the big man. That didn't bother him. It would save him the job of throwing them out. Buying the stuff from him and then trying to sell it on in one of his clubs was a no-no.

Viktor turned to face his posse as the music changed to an old Billy Ocean song. At least the DJ was trying. Most people were sitting at the bar, or at tables in the corners. Perhaps they were ready to call it a night.

Viktor nodded to his team. The two bodyguards, and Arthur, all went in separate directions, while Viktor headed for the bar. Four people immediately jumped up from the stools and departed, leaving a nice gap for him.

When Leon the barman turned around, he jumped back a little.

"Viktor," he shouted. "Good to see you."

Viktor wasn't so sure he meant it. Leon was a bit of a weasel. He would tell you anything to keep the peace. A lot of the time he would agree with you even if it was against his religion. Leon was around thirty years of age, had a good head of black hair, blue eyes and a nice smile. He usually dressed in a white shirt and tight black jeans in an effort to sell more drinks to the female clientele. It never hurt to have an attractive barman.

"We have to talk," said Leon, glancing sideways.

"Yes, my friend, I know," replied Viktor, signalling to the DJ to keep it quiet. He returned his attention to Leon. "All in good time. Let us first deal with business."

"This *will* be your business if it's not sorted."

"Leon," said Viktor, staring straight into Leon's eyes with an expression capable of halting electricity. "Where I come from it is customary to get business out of way first, before discussing anything else on menu. Now, I believe you owe me money."

Leon slipped into the back room without argument. He returned with an envelope, passing it over.

"Thank you," said Viktor. "You have no trouble?"

"Are you serious? Who's going to muscle in on your territory?"

"No one who knows what is good for them." Viktor laughed, inviting Leon to do the same.

Arthur suddenly appeared by Viktor's side and asked for a drink. Leon knew better than to ask what he wanted – or to charge him. "Better make it a double and then I won't keep asking, will I?"

"You drink too much," said Viktor.

"Oh really," replied Arthur. "Yesterday you said I ate too much."

"Eating is not the word for what you do. You consume, my friend, like a blue whale."

"Life is for living, Viktor," replied Arthur, appearing totally unruffled. "It's far too short not to eat or drink the things you love."

"Christ," said Viktor, "you must do a lot of loving."

"Not as much as I'd like," muttered Arthur, turning his head away.

"Arthur," said Viktor, "take the drink and the envelope into the office and check the amount is correct."

"Don't you trust me?" asked Leon, laughing, more out of fear than anything else.

"Who else has access to the office?"

"Well…" Leon hesitated. "Everyone who works here, I suppose."

"Precisely. You I trust. Everyone else, no."

Leon seemed appeased.

"So," asked Viktor. "What you have to tell me? You say we need to talk."

Leon leaned in a little closer. "The police, Viktor."

"What about them?"

"They're all over the club."

"Tell me something I don't know. This is nothing new."

"It is when it's in connection with a girl who was found dead in her apartment and who was in here on the night she died."

The music changed again, to a number from the musical *Grease*. The audience had thinned a little since Viktor had walked through the door.

"Yes, I know about this," said Viktor. "What they say?"

"They're all over here like a rash," said Leon, pretty excited, very animated. "They're asking about what she was doing. Who did she see? When did she leave? Did she meet anyone when she was in here? Did she do anything?"

A man stepped up and asked for two pints of lager. Leon served him quickly, ushering him away from the bar.

"So, what is the problem?" Viktor asked.

"It's making me uncomfortable."

"Why? Are they forcing you to tell them something you don't know?"

"No."

"Are they forcing you to pin something on me?"

"No," shouted Leon, more forcefully.

"Are they asking about me?"

Leon hesitated. "Yes."

"Is okay," said Viktor. "I know all about the police. They've been to see me."

"You?" shouted Leon, as if he couldn't believe what Viktor had said. "What about?"

Viktor tired of the man's stupidity. "What you think, idiot? Which bus service goes to Leeds at midnight? They asked me same as they asked you, about the dead girl."

Leon stepped back – his expression confused. "Did you know her?"

"Fuck!" shouted Viktor, his patience wearing thin. "You sound like them, now. Do I know who she is? Did I speak to her? Questions! Always fucking questions, and more questions. They want to know if I sold her drugs."

"You didn't?"

"Am I stupid? You think I want to draw attention to myself? I have little idiots for that stuff. *They* can sell white powder."

Arthur returned. He must have caught the back end of the conversation because he quickly nodded his approval, passing over the package.

"I have bigger fish to fry," said Viktor. He held the envelope aloft. "This is why I am here, not white shit."

He passed the envelope back to Arthur with an expression that said why the fuck did you give it to me?

Viktor turned back to Leon. "What you know about it?"

"I know who she is," said Leon. "That fit bird on *Emmerdale*."

Arthur nodded his agreement.

"What do you know about her?"

"I don't know anything, Viktor," said Leon shaking his head. "I keep my eyes open and my mouth shut."

Viktor leaned across the bar and gently took hold of Leon's shirt collar, pulling him slowly forward. "Keep it that way. What did she get up to in here?"

"Nothing that I know about," replied Leon, staring at his shirt collar.

"Who was she with?"

"How do I know? I was serving drinks all night."

Wrong answer. Viktor dragged him across the bar top. "I pay you to keep your eyes open. I know you see everything that goes on. Who was she with?"

Leon struggled to speak, due to the tightness of the collar. "She was with her friend, but she was also seen talking to the bloke wearing the white shirt with the red stripe."

"Name?" asked Viktor, relinquishing his grip, allowing Leon to step back and breathe, and smooth out his shirt.

"I don't know his name."

Viktor's eyes narrowed. He wouldn't be played for a fool. "Are you sure?"

"Do you think I'd let you drag me all over the fucking club if I knew what you wanted?"

He had a point, thought Viktor. "You don't know his name? How many times have you seen him?"

"He's often here."

"Who with?"

"No one that I know of," said Leon. "He speaks to some of the girls but I've never really seen him with anyone."

"Find out. I want to know who he is, where he lives, what he does for money, what he drives. I want everything. You understand me?"

"Why do you want to know about him?"

Viktor leaned forward and Leon stepped back. He couldn't go any further because of the cabinets and the optics.

"Because someone has told the police I am involved with girl who died. They saw me with her in the club, and they want to know what I know about her. They want to know if I sold her drugs, if I am responsible for her death. Someone has put a finger on me, and when I find out who, I will put a finger on them."

Viktor paused slightly, before adding, "And my fingers are bigger, trust me."

"I might be able to help you with that one," said Leon, obviously in need to score some points.

"How?"

"The police are not the only ones looking into her death."

"What?" shouted Viktor. "Who else has been asking? The man from last night? Don't worry, we'll take care of that."

"No, not him," said Leon.

"Is someone after my patch?" asked Viktor, menacingly.

"No, it's not any of your competition. None of them are that stupid, Viktor."

"So, who is it?"

"A girl."

"A girl?" Viktor screwed his eyes up. "Which girl?"

"The one she was with. They're usually in here together."

"Who is she?"

"She is only small," replied Leon. "My height." Which was a little over five feet. "She's quite chunky, has long blonde hair and wide frames glasses. Doesn't wear a lot of make-up."

"Fucking hell," said Viktor, staring at the ceiling. "That could be anybody. You have a name?"

Leon waited as another staff member slipped into the office. When the girl left, he resumed the conversation. "Her name is Jodie, Jodie Thomson."

"And what is Jodie Thomson asking?"

"She's looking into her friend's death."

"What? She is police as well?"

"No," said Leon. "She's not the police."

Arthur had now leaned forward, all ears.

"Fucking counterfeit police," said Viktor, through clenched teeth. "Where I find her, this Jodie?"

"I don't know where she lives."

"So how do I find her?" asked Viktor, throwing his arms in the air. "Who am I, David fucking Copperfield?"

Leon slipped out his phone, scrolled through his files and then passed it over to Viktor, with a picture of Jodie.

Viktor showed it to Arthur. "You know her?"

"I've definitely seen her around," replied the big man.

"Good. In that case, Arthur, I want to see her around, and you know exactly where."

Chapter Twenty-three

Once again, the early evening briefing saw the whole team in attendance. Gardener was hoping that someone may have found something upon which they could proceed.

He started with Frank Thornton and Bob Anderson on their quest to find anything on The Casting Couch's Adam Baxter.

"Clean as a whistle," said Anderson.

"There are no strange transactions on his bank accounts," continued Thornton. "And as for the night in question, he was in London."

"London?" questioned Gardener, realizing that the capital was pretty much the centre of the entertainment world, so it would make sense.

"His card transactions bear that out," said Anderson. "He was staying at a place called The Bedford, which is close to Kings Cross."

"And he spent the night in the West End watching *Only Fools & Horses*," said Thornton. "He had a meal at a nearby Greek restaurant, and then went on to a club. He's definitely in the clear."

Gardener had to agree. They couldn't pin anything on Adam Baxter, not that he had held out much hope.

He updated the whiteboard and turned his attention to Gates and Longstaff.

"We have had both Viktor's CCTV, and the CCTV obtained from The Key Club," said Gates. "He left the club when he said he did, and arrived home twenty-five minutes later – which pretty much bears out what he said."

Gardener hadn't expected anything else.

"What we're not so keen on," said Longstaff, "is that we suspect the remainder of Viktor's CCTV has been doctored."

"In what way?" asked Gardener.

"The three days following Sonia Markham's death are sketchy," said Gates.

"There are chunks of it missing," said Longstaff. "It's obviously been edited because he doesn't want us to see everything he gets up to."

"He's not on all of it," said Gates. "So, we cannot account for where he may have gone, or what he may have been up to."

"None of which makes him a murderer," said Briggs. "Especially in light of what Stewart and Sean got from him."

"I must admit," said Reilly. "I did think there was something odd about him giving us a DNA sample and fingerprints."

Gardener nodded. "Almost as if he was challenging us to find something."

"Which he knew we wouldn't," replied Reilly.

"Certainly not for a murder," said Briggs. "This is where he's been clever. He knows we're not looking into any other aspect of his business, just a possible murder. Of which, he knows he's in the clear. And from where I'm sitting, Stewart, it's beginning to look like everyone else is."

Gardener quickly turned his attention to Sharp and Rawson.

"We have found some interesting information regarding his drug dealing activities," said Rawson.

"Go on," said Gardener.

"We caught up with an ex-bouncer who worked all of the clubs Viktor did," said Sharp.

"He reckons most of the drugs come through in Turkish rugs," said Rawson.

"Rugs?" questioned Reilly.

"He's fronting an OCG who are importing Turkish rugs. Apparently, they sew in flexible straws filled with heroin," said Sharp.

"It's part of the manufacturing process," said Rawson, "so it's a nightmare to detect."

"That's clever," said Reilly.

"It all works," said Rawson, "because all the bouncers in the nightclubs are part of the OCG. They control everything that goes into the club and thereby create a captive audience that can only buy their gear."

"But before we get carried away," said Briggs, "we need to keep focused. We're not investigating what he does with the white stuff, we're after him because of a possible connection to Sonia Markham's death – and so far, we've found very little, or to be more precise, nothing. I agree, what you lads have found can be passed on, but it's not for us to get involved."

With a defeated expression, Sharp continued. "Sorry, boss. All the clubs say the same thing; people either speak highly of him or say nothing."

"Someone did let it slip that with Viktor looking after the place, there is never any trouble," said Rawson.

"That suggests a protection racket," said Reilly.

"Which is also illegal," said Gardener. "We all know how they work, usually operating under the guise of an insurance company. Thugs pretending to help local businesses by stopping them accidentally burning to the ground. The inference being, if you don't pay up, they'll be the ones doing the burning."

"Once again," said Reilly, "Viktor will have access to the bouncers – big scary lads willing to do things for cash."

"He'll have them visit some of the locals and make them an offer they can't refuse," said Briggs. "It's normally a cash sum, every month, picked up in person by one of the henchmen, and isn't too much that it puts the business under any real pressure."

"It would be almost impossible to detect, boss," said Rawson. "All the victims have a sense of fear instilled into them, believing if they go to the cops, they'll lose more than just their business."

"Again," said Gardener. "We can't really touch him for that."

"Granted," said Briggs. "If we find something, as I said, we can hand it over. But for us, can we connect him to what we think might be murder? I think not."

"Hold your horses," said Gates.

"Pardon?" said Gardener, immediately latching on to the comment.

"We might have found something," said Longstaff.

Gardener was all ears. "Are you serious?"

"While we were probing the cold cases in the area," said Gates. "And particularly anything connected to the city centre nightclubs and missing girls, we came across some interesting information."

"Regarding Viktor?" asked Gardener.

"He certainly appears to have been mentioned, and spoken to about it," said Gates.

"About what?" asked Reilly.

"It appears," said Longstaff, "that Jodie Thomson's sister, Pippa, died in mysterious circumstances."

"Jodie's sister?" questioned Reilly, sitting further forward. In fact, the whole team had gone deadly silent.

"When?" asked Gardener.

"A couple of years back," said Longstaff.

"Do you have the police reports of what happened at the time?"

Gates nodded. "Give us a minute."

She sorted through a pile of paperwork until she found what she wanted.

"Here we go. Pippa Thomson was last seen alive sometime between 02:00 and 03:00 GMT on 22 December 2022, leaving the Pryzm nightclub in Leeds. A witness who had been working the door said he saw Pippa jump into a taxi at 02:20. Another witness, living opposite, said Pippa arrived home in Yeadon, at 02:45, paid the driver and entered her house."

"Have we spoken to the neighbour?" asked Gardener.

"Yes," said Longstaff. "A guy named Gary Towell. It all checks out."

"Police spoke to the driver of the taxi," continued Gates. "He said he didn't want to drive off until she was safely in the house. He also said she was very well behaved in the taxi, and they spoke all the way through the journey. Pippa was excited about the year ahead because she had been accepted by a London university to study history and would be starting next year, residing in the student accommodation."

Gates picked up more paper from the file. "The next person who saw Pippa was her sister, Jodie."

"Jodie?" questioned Gardener, slightly concerned. "Interesting. Two people close to her have died and she may have been the last one to see them alive."

"Doesn't mean much," said Reilly. "Could simply be bad luck."

"When did she find her sister?" asked Gardener.

"Christmas Day," said Gates. "After lunch. She was quite concerned that Pippa had not returned any of her texts or phone calls."

"How did she get in?" asked Sharp.

"She used her own spare key. She found Pippa face down on the bathroom floor in her own vomit."

"Christ," said Reilly. "That's bad."

"Not a good start to Christmas," said Gardener, remembering his own tragedy at a similar time of the year. "Did you get the post-mortem report?"

"Yes," said Gates. "Usual thing. Toxicology samples were taken. Pippa was found to have potentially lethal levels of cocaine in her system, not to mention several other drugs including flubromazolam, part of the benzos family. The pathologist explained that these were psychoactive drugs, often used as a depressant and generally prescribed for anxiety, or insomnia, and in some cases, seizures."

"Is this where Viktor comes in?" asked Gardener.

"Possibly," said Gates. "The coroner was concerned that Pippa's death had been linked to a designer drug. The problem with those is that there is no way of knowing how strong they are, and are often ordered online from anonymous suppliers because they're not available on prescription.

"There was quite a lot in the local newspapers at the time. Apparently, these so-called designer drugs make their way onto the nightclub scene through local suppliers and dealers – people who have obviously seen a market that they could exploit, by ordering copious amounts themselves and selling them direct, reducing the waiting time for the customer."

"And Viktor was questioned about this?" asked Gardener.

"Yes," said Longstaff. "But to be fair, so were all the major players at the time. Our lads couldn't pin anything on any of them, so they all walked."

"That's very interesting," said Gardener. "Still doesn't get us anywhere with Viktor. What is disappointing is that we've spoken to Jodie. While she was quick to suggest that Viktor may have been responsible, she said nothing about her sister's death."

"Which tells me," said Briggs, "that what's going on between Jodie and Viktor is personal."

"And, as we've mentioned, also makes her an unreliable witness," said Gardener.

"So, what is going on with her and Viktor?" asked Reilly. "So far, there is no proof he had *anything* to do with Sonia Markham's death."

"Perhaps it's time Jodie Thomson was brought in to answer that very question," said Gardener. "As well as a number of others that we might have. Meanwhile, can everyone keep looking into the mispers?"

Chapter Twenty-four

As the Markham family roots were in Skipton, it made sense that Parkinson & Son were the family undertakers. Jodie nearly died when Angela had asked that she join Will and herself to make the arrangements for Sonia. She understood that it was something that had to be discussed, and something that had to be done but she did not feel entitled to be a part of it, nor did she feel she was in the right frame of mind.

Jodie was sitting on one of the three-seat sofas in the main room, whilst Angela and Will were sitting on the other. The room was impeccably clean and the soft tone of the panpipes very soothing, though she couldn't have told you the tune.

Jodie was finding it so hard to concentrate. She wondered if she was coming down with something because she was alternately shifting from feeling warm to growing cold. Her mind constantly wandered, permanently asked questions, for which there were no answers. She'd had trouble sleeping, wasn't eating properly and was often distracted. So much so, she had left her phone at the Markhams' house.

Rodney Parkinson was sitting on one of the high-backed chairs. "Are you okay, Mr Markham?" he asked. "If you don't mind my saying you look as if you've been in the wars."

"I'm fine," he replied. "Walked into a door."

"Oh dear. I've done that myself on more than one occasion," replied Rodney. "Can't say I've walked into one as big as the door you must have found."

Will Markham simply smiled without answering.

Jodie observed the short interaction but found it easier not to join in. She had decided early on she would only speak when spoken to.

Rodney turned his attention to Angela. "Mrs Markham, this must be a very difficult time for you, and what we have to talk about today will be very unsettling. But we'll do our best to make the journey as easy as we can, and if at any point you feel you need a break, please just ask."

Angela smiled and thanked him.

Before Rodney said anything else, the door opened and a young man joined them. Parkinson senior introduced his son, Alec. He was dressed in a tight-fitting black suit, white shirt, black tie and black shoes. Alec greeted everyone and opted for the sofa that Jodie was on so they were sitting quite close.

Jodie smiled, taking in a small amount of detail. He had neatly trimmed black hair, a thin moustache and beard and perfect teeth.

Alec smiled back, placing a folder on the table. He produced a pen and paper for notes.

Old man Parkinson broke the mood. "Mrs Markham, would you like to tell me something about your daughter, Sonia?"

Angela nodded, probably close to breaking point, thought Jodie. She knew *she* was.

"All the family have been here," said Angela. "My grandmother was here only last year. She was one hundred."

"Yes," said Rodney. "I thought I remembered the name. I believe she was a sprightly character even for her advanced years."

Angela laughed. That was no understatement. For her ninety, and ninety-fifth birthdays, she had done a sky dive to raise money for the OPA cancer charity, and was set on doing it again when she turned one hundred. Sadly, it never happened.

Eventually, the Markhams opened up and talked more about Sonia: her life, what she liked and disliked, things she had achieved; all of which, Jodie found increasingly difficult. Angela then passed over a photo in a frame, explaining she would like it placed on top of the coffin throughout the service.

"We can certainly do that for you," said Rodney, taking the photo.

As he studied it, he glanced again at Angela. "Forgive me for asking, but is this the young lady who died a few weeks back? She worked on the TV, didn't she? So sad. I remember reading she'd been out only that evening to a club to celebrate a birthday."

Angela nodded her head several times to all of those points.

Jodie had a tissue close to her face, tears flowing freely, wishing to God she had stayed with Sonia that night, believing that if she had, nothing would have happened.

"The newspaper said that the police are treating it as murder, Mrs Markham," said Rodney. "Have they caught the person responsible?"

Angela, too, had started crying. "No," she replied.

"How terrible," said Rodney. He passed the photo to Alec, asking if he had known the girl.

Alec studied the photo and replied that he hadn't.

The reply was a little too quick for Jodie, which made her pay a little more attention. Alec had blue eyes, a slim nose, and pouting lips. But it was the teeth. She had never, ever, seen teeth as white as his. He reminded her of someone from TV but it escaped her at the moment.

A strange thought crossed her mind, as she wondered why he was wasting his time as an undertaker, when he could quite clearly be a male model.

Where the hell did she recognize him from? She couldn't for the life of her remember, but it was very quickly starting to bug her.

They passed another half hour talking about the service, what the parents wanted, the music, the coffin itself, and the transport and where they would like the coffin to go from.

All the while, Jodie was mostly switched off. She caught herself staring at Alec more often than she should. He, in return, shot a couple of furtive expressions back.

Rodney suddenly turned to Alec and questioned him again, regarding the newspaper reports, and about the name of the club Sonia had been in.

"It says the police are asking for witnesses. Don't you go there, Alec?" Rodney asked. "To that club?"

"I've been a couple of times."

"Were you there that night?"

"Don't you think that if I was, I would have remembered?" said Alec.

"I'm sure you would have done, son," smiled Rodney. "It was just a thought." He turned to Jodie. "Were you there, Ms Thomson?"

"I was, yes," she replied.

"Must have been awful for you, too," said Rodney.

"I've had better nights," said Jodie.

She noticed an expression of thunder from Alec toward Rodney, as if he was trying to tell him to shut the fuck up about the club, without actually saying as much.

And that's when it hit Jodie, like a brick in the face. She suddenly realized that the undertaker sitting beside her *had* in fact been in The Key Club on that very night.

If she was not mistaken, he was the man that Sonia had been kissing, the man who had her all hot under the collar.

She was absolutely bloody sure of it. There couldn't be two of them. It had to be him. But if it was, why hadn't he come forward when the police had been asking for witnesses?

If she *was* right, what should she do? She couldn't say anything here and now. Her mind went into overdrive. Also, if she was right, that could mean Viktor the drug dealer had had nothing to do with Sonia's death.

That was more than possible. To be fair, Jodie had only put him in the frame because she hated him, especially for what he had done to her sister.

But then maybe Alec had had nothing to do with Sonia's death either.

So why not come forward and help?

Jodie might have it all wrong. Perhaps in her grief she thought it was Alec, when it wasn't. As far as she could remember, the man kissing Sonia wasn't called Alec. His name was Alan.

What if she'd heard it wrong? What in God's name was she going to do now?

Chapter Twenty-five

Later, at home, Angela made the tea while Jodie sat at the kitchen table, still totally and utterly confused. She loved the room because it was so homely. Everything was decorated with pine. Fresh flowers had been placed in the middle of the table, which was constantly set with place mats and coasters. Everything smelled fresh and clean.

Angela placed the teapot on the table, underneath a woollen cosy. She slipped back to the cupboards, opened one and pulled out a biscuit caddy before returning to the table.

Jodie checked her phone. She had three missed calls, two of which were from a number she recognized as the police. What the hell did they want? *She* certainly didn't want to speak to *them* at the moment, not with what was going on in her head.

Angela sat down, set out everything and poured tea for them both. Will was out. She passed the tea over to Jodie. "Help yourself to biscuits, love."

Jodie sipped on the tea, still oblivious to the world.

"What's on your mind, Jodie?"

Jodie glanced upwards. "I'm okay, just a bit stressed. You know, with everything that's going on. It's bad enough for me, but it must be bloody awful for you."

"It's more than that," said Angela.

Jodie should not take Angela for a fool. She was a very intelligent woman and appeared to be holding the family together, but Jodie desperately wanted to avoid the subject.

"I just keep going over everything in my mind, getting nowhere," said Jodie. "Why the hell did it happen?"

Angela sipped her tea, and fished a rich tea biscuit out of the caddy. She sighed heavily. "Because it did, Jodie, love. When it's your time to go, it's your time."

Jodie stared at Angela. Sonia's death had taken its toll on her. She had aged about ten years in a matter of weeks. Yet somehow, she still had her faith. Maybe that's what kept her going. "You're a big believer in all that, aren't you?"

"Of course I am," replied Angela. Her expression told Jodie she found it disturbing that someone would think she might have lost her faith because of what had happened.

"But how? Why?" questioned Jodie. "What if you get on a plane and it's the pilot's time that's up? He doesn't just go on his own, does he? He takes everyone else with him."

Angela smiled. "It doesn't work like that."

"What do you mean?"

"You have to look at the bigger picture, Jodie, love. It isn't just the pilot's time that's up, it's everyone. Everyone who's on that plane. It's their time as well," said Angela. "That's the bigger picture. We'll never understand what's in the Lord's mind, we just have to accept it. I won't lie to you and tell you that I'm fine with the decision. I find it hard to accept that it was Sonia's time, but it was. The Lord wanted her."

"How can you still go on believing in the Lord when he does awful things like that; takes people before their time?" asked Jodie. "He even takes babies. What kind of a God can do that?"

"The kind that we'll never understand. Because we don't have the capacity to. There's an even bigger picture that we can't see."

"I don't think I'd want to. And yet, still, you have faith, after everything that's happened."

"Yes, I have," replied Angela. "And I'll see Sonia again, when it's my turn to go. But at the moment, what's important is you, and I know you're suffering, so why don't you tell me what's going on in that pretty little head of yours. You did really well today, at the funeral home. You answered a lot of things that we couldn't. You sorted out her choice of music. You were a great help, but something was bothering you. What is it?"

Jodie hesitated, running things through her mind. "Oh, it's nothing."

Angela finished her biscuit and had another. "I won't ask again. I know you too well. You will have to tell me, you know."

Jodie did know. Her back was against the wall. If she refused now, or she left without saying, she felt as though she would be insulting Angela, and Sonia's memory. She had no choice.

"I think I recognized Alec."

"The young man, you mean? He was definitely a treat for the old eye."

"I think it was Alec who was kissing Sonia in the club that night," said Jodie.

There, it was out. Now what?

"Our Sonia?"

"Yes," said Jodie. "I'm sure it was him. Only she said that his name was Alan, not Alec."

"Maybe you misheard."

"I thought that," replied Jodie. "But when she was telling me, we were in the toilet, well away from all the loud music. There is no mistake, the name he used was Alan."

"Well maybe it was someone *called* Alan, who looks like Alec."

"Are you serious?" asked Jodie. "Do you honestly think there are two blokes who are that drop dead gorgeous living in Leeds with very similar names? No, it was him. And either Sonia had his name wrong, or he told her it was Alan when it wasn't."

Angela seemed deep in thought before she said. "It's pretty serious, this."

"I keep wondering," said Jodie. "Did Alec, or Alan, have anything to do with Sonia's death? Did *he* give Sonia drugs?"

"I'm not sure she had taken drugs, Jodie," said Angela. "After all, the police haven't found any in her system. They say she had something called the Nipah virus. And should that be the case, this is not murder, is it?"

"I still wouldn't rule out drugs," persisted Jodie. "There's some dodgy stuff out there." She suddenly leaned forward. "Maybe Alec is working with Viktor."

"How can he be?" argued Angela. "He's a funeral director, for pity's sake. He works for God. I doubt very much that he would be involved in anything like that."

"Just because he's a funeral director doesn't mean he can't be involved in drugs, or owt dodgy," retorted Jodie. "After all, he goes to nightclubs, doesn't he? You heard his father mention that. He actually asked him if he'd been in the club that night, and if he remembered Sonia. He said he hadn't. Did you see his face when his father asked that?"

"I can't say I did, no," replied Angela. "I was too busy taking in what Mr Parkinson was saying."

"Well, I saw it," said Jodie. "He wanted the floor to open up underneath him. No, I'm telling you, he was in that club. And he was kissing Sonia. And now she's gone."

After some obvious debate inside her own mind, Angela spoke to Jodie. "It's very unlikely. I really can't see what you've said as being right, Jodie. I don't mean that you're lying, but maybe you're mistaken in what you're thinking."

"What do you mean?"

"Well, suppose he *was* in the club," said Angela. "Nothing wrong with that. Suppose he *was* kissing Sonia. Nothing wrong with that, either. She was happy, you said so. But that's where it must have ended. Sonia left the club alone, and she got home alone, and there was no one in the apartment with her when she got home, or when she died. And the police don't seem to have any evidence that there was. I had a long chat with that nice Mr Gardener, and he told me all of this."

"Then why didn't Alec – or Alan – come forward, with the information, when the police were asking? He was in that club, and I know he knows something about what went on, but he hasn't said a word."

"I don't see what he could know," replied Angela. "And maybe he doesn't know anything. Like you said, he would have come forward. If you're *sure* about this, Jodie, you must give the information to the police, let them deal with it."

Jodie sighed heavily. "You're probably right. This is all too much for me, and I'm not the right person to find the answers. I certainly haven't found any so far."

Angela's expression darkened. "What do you mean? Have you been investigating this on your own?"

"A bit," replied Jodie, sheepishly.

"What's a bit?"

"I've been to the club, asked questions about the drug dealer."

Angela put her face in her hands. "Oh God, Jodie, you need to be careful. You remember what happened to Will when he tried to sort things out, and what advice they gave him?"

Jodie remained silent for a minute or so. "I've been stupid, haven't I?"

"Look," said Angela. "This Alec, or Alan, or whatever his name is, might be completely innocent, but they will see that. You must tell them, and leave them to deal with it. I really think you should phone them now."

After some thought, Jodie replied, "No. I'll do better than that. I'll go over there now and talk to that detective."

She rose from the table.

Chapter Twenty-six

Due to the pressure of the case, the best that Gardener and Reilly could offer their better halves, and Malcolm, was a half day at Tropical World, with Gardener feeling incredibly guilty that that was all they could do, because he really should have been spending time in the office.

So far, however, every single avenue they had pursued had come up with a dead end. Little things had transpired but there was no concrete evidence against anyone, or anything to support the theory that Sonia had actually been murdered, which meant, it would go cold case anytime soon – unless something turned up.

Once the girls had found the only table big enough to accommodate all of them, against his better wishes, Gardener took Reilly to the counter with him. The bill could prove astronomical depending on how hungry his sergeant was.

When they had their food and everyone was comfortable, it was Laura who spoke first.

"I've really enjoyed today. I can't remember the last time we had a day out." As she said this, she was glancing at her husband, but he was already otherwise engaged with a large sandwich.

"It's been brilliant," said Vanessa. "And so nice to finally meet you."

"Likewise," said Laura. She turned to Gardener's father. "Have you enjoyed yourself, Malcolm?"

"Yes, thank you. It's made a real nice change to get out of the house for bit. And I certainly couldn't have asked for a better place to visit. There is so much to see and do in here."

Laura smiled and turned to Vanessa. "And I think that you guys look fantastic together."

"Oh, thank you," replied Vanessa

Emboldened, Laura continued. "I never thought I'd see the day when someone finally captured this man's heart again."

Gardener flushed. He knew what was coming.

"Me neither," added Malcolm.

"It took some doing," said Vanessa, staring at him.

"I'll bet it did," said Laura.

Glancing at Gardener, Vanessa said, "We're getting there, aren't we?"

"We seem to be," replied Gardener. "Though I'm not exactly sure where there is."

"Neither am I," said Reilly. "And we've been at it years."

"Oh, here he goes," said Laura. "We're going to get the hard-done-by routine."

"Hardly surprising, dearest," said Reilly, glancing at Laura, "with what I have to put up with."

"You should try the view from my side."

"I've wanted to, believe me. It must be such an improvement."

"Sean Reilly!" exclaimed Laura. "I don't know how you dare. You wait till you get home."

"She'll give in, she always does."

Gardener and Vanessa were laughing. Once again, staring at Gardener, she said. "And it's great to see this one enjoying himself as well. He works too hard."

"I've been telling him that for years," said Malcolm. "But he's never listened to me."

"You don't have the magic touch, Malcolm," said Vanessa.

Reilly jumped in. "What she means is, you don't look like her."

They all found the comment amusing. The only other occupied table in the tea room settled their bill and left. A waitress cleared the table and returned to the counter at the other end of the room.

"Talking of work," said Vanessa. "How is the latest case progressing?"

"It isn't," replied Gardener. "We're at a standstill."

"Unless anything about the mispers comes to light," added Reilly.

"Even if they find something, Sean," said Gardener. "Connecting everything could be a problem."

"You mentioned something about Fitz connecting the case to a virus of some sort," said Vanessa.

"It's what he seems to think."

"So what did he actually find?"

"As I understand it," said Gardener, finishing his sandwich and his tea, "the main thing he was concerned about was encephalitis."

"The brain swelling," said Vanessa, "which could be a number of things."

Gardener poured himself some fresh tea, offering the pot to anyone else, which Malcolm took.

"He did mention that. But when you couple it with what we *have* managed to find out it becomes more focused."

"Her friend, Jodie Thomson," said Reilly, "reckoned that Sonia Markham complained of one or two symptoms that made it look like a cold."

"She apparently had a headache," continued Gardener, "a cough, and a sore throat."

"Which could simply be the flu," said Vanessa. "Did Fitz say which virus he thought it might be?"

"The nearest thing he could compare it to was something called the Nipah virus."

"Nipah?" repeated Vanessa. "Did she suffer any vomiting, or difficulty breathing?"

"Not sure about the breathing but she certainly wasn't vomiting," replied Gardener.

Vanessa was topping up the tea for herself and Laura.

"As a matter of fact," said Reilly, "the food she'd prepared herself went untouched."

"It's a very rare virus," said Vanessa. "Having said that, those kinds of infections are expanding globally. Any idea where she picked it up from?"

"No," said Gardener. "Not yet."

"If she picked it up somewhere, then it's not murder," said Reilly.

"But you think otherwise?" questioned Laura.

"We do," said Gardener. "But I can't put my finger on why. If it was drug-related, I'm sure we'd have found some evidence to support it. But there is nothing."

"And if it's the Nipah virus," added Reilly, "then why haven't we seen more evidence to support *that*? Why have we not got a pandemic on our hands?"

"Maybe Sonia Markham is the first," said Laura.

"Maybe so, but she died a few weeks ago," said Vanessa. "If we were on our way to a pandemic, we'd have seen more cases by now. If it's not drugs, and it turns out not to be the Nipah virus, then where does that leave you?"

"Up shit creek," said Reilly.

"Looking for another case," said Gardener.

Vanessa raised her hand in the air. "Wait a minute."

Gardener glanced at her. "Has something just come to mind?"

He waited as she grabbed her phone.

"Maybe," said Vanessa. "And believe it or not, it's something involving this place."

"Here?" said Gardener. "Tropical World."

"Yes," replied Vanessa, scrolling through her phone. "I'm just trying to remember what it was."

"Surely if something had happened here," said Gardener, "wouldn't it have been big news? I certainly don't remember anything."

He turned to his father. "Dad?"

"Nothing comes to mind for me."

"It happened around eighteen months ago," said Vanessa, glancing at Gardener. "I'm sure that a girl who worked here succumbed to a virus of some description. But I don't think she caught it here. Problem is, I can't remember enough about it."

She checked her phone again before glancing upwards. "Look, I don't mean to ruin the day, but I think you should strike while the iron is hot. Go and speak to the manager. I'm sure if you flash your warrant cards, he or she would be more than happy to help."

Gardener glanced around the table. It could be something or nothing, and if he was on duty, he would follow it up.

"Do you guys mind?" he asked.

Each of them said they didn't. The ladies still had their drinks and a cake each, so they were happy to sit and talk for a while. Malcolm was fine with that.

"What do you think, Sean?"

"I don't think we should pass up an opportunity, boss."

It took them another thirty minutes to track the manager down. When they did, they were shown into an office overlooking the grounds.

Sandra Pearson was middle aged, her grey hair was tied in a bun, and she wore wire rimmed glasses.

"How may I help you?" she asked.

Despite being off duty, the pair of them did have their warrant cards. Pearson asked them both to take a seat and Gardener explained the reason for their visit.

"Dear me," said Sandra Pearson. "I remember reading about that girl in the newspaper quite recently. And you haven't found the person responsible?"

"Not yet," said Gardener.

"Well, I'm not sure how I can help."

Gardener explained the conversation they had all had around the table about forty minutes ago.

"Oh, I see," said Sandra Pearson. "As a matter of fact, I certainly do remember the girl in question. It was very strange."

"Can you tell us what happened?" asked Gardener.

"If you think it will help."

"We don't really know," said Reilly.

Sandra Pearson turned to her computer, tapped around on the keyboard and brought up what she needed.

"One of the things we pride ourselves on here at Tropical World is we like to encourage people, we want them to do well. It's not a job for just anyone, you really have to love what you're doing because the animals and birds that we deal with are not your run-of-the-mill household pets."

"We noticed," said Reilly.

She smiled. "We decided to run a job placement many years ago, which works very well. We send one of our staff to a zoo in the Philippines and they send one of theirs here. The visitor is put up in basic accommodation, with meals included and we both learn a lot from the scheme."

She tapped more keys, leaving Gardener to wonder at the possible breakthrough they had been needing.

"Eighteen months ago, we had a very high achiever called Lucy Brown. She was nineteen, and she lived with her parents in Pudsey. When she came to work for us, she had recently passed her driving test. Her father had bought her a small Fiat 500, so she was very independent.

"I remember Lucy loved working with animals," said Pearson, her gaze akin to a proud mother. "She was more than happy do anything you wanted her to do, working all hours. We thought she deserved to get something more out of the job, so we inquired about a placement and once it was all sorted, we sent her."

"To the Philippines?" said Gardener.

"Yes. She really enjoyed herself, worked equally as hard over there as she did here. In fact, the zoo in question spoke to us because they wanted offer Lucy a full-time position. We didn't want to lose her but we couldn't stand in her way, either. Eventually, all the paperwork was sorted and everyone agreed. She was only coming back here for a month to sort everything out."

"What happened?" asked Gardener.

"Well, although Lucy Brown contracted a virus of some description, she did not do so in the UK. From what we know, she picked it up from infected fruit on the final day of her placement in the Philippines before flying home. She was feeling ill when she arrived in the UK, immediately went home and did not report for work in Leeds again. She died at home five days later."

"She never actually came back here?" asked Reilly.

"No," replied Sandra Pearson. "It was a very upsetting time."

"Do you have the names and address of her parents?"

"I'm not really supposed to give out that kind of information," said Sandra Pearson. "But on this occasion, I can't see it will make a lot of difference."

Gardener was pleased about that. The last thing he wanted was a tussle with a jobsworth.

Sandra Pearson printed out the details and handed them over to Gardener. Rhona and Geoff Brown lived on Lidgett Hill in Pudsey. He passed the details to Reilly.

"I remember Geoff meeting his daughter at the airport to give her a lift home," said Sandra Pearson. "He knew at that point something was wrong because Lucy had no colour and she complained of feeling unwell. She was aching all over, had a headache and had developed a cough.

"He took her straight home. Her mother certainly didn't like what she saw either, and told Lucy to go straight to bed, where she would bring her up a hot drink. Lucy did manage to drink it, said it hit the spot, but then turned over and went to sleep. She did not come down for an evening meal, and when she showed for breakfast, she appeared no better.

"Her mother said there was a bit of trouble because Lucy wouldn't hear of the doctor being called out. She said it was probably just a cold. That's definitely the Lucy we knew. She never had a day off in all the time she worked here – not a sick day, anyway.

"The next day she was even worse, she was disorientated and confused and her mother believed that it was more than just flu. The surgery said no doctor was available until the next day and that if her parents were really worried, they should take Lucy to A&E."

Sandra Pearson stopped talking. Gardener noticed her eyes filling up.

"They never had the chance," continued Sandra Pearson. "Rhona found Lucy the next morning. She had passed away. The family was distraught. Relatives rallied around and Lucy's body was taken away for a post-mortem."

"Did you ever find out what that virus was?" asked Gardener.

"I'm afraid I didn't," replied Sandra Pearson. "I never heard anything from the results of the post-mortem."

The two detectives talked a little more with Sandra Pearson before thanking her for her time and efficiency. As they were leaving the office, she asked them if they would call back to see her if they managed to solve their case, especially if it had anything to do with their ex-employee.

Outside, they made their way back to the tea room.

"What do you make of that, boss?" asked Reilly.

Gardener thought for a moment before replying. "That we may have an even bigger problem on our hands."

"What makes you say that?"

Gardener stopped and stared at his friend.

"There is one question running through my mind right now. How does a girl who died eighteen months ago from a virus of some description, have anything to do with what's happening today?"

"I've no idea," said Reilly. "But now we need to do what we do best, and investigate the matter further."

Chapter Twenty-seven

After lunch the following day, Gardener and Reilly were in the office with Fitz.

"What the devil brings you two here?"

"The coffee," replied Reilly.

"Oh God," said Fitz, slipping his head into his hands. "That's the new stock of snacks about to take a battering."

"You love us coming here, my friend," said Reilly. "What would your day without us be?"

"Cheaper," replied Fitz.

When they were seated, Fitz asked them again what he could do for them.

"We'd like to pick your brains," said Gardener.

"Is this to do with Sonia Markham?"

"Yes," said Gardener. "We managed to find out something yesterday, completely by accident. We felt the need to follow it up. But before we get into that, do you have anything further to say on that score?"

Fitz pushed his glasses further up the bridge of his nose and tapped his keyboard. "We're pretty certain now that she did contract the Nipah virus. All the signs are there. They ran a series of tests, specifically aimed at finding out."

It wasn't what Gardener wanted to hear.

"Then why haven't we had more cases?" asked Reilly.

"Can't really answer that," said Fitz, "but it is unusual. Tell me what you've found."

Gardener explained they were following up on information from a place called Tropical World.

"Isn't that the zoo at Roundhay?"

Gardener nodded.

"What took you there?" asked Fitz.

"A day out," said Gardener. He then went on to recall what had transpired.

"That is interesting," said Fitz, after listening closely.

Gardener asked if it was possible to see the post-mortem on Lucy Brown.

"We can try. If it was done here, it should be on the system."

"What if it wasn't done here?" asked Reilly.

"I should still be able to find it," replied Fitz. "Might just take a little longer. Do you have her address?"

Gardener passed it over.

Fitz tapped away at his keyboard.

As Gardener waited, he found his nerves fraying. If they *had* found something, it could change the case. Even if they hadn't, he felt that the case was about to change anyway.

"Here it is," said Fitz. He must have hit the print button because the machine fired into life.

After Fitz had the printout, he studied it carefully for quite some time, winding up Gardener even further.

Finally, he put the report on his desk. "Interesting, but to be honest, the results of Lucy Brown's post-mortem don't reveal anything unexpected."

"Does it say what she died of?" asked Gardener.

"Not particularly," said Fitz. "It was put down to a virus of some sort. I will say what's interesting about it is, it was almost like reading the post-mortem for Sonia Markham."

"So, they both died of the same virus?" asked Gardener, hopefully.

"I can't really say," said Fitz, "but there are similarities. Hold on a second."

Fitz played around with the keyboard some more, and then said. "I thought I didn't recognize it. I didn't do the PM on this one. I was away."

"Who did?" asked Gardener.

"It was a locum," replied Fitz. "Brought in from somewhere in Glasgow."

"Couldn't they get anyone closer?" asked Reilly.

"Doesn't always work that way." Fitz studied the report some more. "Nothing has flagged up."

"But Lucy Brown had been to the Philippines," said Gardener. "And this Nipah virus is well known over there. Surely something must have come to light."

"Not necessarily," replied Fitz. "A pathologist wouldn't screen for any infection unless there were signs that an infection was present before death. He or she would then need to have an idea as to what that infection is likely to have been before they look for it.

"The public seem to think that you just run a general test which shows up any problem, but medicine doesn't work like that. Viruses can only multiply in living cells. If they do not find a living body to re-infect, they usually die within minutes, sometimes hours. The whole reason for infecting someone or something is to reproduce and continue their life cycle. The symptoms, or damage done to the host body is incidental – a by-product of using the host cells to reproduce."

"Did it even mention a visit to the Philippines?" asked Gardener.

"I can't see anything," replied Fitz. "To decide to look for a particular cause of infection, the symptoms would have to suggest an infection with that particular bacteria or virus. If the pathologist did not know the medical history prior to death, they would not think to screen for a particular virus or bacteria.

"In this case, there is a need to defend the man. If he didn't know the patient had recently travelled to the Philippines, or anywhere the virus is endemic, he would not even contemplate looking for it in his patient. And that is assuming the pathologist is informed about the Nipah virus – I am sure many wouldn't be.

"A microbiologist might well do so, but they are only involved when specifically asked by the pathologist – again not a routine thing. That's one way of explaining why your pathologist is more likely to miss the infection than to identify it anyway – however experienced they are. A microbiologist might identify it in a living person if they are on the ball."

Gardener glanced at Reilly. "Doesn't get any easier, this case, does it?"

"You're telling me."

"In all fairness," said Fitz. "From what I can see, the man had been on his feet for eighteen hours, and it was the final one of the day. The connection between the two is a 'slight swelling of the brain' but there is nothing to indicate it was the Nipah virus. There was nothing in the file informing the locum that Lucy Brown had been away for a month on a work placement."

"But both of them could have died because of the same virus?" pressed Gardener, not quite sure where he was going with it.

"It's very possible," said Fitz.

"But because we now know that Lucy Brown had been to the Philippines for that placement and had caught the virus there," said Gardener, "we could do with finding out if both girls succumbed to the same virus."

"But our girl hasn't been to the Philippines," said Reilly.

"That's what's worrying me."

"There is only one way of finding that out, gentlemen," said Fitz. "But I'm not sure your lord and master will want to go to the trouble and the expense."

Gardener had already thought about what Fitz was going to suggest. "You're talking about an exhumation and a second post-mortem, aren't you?"

Fitz nodded. "That really is the only way to find out. But I have to tell you, it's not very nice."

Gardener had never asked for one. "What's involved?"

"Depends," said Fitz. "If it's from a churchyard – consummated ground – you'll need a church licence from the local bishop, assuming it's Church of England. If it's not from a church cemetery then you'll need a Home Office licence."

Gardener could see the expression on Brigg's face already.

"But!" said Fitz. "And this is the problem. If you're taking the body out of the church ground and putting it into a non church ground you need both licenses! You will also need a health officer present. It needs to be done at night, the grave needs to be screened off, you need to put the body and coffin into a sealed box, the whole site gets decontaminated, and then put back the way it was before you arrived."

"Jesus," said Reilly, rubbing his hands down his face.

"It's also good practice," said Fitz, "to inform the coroner – but oddly not a requirement. And none of this can be done without family consent. And I will almost certainly hate the pair of you for a very long time."

"Nothing new there, then," said Reilly.

"Bodies are no fun to work on when they're putrefied."

Gardener shook his head. "We're caught between the devil and the deep blue sea here."

"Why?" said Reilly.

"To be absolutely sure, we have to consider it. But the important question still remains."

"Which is?" asked Fitz.

"How does Lucy Brown's death, eighteen months ago, from the Nipah virus, have anything to do with Sonia Markham's death today?"

Chapter Twenty-eight

As early evening approached, Gardener had the whole team in the incident room. Though he had something to share, he was not hopeful that Briggs would go for it, without some hard evidence. As it stood, Sonia Markham had caught a virus and died. She had not been murdered. Gardener needed a little bit of luck if he was going to confirm his suspicions; maybe the team would help.

As he was about to start, the door opened and desk sergeant Dave Williams stepped in, waving a report around. "Am I right in thinking that you guys are still looking for Jodie Thomson?"

"Yes," replied Gardener. "Is she here?"

"No, and I'm not quite sure where she is."

"What do you mean?" asked Reilly.

"We've had a call from the bank to say she was not in work today, and they can't get hold of her. And now we've taken a call from the concierge of the apartment block, and he hasn't seen her for three days."

"Have you called the Markhams?" asked Gardener, the whole team riveted on the conversation.

"Yes, twice," said Williams. "No answer."

"What about her parents?" asked Briggs.

"Called them. They say it's not unusual for them not to see Jodie for anything up to a week."

"*Her* phone?" asked Gardener.

Williams nodded. "Goes straight to voicemail."

"This doesn't sound good," said Gardener, trying to think ahead. "Keep calling the Markhams, she could be with them, they may all be out somewhere. Keep trying her phone, and keep calling her parents to see if they have any news. Ask them to call as soon as they hear anything. And can you send someone over to The Quays? Get the concierge to let you into her apartment. God forbid she has ended up the same way as Sonia Markham."

As Williams left, Gardener stared at Briggs but nothing was said between them.

Gardener started the meeting, explaining what he and Reilly had found out at Tropical World, and then what Fitz had to say on the matter; namely that an exhumation may be necessary.

The expression on Briggs' face told Gardener all he needed to know. He was unhappy with that suggestion.

"Is this really necessary?" he asked.

"It's possible that her death may have something to do with what's happening now."

"How?" asked Briggs.

"It's just an idea that's popped into my head," said Gardener, before adding. "Maybe somebody has harvested this bloody thing in a lab, and now he's letting it loose on random people to see what happens."

"That's a bit far-fetched," said Briggs.

"But not impossible," said Reilly. "We've dealt with some strange people over the years."

"We still are." Rawson laughed whilst glancing at Reilly.

"If that's the case," said Gardener. "We could be in real trouble, but an exhumation could be a way for us to make absolutely sure that the two cases are connected… or that they aren't. And if someone *has* found a way to keep this thing alive in lab conditions, we need to find them."

Briggs shook his head. "I understand the way you're thinking, but have you any idea what's involved in an exhumation?"

"I do now."

"Then you'll know why I'm not happy about it," retorted Briggs. "I'll need more evidence than you've brought me."

Gardener couldn't argue.

Briggs continued. "What about the mispers you've all been looking into? Has anyone found any evidence to support why we should continue with this investigation?"

Gardener glanced at the team.

Gates saved the day. "Actually, we've found four cases that merit further investigation."

Gardener could have kissed her. "Four?"

"We believe so," said Longstaff.

"We've definitely found *something* that just might connect some dots."

Briggs stood up, walked to the side of the room, poured himself some tea and sat back down. "You'd better start then."

"The first missing girl on the list that caught our attention," said Gates, "is a lady called Katherine Field."

"When did she go missing?" asked Gardener.

"Last December," said Longstaff.

"Okay," said Gardener, parking himself on the edge of the table at the front of the room. "Tell us what you have."

Longstaff consulted her notes. "Katherine was twenty-nine years old, lived in barn conversion with a double garage on White Hills Lane in Skipton. She had recently divorced her husband and was living with her parents, hoping to find somewhere once the settlement came through.

"She was a nurse at a local care home called The Feathers, about two miles outside of Skipton. As it was very close to her birthday, her parents had encouraged her to have a night out with her friend, a lady called Marsha West, who also lives in Skipton."

"Have you spoken to Marsha West?" asked Gardener.

"We have," said Gates. "Everything checks out. Marsha works for one of the local building societies.

Here's what she told us. The pair had been friends since childhood and had a lot of common interests. The difference was, Marsha was happily married.

"The night in question was Saturday 5th December. They took a train from Skipton in the afternoon, landing in Leeds at around four o'clock, and from there, a bus into Wakefield for four-thirty, where they then went to the Premier Inn on Paragon Business Park, on Herriot Way, and checked in for a twin room."

"They had something to eat at six and hit the pubs at seven," continued Longstaff. "By ten o'clock they had been in a number of them before finally ending up in After Dark, a nightclub on Westgate, where they stayed.

"Marsha said she wanted to call it a night at midnight but Katherine was really up for letting her hair down. She persuaded Marsha to go back to the hotel and that she would be absolutely fine because she'd met a really nice guy. He said he would see her back to the hotel, as it was on his way home. That was the last Marsha saw of Katherine."

"What happened?" asked Reilly.

"Marsha woke up the next morning," said Gates. "She immediately noticed that Katherine's bed had not been slept in. She tried not to worry too much, sent her friend a text and slipped down to breakfast.

"By ten o'clock, when it was time to check out, Katherine had still not returned, nor had she answered the message. Marsha was becoming really concerned. It wasn't like Katherine, and besides, she had a six-year-old daughter to look after."

"Marsha called Katherine's parents but they had neither seen nor heard from her," said Longstaff. "Marsha said she was coming back to Skipton and if they had heard nothing by the time she returned, they would phone the police."

"And did they?" asked Briggs.

"Yes," said Gates. "The police turned up, took statements and followed up everything they could."

"The trail went cold," said Longstaff. "And as of now, it's still a cold case. Katherine Fields had not been seen or heard from again."

"And do we have all of those police files?" asked Gardener.

"We do," replied Gates. "Phone records showed a number of calls and texts to Katherine's phone, all of them unanswered. Most of them were from Marsha, some from her parents and others from friends."

"And why do we think that this might have a bearing on what we're looking into?" asked Gardener.

"Our mutual friend, Viktor, had been seen in the After Dark nightclub on the same night as Katherine Field. Earlier in the evening, they were seen talking. No one was prepared to come forward and state what he was up to, but it didn't take a genius."

The room grew silent, before Briggs broke that silence. "It might be a link but it's tenuous."

"Maybe," said Reilly. "But it's enough for us to drag Viktor in for questioning."

"Let's go back a bit," said Gardener. "Who was the really nice guy that she'd met? Did Marsha get his name?"

"We spoke to her about that," said Longstaff. "She remembered him being slim with black hair and said his name was Andrew."

"Did the local police follow up on that?" asked Gardener.

"They tried but there wasn't enough information," said Gates. "They didn't have his surname. No one really knew him."

"A couple of people mentioned they had seen him in the club before," said Longstaff, "but only once."

"Slim, black hair?" said Gardener. "Sound familiar? Okay, maybe we have a pattern developing here. Viktor has come up in our case with Sonia Markham, and so has a slim man with the black hair. I'll grant you, it's cotton thin, but it's something. We need a lot more. Do we have anything else?"

Chapter Twenty-nine

It fell to Thornton and Anderson. Both detectives consulted notes and took it in turns to fill the team in on the details.

It was a very similar story with Amelia Simms the second girl to go missing in unusual circumstances some three months later, in March. Amelia was twenty-one years old and also lived with parents, Ken and Emily in a small three-bedroom bungalow on Earl Street, off Spring Garden's Lane, Keighley. She was a counter assistant at Boots chemist in the town. She had a younger brother, Keith, who was studying climate change at one of the colleges in Cambridge.

The family never really had much money but a small win on the lottery when no one had claimed a penny for a full month, gave them enough to buy a bungalow and book a holiday on a ship. The cruise was to include both children to celebrate the couple's twenty-fifth wedding anniversary.

Although they had realized the trip had fallen on Amelia's twenty-first birthday, they still thought she would be excited enough to go. However, she preferred to celebrate her twenty-first with her friends. After a major discussion between the family and then the travel agency, they managed to postpone the cruise for a month, because there had been another cancellation.

Emily had taken Amelia into Leeds for the day and bought her something to wear for the evening. They'd had dinner out, before returning around three o'clock, when

Amelia hit the bathroom – for two hours, but it had been worth it. Amelia had a very slim figure, jet black shoulder length hair with blue eyes, yet still, she had no boyfriend.

She left the house at five to meet with friends for pre-food drinks in The Livery Rooms, a local Wetherspoons, before heading to Azeem's Indian restaurant on South Street, for a proper meal in anticipation of the night ahead. Her friends were Jenny Seabrook, Carla Winston, and Eva Ronson. They were all sensible girls; no tricks had either been played or lined up.

They left the restaurant at ten and were seen in Bar 61 on Church Street at ten-thirty, before hitting the K2 nightclub, which is close by on the same street. That was the last that anyone actually saw of her. As usual, in nightclubs, people separate and either talk to other people they know, or are chatted up. Jenny said she last saw Amelia talking to a guy at midnight. Carla said she was still talking to the man twenty minutes later, and Eva said they both spoke in the toilets a little after one o'clock. Amelia said she had had offers from three different men that evening, but the first one she spoke to, called Ashley, seemed the nicest.

Amelia had had a bit to drink and she could only remember black hair and nice teeth. He worked for himself but he hadn't said what – at that point. The girls left the toilet and never saw each other again. Sometime around two o'clock, they panicked because they all met up in the lobby area and no one had seen Amelia for quite some time. One of them went back in to search for her, which was easy, because most people had left by then. Amelia was nowhere to be seen. They tried calling but her mobile went unanswered. They left messages. The last thing they wanted was to alert her parents at that time in the morning. But they did so later that same morning.

Eva had taken it upon herself to contact everyone at nine o'clock. No one had heard anything. Amelia's phone remained unanswered. Eva called Amelia's brother, Keith;

he'd heard nothing. She then called Ken and Emily, who said, after checking, that her bed had not been slept in. The police were called. They issued a crime number but the case went cold.

The only possible lead they had was the CCTV outside the club, which picked her up leaving with the man she had been talking to –black hair, smartly dressed – but it may not have been the same man. The pair of them staggered up Church Street, out of view of the CCTV. Witness statements were very thin on the ground. Two more sightings shortly after that put her on Mornington Street, still with the man, but another said they saw her heading towards Earl Street on her own.

"So," said Anderson. "Anything could have happened, but without CCTV and witnesses they were struggling. A press appeal revealed nothing. She has not been seen since."

Thornton continued. "Phone calls and text messages to Amelia's phone remained unanswered. They were mostly from Jenny, Carla, and Eva – not to mention her parents and her brother, Keith. The police did a very competent job tracing everyone they could find from the club on the night in question, but that did not include the man she had been talking to. Everyone was tracked and interviewed. Nothing came of it and the trail went cold, and has remained cold."

"Once again," said Gardener, "we have the man with black hair. Do we have Viktor?"

"Viktor was seen in the K2 earlier in the evening," said Anderson. "And outside at around one-thirty. Someone said he had left with a girl who was slim and had shoulder length black hair – but it could have been anyone."

Gardener definitely wanted him in, wondering whether or not he was interviewed at the time. If he wasn't, he should have been.

"Viktor, and a man with black hair called Ashley," said Gardener. "Who may also have the name Andrew, and very possibly Alan. Who's next?"

Rawson and Sharp indicated that they too had something similar.

Dawn Roberts was the most recent of the four girls that went missing; in September.

Dawn was twenty-six years old and came from Wakefield. She was given up for adoption almost immediately after she was born, and taken into the care system, where she stayed until she was fourteen, until she literally ran away one night. She had spent time in three care homes during those years, each of them within a twenty-mile radius, and in each case, Dawn Roberts suffered abuse.

Despite a bad start in life, Dawn was attractive, slim with blonde, shoulder length hair and blue eyes. Records subsequently show that her abuse started when she was seven years old, when one of the male care workers had taken a real shine to her and used to visit her room.

Until that point, Dawn had remained reasonably balanced despite the bad start. From then on, she became withdrawn, didn't speak much to people, and didn't eat a great deal. That pattern followed wherever she went until she could take no more. But a life on the streets did little to improve her situation and the only person she could call a friend was twenty-year-old brunette who went by the name of Angel.

At some point, and it really isn't clear when, Angel introduced Dawn to her pimp, and then it went even further down hill. It's believed that Dawn went on the game at sixteen. Where she lived and where she went was impossible to keep a track of, but the last that anyone really knew about her, she had a place in Park Lodge Lane on the Eastmoor Estate in Wakefield.

The last real sighting anyone had of Dawn Roberts was the night of the twenty-first of September, sometime around midnight. She had been thrown out of the Reflex nightclub on Westgate for soliciting.

A report at twelve-thirty on the same evening said she was seen jumping into a car on Leeds Road, close to the Wakefield College, with a possible punter. Where the car finished up, no one knows. CCTV tracked it heading towards the M1 motorway. It was a blue Ford Mondeo but they had since discovered that the registration plate on the car was false. The last known sighting was on the M1 going towards Leeds but at some point it must have either pulled off, or into a service station. Then, very likely, the plates were changed.

The police had her down as a misper. They talked to her neighbours, who couldn't tell them much because she kept to herself. They never found the girl known as Angel, or the pimp she was believed to have worked for.

"Why is she a link to the others?" asked Gardener.

"Because she was seen having a fierce argument outside the club with Viktor," said Rawson, "where she stormed off down Westgate toward the centre of town."

"Now we're down to just Viktor," said Gardener. "There doesn't appear to be a slim man with black hair whose name begins with an A."

"You said four," said Briggs, who had remained quiet for some time, which Gardener took to be a good sign. "We've only had three."

"Their last movements indicate that all of them frequented clubs that Viktor was known in, and seen in on those nights," said Sharp. "Save one."

"And why her?" asked Gardener.

"Well, here is where we have another bit of a mystery," said Gates.

Chapter Thirty

"Just what we love," said Reilly. "A mystery."

Gardener signalled for Gates to continue.

"Diane Drayton was the oldest of the four girls to have gone missing in or around the Leeds area. This one was in June of last year, and remains unaccounted for.

"She lived in Station Lane, Woodlesford, which is near Oulton, just outside of Rothwell, with her husband, Phillip, and her eight-year-old daughter, Debbie."

"She was attending the funeral of a work colleague, Cynthia Keane," continued Longstaff. "Who had been taken rather suddenly one night on Boar Lane in Leeds when she was knocked over by a car.

"Cynthia was alive when the ambulance was called but died on the way to hospital. Most of the firm were actually given the day off to attend the funeral, which was held in Rothwell at the crematorium, before moving on to the Bridge Farm Hotel on Bullerthorpe Lane for the wake."

"Like most of the people there," said Gates, "Diane was upset at the funeral but had rallied round at the wake. She seemed in good spirits and was in fact last seen talking to a young man called Alec Parkinson, the undertaker who had played quite a large part in all the proceedings.

"Here's the bit you'll like," continued Gates. "The one really surprising fact was that Viktor was seen in the pub that day, but it wasn't confirmed whether he was a guest at the wake or there for another reason."

"What other reason could there be?" asked Briggs.

"Surely he wouldn't be trying to sell drugs at a wake?" asked Reilly.

"I wouldn't have thought so," said Rawson. "But you know what these people are like."

"Let's assume for the time being that he was there as a guest," said Gardener. "Maybe he was a family friend, or something."

"Are you serious?" asked Rawson. "Who has a drug dealer for a family friend?"

"Fair point," said Gardener, indicating for Gates and Longstaff to continue.

"The guests at the wake remember Viktor being there, but none of them spoke to him for any length of time," said Gates. "Most people had left the wake by four o'clock in the afternoon, but Diane Drayton had been spotted by one of the bar staff as pretty much one of the last to leave, along with Alec Parkinson.

"All interviews were followed up at the time. According to his statement, Parkinson confirmed that he had left with Diane, but he only walked as far as the car park."

"Apparently," said Longstaff, "he received a phone call, which checked out. He had to leave, and she left to walk home in the opposite direction."

"She obviously didn't make it," said Gardener.

"No," said Gates. "And it wasn't clear exactly what had happened to her."

"Where did Parkinson go? Did the statement say?" asked Gardener.

"Back to the funeral parlour, on business," answered Longstaff.

"Out of curiosity, did anyone check that against any CCTV on the route?"

"What are you thinking?" Briggs asked Gardener.

"Nothing really. Just crossing the 't's and dotting the 'i's."

"CCTV did show her leaving the pub, and walking off in the direction she lived," said Longstaff. "Her house was three miles away, and given it was a lovely afternoon, she walked instead of taking a taxi."

"Trouble is," added Gates. "It's not clear what route she took. There's more than one, but the likelihood is, at some point she would have walked the canal towpath as it was much more pleasant. There is no CCTV along the canal path and there were no witness statements confirming that anyone had actually seen her, so what happened no one knows. But she did not turn up at home as expected."

"Her husband raised the alarm later in the day," said Longstaff. "The police attended, took a statement, issued a crime scene number, and said that if she had not returned the following day, they would start an investigation.

"The husband was cleared of any wrongdoing and detectives have left the case open, but Diane has not been seen since."

"Once again," said Gates. "No calls and texts were ever answered after the time she went missing – most of which were from her husband and daughter, and one or two from the police involved."

"And," said Gardener, "once again, the common link in all of these cases is Viktor."

"Seems to be making quite the appearance, doesn't he?" said Reilly.

"What was your opinion of him?" Briggs asked Gardener.

"Very sure of himself," said Gardener.

"With his money he has every right to be," said Reilly.

"I was thinking more about the prints and the DNA sample," said Gardener.

"I realize you didn't stay that long with him," said Briggs, "but did you get the sense he was hiding something?"

"Absolutely," said Gardener. "What exactly are you referring to?"

"Something you said earlier," replied Briggs. "About possibly harbouring a virus."

"Nothing would surprise me," said Reilly.

"It's a big house, sir," said Gardener to Briggs. "Lots of rooms. He could be up to all sorts in there."

"Okay," said Briggs. "It was just a thought. Might prove to be lucrative." He turned to the team. "Is there anything else on these mispers?"

Gardener said he had something else to ask, and turned to Gates. "You mentioned something very interesting there. An undertaker by the name of Parkinson?"

"Yes."

"I know what you're thinking," said Reilly. "When we spoke to Sandra Pearson, she mentioned that Lucy Brown had been taken to Parkinson's, in Skipton."

"It's a connection that might help," said Gardener. "Maybe we should go and have a word with Alec Parkinson – try and kill two birds with one stone. We can ask him if he remembers anything odd at the wake with Diane Drayton, perhaps hammer another nail into Viktor's coffin, if you'll pardon the pun. And see if he remembers anything at all about Lucy Brown."

"It's definitely worth pursuing," said Briggs, "especially as we seem to have made some sort of headway."

"That could be worrying," added Reilly.

"Why?" asked Briggs.

"He might have been working with her," said Reilly. "Preparing her, but he won't have known anything about a possible virus."

"Oh God, that sounds creepy," said Longstaff. "That job sounds bad enough, dealing with dead people on a daily basis, but not knowing that they may have died of something infectious. Christ, you could catch all sorts."

"I wouldn't have thought he'd catch anything from Lucy Brown," said Gardener. "She was dead."

Briggs agreed. "Surely if she was dead, so was the virus. But it would be worth checking with Fitz. Some of this shit might still be alive even if the host is dead. And I'll make reference to your earlier comment here about someone harvesting a virus in a lab. What if he or she has created a hybrid that is still capable of living after the host has died?"

"God forbid," said Gates.

"Okay," said Gardener. "In view of what we now know, let's have another press release with photos of the missing girls."

"Let's go one better," said Briggs. "I think we should have a press conference in front of the cameras. It'll have more of an impact."

Gardener wasn't keen but he could see the sense it made.

At that point Dave Williams walked in and announced that Jodie Thomson was not at her apartment block, which now officially made her a misper.

Gardener asked for someone to bring Viktor in.

Chapter Thirty-one

The following morning, Reilly pulled the pool car off Otley Road, drove through the open wrought-iron gates and headed left down a small drive. Within the grounds were lots of shaped bushes and plenty of green vegetation.

Exiting the vehicle, Gardener noticed a very picturesque two-bedroom cottage, with creeping ivy, leaded windows, a thatched roof, and a traditional wooden door within an arch that had a gas mantle for a light inside the porch.

"Definitely the right setting for a funeral home," said Reilly, standing next to him.

"Have you noticed how quiet it is?" Gardener asked his partner. "You can't even hear the traffic on the main road."

"Must be worth a bob or two," said Reilly.

Above, the early morning sky was blue and cloudless, with little in the way of a breeze to stem the burgeoning heat.

To the right-hand side of the property, slightly in front of the wall, Gardener noticed a coal chute, obviously leading into a basement.

"Look at that," he said to Reilly.

"Christ, I haven't seen one of those for years," replied Reilly. "Great idea, though, saves you getting all that shit and muck all over the place. They still have them back in the old country."

Before anything more was said, the door opened and Gardener found himself staring at a smartly dressed young man in pale blue chinos and a thin blue jumper.

"Please," said Alec Parkinson, "come in."

As they passed over the threshold, the SIO noticed Parkinson had neatly trimmed black hair, with a thin moustache and beard. He reminded Gardener of someone but he couldn't think who.

Parkinson led them through the hall and into an incredibly clean kitchen before taking them out onto a patio with a table and chairs and an umbrella. The garden wasn't particularly big, but the grass was cut short, and all the hedges had been trimmed, and there were plenty.

"This place must keep you busy," said Reilly, taking a seat.

"Not me," said Parkinson. "We have a gardener who does the whole place. Takes him ages but, as you can see, he does a great job."

Once they were both seated, Alec Parkinson left the patio before returning with drinks.

"What can I do for you?" he asked.

Gardener wasn't sure whether he was talking to Parkinson the man, or the funeral director. It all seemed a little clinical. He was well spoken but his voice had a camp tone to it.

He explained what they were investigating and why they had been led to him. He showed Parkinson a photo of Diane Drayton, and asked if he could remember her.

"Yes, I do," said Parkinson, pouring himself a coffee. "She was lovely, but very down about her friend." He never really stopped for breath. "Well, who wouldn't be? Funerals and wakes are not the nicest of places, are they?"

"How do *you* cope?" asked Reilly. "You deal with it on a daily basis."

Parkinson gazed upwards before speaking. "You become immune to it. You have to switch off, otherwise it would get too much."

Gardener brought Parkinson back to Diane Drayton, asking what he could tell them about the day in question.

"I'm not too sure," said Parkinson. "It was quite a while ago now. I remember talking to her later in the afternoon. She looked lonely, and sad. She said she was married and had a daughter. She spoke about them both."

"I take it her husband wasn't at the funeral or the wake?" asked Gardener.

"No," replied Parkinson. "He couldn't attend because their daughter wasn't too well. I don't think it was anything serious, but he had stayed home to care for her. She phoned him a couple of times; seemed the daughter was asleep, so he encouraged her to stay put, reminisce about her friend."

"As far as you can remember," asked Gardener, "other than the funeral, did you have the impression anything was bothering her?"

"I felt really sorry for them," replied Parkinson. "She was nicely dressed but the clothes were quite old – good quality, mind. I had the impression they were struggling a little. Didn't have a lot of spare money, but they had each other."

They talked some more but it was quite clear to Gardener that there wasn't a lot to be gained from what went on at the wake. It was the usual thing; people turned up, had a drink, had some food, remembered the person they had lost, and eventually returned to their lives, probably taking it for granted that they still had one.

Gardener showed Alec Parkinson a picture of Viktor. "Do you know this man?"

Parkinson took a glance. "Yes. I know all about him and what he does, and I hate him for it."

"How do you know him?" asked Reilly.

"Not so much him," replied Parkinson. "I've had plenty of his victims in here. He sells them drugs, gets them hooked, they end up a mess, sadly die, and we have to make them presentable. People like him need to be stopped. Why do you ask about him?"

"We believe he was at the wake," said Gardener.

"He was," said Parkinson.

"You wouldn't know why, would you?" asked Gardener. "Was he a friend or a relative of anyone there?"

"To be honest," replied Parkinson, "I don't know. I remember thinking it was odd that he should be there. I suppose he must have known someone. Unless he came to sell some of that garbage he peddles. Be the right place for it, wouldn't it? Plenty of sad people around that day. Maybe one or two of them would be in need of a pick-me-up."

"Did you see Diane Drayton talking to Viktor at all?" asked Gardener.

Parkinson thought about the answer. "Not in the time that I was there. I'd be surprised. She didn't seem the type, and she certainly didn't appear to have the money to waste on that stuff. But I wouldn't be surprised if Viktor had something to do with her going missing. He was there when it supposedly happened."

"Where?" asked Gardener, the hairs on his neck prickling.

"I actually remember seeing him in the car park as we were about to leave. He was at the other end, on his phone."

"Was he there when you left?" asked Reilly.

"Yes."

"Where did you go?"

"I had to come back here for another appointment," replied Alec. "The wake had gone on quite a bit and I'd lost track of time, so my dad was chasing me. It was a shame, I really liked Diane." He leaned forward quickly and placed his tea on the table. "Not in that way. She was just a really nice person who was having a tough time of things."

"So, you left," said Reilly. "And Viktor was still in the car park?"

"As far as I can remember."

"Did you actually see Diane *leave* the car park?" asked Gardener.

Again, Parkinson thought about the answer. "Well, I saw her walk in the opposite direction to me, which I assume was where she lived. But I was leaving, so I can't really tell you any more than that. I can't say if she did leave."

"So you wouldn't have seen if Viktor had approached her?" asked Gardener.

"No," replied Parkinson. "By that time, I was probably a couple miles down the road."

Gardener remembered asking for the CCTV from the afternoon in question, but it was too far back and had been wiped.

If Viktor had anything to do with Diane Drayton's disappearance, he was not going to find out here.

Gardener decided to ask Parkinson about Lucy Brown. He explained what he knew. He appreciated it was a long time ago but he wondered if Parkinson remembered her.

"Oh my God, yes, I do remember," he replied, becoming quite animated with his hands. "We had a long chat with her parents. They said she'd been abroad prior to passing. Apparently, she picked something up, which killed her."

"Did they say what?" asked Reilly.

"I think a virus was mentioned but they didn't know what. I think perhaps maybe they thought it might be their duty to inform us, just in case, so to speak. I remember wanting to ask if it was contagious, but you can't, can you?"

"I think it might have been excusable in your position," said Reilly.

"It's not right, though, is it?" said Parkinson. "Those poor people were burying their daughter. That should never happen. You shouldn't be going to the funeral of your children. I think that's the worst part of this job. You asked me how I coped, and I said you just switch off. Bloody hard when it's children, though. I realize she wasn't a young child, but she wasn't old, either. She had her life in front of her and yet there she was, cut down by something you can't even see."

"How did you feel about working with her?" asked Reilly. "Knowing about a possible virus."

"We always take precautions," said Parkinson. "We have protective gear. Not something you think about, is it? Laying someone out and wearing a NASA space suit."

The comment raised a laugh. They spoke a little more about Lucy Brown and when Gardener thought there was little more to be gleaned in that direction, he thanked Parkinson for his time.

Back outside the front door, Gardener turned and asked one more question, about Parkinson's social life. Did he ever go to clubs?

"Gentlemen," replied Parkinson. "I'm an undertaker. What would I be doing in the nightclubs?"

Chapter Thirty-two

Jodie glanced around. She had absolutely no idea where she was or how long she had been here.

In all honesty, wherever here was, wasn't that bad. The room was spotless, carpeted, frames on the walls, smelled clean. She had a bed, a chair, and a dressing table, believe it or not, and a small bathroom. If it was a prison, she could hack it for a while longer.

What she did not have was a TV, radio, computer, or her phone; no contact with the outside world at all. She did have some piped music to stop her going nuts. Someone had also brought her food and drink, and it had been quite nice. The door, however, was firmly locked.

The last thing she could remember was leaving the Markhams' house after talking to Angela about Sonia's funeral arrangements, and a further discussion about Alec Parkinson.

She really couldn't work that little problem out. She couldn't prove Viktor had been responsible for Sonia's death, any more than she could prove it for her sister Pippa's demise. It was simply something she believed from all of the rumours, and all of the stories she had linked together.

But she had no proof.

Nor could she prove Alec Parkinson had had anything to do with it. The only thing she could say was that he had been kissing Sonia. It's unlikely you'd kill someone with a kiss. And from everything she had seen and heard, neither

Alec nor anyone else had followed Sonia back to the apartment.

So what the hell *had* happened?

She thought again of leaving the Markhams'. She had declined a lift from Will, saying instead she would prefer to walk to the bus stop and make her own way from there, clear her head, give herself some time to think about what she was going to say to the police. She never made it as far as the bus stop. A car silently glided up behind her; so quietly in fact that she barely heard the bloody thing.

She actually managed to make a quarter of a turn, because she felt someone was there. But that was it. Her world went black and silent and she woke up here.

So, who exactly had her? She didn't think it could be Viktor, not after everything she had heard about him. But then, who else would want her off the street? It had only been Viktor's business she had been meddling in.

The lock in the door clicked, the handle turned and the door opened. Lo and behold, it *was* Viktor. Over six feet of solid muscle, with jet-black hair, cut short. His face was lined and weather-beaten, with a scar, running from his right ear to his mouth. She didn't want to think about how he had managed that. She certainly wouldn't have the nerve to ask.

At least fatty wasn't with him.

Viktor stepped into the room, closed and locked the door and stood in front of it. "You ready to talk?"

Jodie said nothing which was possibly the best option – for now.

"Funny that. You talk a lot around the city about me. Yet here I am, in front of you; I give you a chance to speak, and nothing."

He turned to leave. "Okay, I can wait."

"Wait," said Jodie. Despite not wishing to admit it, he made sense. But what was going to happen when she talked? "Where are you going?"

"You want to ignore me, I leave."

"You can't just leave me here," she shouted.

"You want to put bet on it? Something wrong with the place? Not to your liking? Maybe we could put you in the Hilton. That suit?"

"Look, where am I?" She never thought for one minute he would tell her but it was worth a stab.

"How about we start with who you are?" he replied, now facing her, even though his manner was not threatening. "Why are you asking about me, you want a date?"

"In your dreams," muttered Jodie. "Why should I tell you? You're only going to kill me, like Pippa."

"Pippa?" he asked, with an expression of confusion, his face screwed up. "Who is Pippa?"

"Don't tell me you don't know," said Jodie, rearranging herself on the bed.

Viktor leaned forward. "What am I? A mind-reader? How do I know what you're talking about unless you tell me?"

Jodie lost her temper, screamed at him. "Someone told me you were responsible for Pippa's death. So don't bother denying it."

Viktor moved toward her and she stepped back. "Calm down, lady. And tell me again, Pippa who?"

Her back was against the wall. There was nowhere to go, and perhaps nothing to lose. "Pippa Thomson? Pryzm, in Leeds. Two years ago."

Viktor threw his hands in the air. "That narrows it down. When, exactly?"

"I just told you."

"When?" shouted Viktor. "Stupid woman. What time of year?"

"Christmas, 2022," shouted Jodie, back at him.

"Not me."

"You would say that."

"Because it's true," said Viktor, moving to within feet.

"You wouldn't know the truth if it *hit* you in the face," shouted Jodie, with some real venom.

"You don't know me," shouted Viktor.

"Everyone knows who and what you are and what you do."

"No," corrected Viktor. "Everyone thinks they know who and what I am. They know nothing. They see a successful foreign businessman and they don't like it. No one knows anything about me."

"Is that because they can't prove anything?" shouted Jodie. "Because you've covered up all your dirty little secrets?"

"What is there to prove? I am not a killer. I am not a drug dealer. I do not break your laws. I pay tax in your country. I employ people and provide a living for them. Did you know any of that?"

"Words are cheap, you can say anything you like, and you can make yourself and others believe it. But I know what I've seen, and it was your scummy white powder that killed my sister."

Viktor moved a step closer, clearly becoming angrier. Had she hit a sore nerve?

"You don't *know* anything," he shouted. "You only listen to what people tell you. I did not kill your sister. I did not make your sister take whatever it is she took."

The vision returned to Jodie's memory like a slap in the face. Pippa lying face down on the bathroom floor, covered in vomit. Her skin blue, all life drained from her.

Unable to take any more, Jodie flew at him in a rage, landing her fists on his chest and one lucky strike in the face.

He stepped back and brought his arms up in defence. "What are you doing?"

"No," she raged. "You just sell it and get them hooked and then they can't stop, can they? You're scum, all you drug-dealing bastards." She wasn't going down without a fight, despite knowing she would lose.

He slipped back, twisted and turned and then grabbed her arms and pushed her back onto the bed. Finally, he said, "Stay there. How dare you punch me, in my own fucking house?" His eyes had grown wide, as if it was okay to punch him but not in his own house.

"That's where we are, is it?" asked Jodie. Not that it would do her any good if he told her exactly *where* it was. No one knew; so no one was coming to find her.

He straightened his suit. "I tell you. I don't sell drugs. I can't afford to get mixed up in that shit. Maybe people who work for me sell it. I can't keep on top of every operation."

"That's a good one," said Jodie, sobbing. "Not heard that before."

He stood over her. "You say, Christmas 2022?"

Jodie nodded.

He stepped back. "Couldn't have been me. I was not in the country at time."

"Oh, how convenient," shouted Jodie.

"I tell you," Viktor shouted, "I was not here. I have had enough of this. I'll show you."

He stepped further back and reached into his jacket pocket.

Jodie immediately panicked. She thought he was going to pull a gun on her, that her time was up. She was going to die in God knows where and no one would ever find her.

She stood up, quickly. "Oh Jesus, I'm sorry. Don't kill me."

Viktor stared at her, his arm still inside his jacket. "What the fuck are you talking about? I just told you I don't kill people; and certainly *not* in my house. I'd have to get rid of body. Fucking mess."

"What the hell *are* you going to do?" she asked.

"Prove I wasn't here." He suddenly stared at the wall and waved his right arm in the air and then glanced back at her. "Why am I bothering? What I have to prove to you? It is my house. You are guest and you treat me like shit."

"*Me* treat *you* like shit," shouted Jodie. "You're not the one locked up."

"Good job I did," said Viktor. "Fucking joint would be wrecked if you were free. Anyway, shut up, I'm bored. I didn't come in here to be assaulted or questioned. I want information and you're going to give it to me."

He leaned over and showed her his phone, scrolling through and locating the pictures from Christmas 2022.

"Where the hell is that?" she asked.

"Latvia, with family, on the ski slopes."

He scrolled through and showed her dozens, all timed and dated, all showing Viktor and a load of people she didn't know – apart from Arthur.

Everyone appeared to be having fun. Most importantly, they were dated.

As Viktor was about to pull the phone away, Jodie suddenly asked. "Who's that one of?"

Viktor checked. "Sorry, no one. She's local, not Latvian. No one you would know. Right, sit down. I talk, you listen. Then you talk. You get me?"

She nodded.

"Good. I have better things to do. I did not kill your sister and I do not know who did. But I can find out. Is that why you have been asking around, about my business?"

"Not entirely," said Jodie.

"Fuck." Viktor threw his arms up again. "There's more?"

Jodie explained what had happened to Sonia Markham and why she was asking about him.

"That is why I have the police all over me like fucking rash," said Viktor.

"My heart bleeds for you."

Viktor leaned over her and Jodie shrank back, at least as far as the wall would allow. "Shut your mouth. You have too much to say for yourself. Okay, I did not kill your sister, and I did not kill Sonia whatever her name is. I can prove my innocence to the police, and to you, and get you off my back. You mad cow. So here is the deal."

"Deal?" shouted Jodie. "You think I'm going to deal with you?"

"Do you have a choice?" asked Viktor. "Do you want to live?"

That sealed it. Jodie didn't like the sound of that. "What do you want to know?"

"Tell me what you know about your friend's death, and who you think is guilty. I will sort it."

"How the hell are you going to sort it?"

"What?" said Viktor. "You think I'd tell you? It's my problem. Not yours."

"How can I believe you?" Jodie asked.

"You can't."

"How can I trust you?" asked Jodie. "You're a gangster."

"You can't trust me, either," said Viktor. "And no, I'm not. Don't call me that. Take a look around. What are your choices?"

Jodie didn't say anything.

"Speak up!" shouted Viktor. "I don't want you here for fucking ever. What are your choices?"

"I don't have any," said Jodie, sullenly, the proposition sinking in. What was to stop him killing her once he had the answers?

Nothing. But still, she didn't have the cards stacked in her favour. All she had was faith. And she doubted that would be enough.

"Finally," said Viktor. "You've worked it out. Start talking."

Chapter Thirty-three

Following their interview with Parkinson, Gardener and Reilly had spent the remainder of the day at the station, trying to piece together any further information about the mispers. He needed to update his team with what little he'd discovered, and he wanted to know what – if anything – had surfaced in relation to Viktor and Lucy Brown.

Briggs was the final person in the room. He slipped over to the tea urn and poured himself a cup before taking his seat.

Gardener started by covering his meeting with Alec Parkinson.

"That's a pity," said Briggs. "I suppose the fact that he remembered Diane Drayton was a bonus."

"It might have been if he'd stuck around a little longer," said Reilly.

"I'm surprised he remembered the Lucy Brown incident," said Anderson. "It must have been the mention of a virus that jogged it."

"Still doesn't help us," said Gardener. "Even if Sonia Markham died of what Lucy Brown had, we're still no nearer to working out how she contracted it."

"Or if it killed her," said Reilly.

Gardener turned to Anderson. "Talking of Lucy Brown, did you manage to visit her parents?"

"We did," said Anderson. "But they won't be able to help you."

"They won't give their permission for an exhumation?"

"They might have done," said Anderson, "had she not been cremated."

Gardener had not really thought about that one. He'd covered most possibilities in his head but he hadn't thought of that.

He sighed. "That's scuppered us."

"Not necessarily," said Briggs. "I still wasn't convinced that it was the path we needed to tread."

Gardener was disappointed but he needed to move on. He couldn't let it affect him.

He asked Sharp and Rawson if they had managed to contact Viktor.

"I'm afraid not, boss," said Sharp.

"It's not that we haven't tried," said Rawson. "He's not here."

"Not where?" asked Gardener.

"Not in the UK," said Sharp, "according to his cleaner at the house."

The hair on Gardener's scalp bristled. He did not like that one bit.

"Not in the UK," said Reilly. "Where the hell has he slipped off to?"

"Of all places," replied Sharp, "Turkey."

"When did he go?" asked Gardener.

"About three days ago, Friday," said Rawson.

"He's obviously gone to sew up some more drug consignments," said Reilly.

"Literally," said Gardener, thinking of the story about the Turkish rugs being used to bring the shipments in. "He flew on Friday?"

Rawson nodded. "Manchester."

"Did the cleaner say when he'd be back exactly?"

"About a week, she said," replied Sharp.

"How convenient," said Briggs.

"I take it you asked about the flights and checked the details?" Gardener asked.

"Definitely," replied Rawson. "We asked one of his ugly sisters to get us the details. We contacted the airline, gave them everything, and they confirmed that he flew out on Friday morning."

"He never mentioned that when we spoke to him, did he?" asked Reilly.

"To be fair, Sean," said Gardener, "he wasn't under arrest, so he didn't have to surrender any details. But I know what you mean. I doubt this trip came as any surprise to him. I wonder if the airlines will tell us how and when it was booked." The SIO was slightly disappointed, in himself. After interviewing Viktor, he should have asked him not to leave the country.

"Not likely," said Briggs. "Not without a number of warrants. You know what they're like with data protection."

Gardener was stumped. There was nothing he could do. "We'll just have to hope he does return." He asked Rawson if they had the return flight details.

"We do. Friday morning."

"In that case, make sure you're at the airport in good time, and see if they will give you any access to CCTV."

"What are we looking for?" asked Sharp.

"The day he left," said Gardener. "Let's make sure it is him, and he's not doing what some of these European presidents do, using a double."

"You reckon he's that dangerous?" said Gates.

"Not dangerous," said Longstaff. "Maybe vulnerable, frightened that someone is going to take him out."

"He may also be up to no good," said Gardener, "and putting us off the scent. He might not be in Turkey at all, but up to something dodgy here. Anyway, no point in worry about that now. Go to the airport on Friday and pick him up straight from the plane if you have to."

Gardener turned to Briggs. "Can we have a couple of operational support officers keeping an eye on his place? See who comes and goes, see who might be lying to us."

"I'm sure we can manage that," said Briggs. "Leave it with me."

"Has Arthur gone with him?" Gardener asked Sharp.

"Apparently not. He's cooking up a storm in the kitchen."

"Okay," said Gardener. "All eyes on Viktor and his house."

He updated the boards before turning and asking if there was any news at all on Jodie Thomson.

No one had anything on Jodie's whereabouts, leaving the SIO very apprehensive.

"She is not at her apartment," said Gates. "Nor with her parents, or with the Markhams, or at work."

"All of whom are now – quite naturally – worried about her," said Longstaff. "Judging by the amount of calls we've had."

"Nothing on her mobile?" asked Gardener.

"Straight to voicemail," said Anderson. "We're all on it."

"However," said Gates. "I spoke to the Markhams shortly before we came in here and Sonia's mother, Angela, dropped a bomb into the conversation."

"Go on," said Gardener.

"Angela told me that the last time they spoke to Jodie, which must have been the day she went missing, she was on her way to the police station to speak to us."

"What about?" asked Gardener.

"She had remembered the man who was kissing Sonia Markham in the nightclub, three days before she died."

"That is interesting," said Reilly. "I wonder if it has anything to do with her going missing."

"Who is this mystery man?" asked Gardener.

"Alec Parkinson."

Gates said nothing more, allowing the room to sink into silence.

"Alec Parkinson, the undertaker?" asked Gardener, struggling to believe what he was being told.

"Yes," said Gates. "He was the man in the club who was kissing Sonia."

"And she knows this, how?" said Gardener.

"Because the Markhams took Jodie with them to see the undertaker to arrange Sonia's funeral. Apparently, Jodie had been quiet for most – if not all – of the time they were there. When Angela questioned her about it, she said she was pretty certain that Alec was the man in the club with Sonia, and she didn't know whether or not to say anything."

"Looks like good old Angela persuaded her otherwise," said Reilly. "Maybe she saw sense after what had happened to her husband."

"That's precisely why she said Jodie had to say something," replied Gates. "That she should let us deal with it, whether or not there was anything to the revelation."

"So why the hell didn't he say something when we asked him?" asked Gardener.

"What *did* you ask him?" asked Briggs.

"Just a quick question about his social life and whether or not he visited the clubs?"

"And he denied it?" continued Briggs.

"Never said one way or another," answered Reilly.

"Meaning what?" asked Briggs.

"What he actually said was," replied Gardener. "I'm an undertaker, what would I be doing in nightclubs?"

"Very evasive," said Briggs. "So, is he our mystery man on all the other occasions?"

Gardener studied the board, trying to piece together any information he could.

He turned to the team. "Let's assume Alec Parkinson is our man, and is in some way connected to Sonia Markham's death. And maybe we can put him at the scenes of the girls who have gone missing – at least two of them."

"Three now," said Longstaff. "He was at the wake, and Diane Drayton went missing from there."

"Good point," said Gardener. "Leaving us with two people connected to the girls who have gone missing, and Sonia Markham's death. What is going on? Are they working together? Is one trying to set up the other for some reason?"

"I can understand Parkinson trying to set Viktor up," said Reilly. "He clearly doesn't like him."

"So maybe Alec Parkinson has been following Viktor all over Leeds for some personal reason, wanting to set him up with us, so that we drag him in and pin everything on him. Even if that is the case, we are a long way from proving anything."

"Maybe Viktor really is innocent," said Briggs, "and Parkinson isn't."

Gardener turned and studied the board again before turning back to Gates. He'd had an idea.

"This is a long shot, but is there anything in any of the witness statements that mentions the man with black hair, who is slim, and who has a number of names beginning with A that could link Alec Parkinson?"

"Apart from the fact that he has a name beginning with A?" asked Briggs.

"Precisely," said Gardener.

The room descended into silence whilst Gates and Longstaff worked the keyboards of their laptops feverishly, banging in a variety of keywords.

Five minutes was all it took.

"I have something," said Longstaff.

"Which word did you use?" asked Gates.

"Undertaker."

"What do you have?" asked Gardener.

"Two witnesses in The Key Club, connected to the Sonia Markham case," said Longstaff. "We have Sally Spencer and Natalie Simpson, both from Armley. Separate statements but both mention the undertaker word."

"Go on," said Gardener.

"Sally Spencer must have seen something, or spoken to someone who had had a liaison with him because she made the point about a creepy undertaker who had been in the club that night, and every other night that one of the girl's went missing."

"Did they say anything more specific?"

"Sally said, and I quote: 'I mean, who wants to dance or have a drink with someone who works with dead people?'"

"And Natalie?"

"'Who the fuck wants to sleep with an undertaker? Touching dead people all day and then pawing you.'"

"When were these statements taken?" Gardener asked.

"To be fair," said Gates. "It looks like they only came to light yesterday and they're still being processed."

Gardener was a little troubled that they had not been processed faster, but the force was understaffed.

But he now had another direction in which to send the investigation, particularly as it would seem that Parkinson could have been leading them up the garden path.

"We now have two possible suspects: Viktor and Alec," said Gardener. "But I still can't see how Parkinson could be involved to such a degree," said Gardener.

"I'm with you, Stewart," said Briggs. "If Alec Parkinson is involved, *how* is he involved?"

"To answer that question," said Gardener. "We would need to find the missing girls before we could start to connect all the dots."

"Was Alec Parkinson involved with Lucy Brown?" asked Reilly.

"Even if he was," said Briggs. "Lucy Brown died eighteen months ago. Yes, she had a virus of some sort, but we still don't know exactly what, or even if Sonia Markham had the same virus."

"He *could* have been involved with Lucy Brown," said Gardener. "But we know for a fact that she did not catch the virus from him."

"Maybe not," said Rawson. "But did he catch it from her?"

"How could he?" asked Gates. "She was dead."

"Doesn't mean he couldn't have caught it," said Rawson.

"I don't see how," said Longstaff.

"Use your head," said Rawson. "It's something that's rarely talked about but it does happen."

The room grew silent again, before Longstaff said. "What does?"

"Are you suggesting what I think you're saying?" asked Briggs.

Gardener stared at Rawson. "Are you actually proposing that Alec Parkinson had sex with Lucy Brown, which was how he caught the Nipah virus, or whatever else it was?"

"Yes," said Rawson. "But what I'm asking is, did he have sex with her before or after she died?"

"Oh fuck," said Gates, covering her mouth, as did some of the others.

"Oh Jesus," said Longstaff.

"Let's hope it was before," said Thornton. "Because if it was after, it could only mean one thing."

"It couldn't have been before," said Gardener. "She had been on the placement for a month, returned home and was picked up at the airport by her father and went straight home and died there. It's not possible he could have had sex with her *before* she died."

"Oh, my, God," said Gates. "I really can't believe what I'm hearing here. What the hell kind of monster is he?"

"A necrophiliac," said Reilly.

Chapter Thirty-four

"You want to discuss what?" asked Fitz.

"Necrophilia," said Reilly, "amongst other things."

Fitz glanced at Gardener. "That's what I thought he said."

They were in the pathologist's office, with coffees and biscuits in front of them. Gardener explained what had transpired in the incident room.

He felt he needed a better understanding of the complaint. And to try to work out how his suspect may have caught the Nipah virus, if indeed he had, from Lucy Brown. Should that be so, how was it having a bearing on *his* case?

Fitz took a sip of coffee. "You'd better fasten your seat belts. Being a pathologist, it is something I've studied. As you've already discovered, necrophilia involves a person who gets sexual pleasure from having sex with the dead. It can be seen by itself, or in association with a number of other paraphilias: sadism, cannibalism, vampirism."

"Vampires?" said Reilly. "Dracula, you mean?"

Fitz nodded. "More a case of the practice of drinking the blood of another person or animal. Then you have necrophagia – eating the flesh of the dead."

Gardener put his coffee and biscuit back on to the desk. He had a feeling the subject was about hit new heights.

"Necropedophilia," continued Fitz. "Which is a sexual attraction to the corpses of children, and necrozoophilia – sexual attraction to the corpses of or killing of animals –

also known as necrobestiality. Necrophagists actually feed on decaying dead bodies to get sexual pleasure."

"Christ," said Reilly. "Never knew there was so much to being a pathologist."

"Or a necrophile," added Gardener.

Fitz continued. "None of what I'm going to tell you is pleasant. A vast spectrum of necrophagists is seen – from those who merely want to lick the genitals or breasts of a dead person – to persons who just want to devour specific parts, to necrophiles who would eat a whole body. Necrophilia is mostly seen in males. It is possible for a necrophile to have normal sexual relations with living beings.

"More modern necrophiliacs include Scottish serial killer Dennis Nilsen, and Englishman David Fuller, who is perhaps considered the worst offender of this kind in English legal history.

Gardener's head was spinning. A lot of information had come his way in such a short space of time. As Gates had asked, what kind of a monster were they dealing with?

"Assuming all of this has happened, *could* Parkinson have caught the virus from Lucy Brown?"

"It's possible," replied Fitz. "Depending on the virus, but most viruses die when the host dies, which is what usually happens with the Nipah virus, which we know this to be. I suppose it would literally depend on how quickly the act had been carried out."

"What the hell drives someone to do that?" asked Reilly.

"A number of factors will come into play," said Fitz. "Poor self-esteem, perhaps due in part to a significant loss. Does he still have both parents?"

"As far as I'm aware," said Gardener.

"They are very fearful of rejection by others," said Fitz. "So they desire a sexual partner who is incapable of rejecting them. They develop an exciting fantasy of sex with a corpse, sometimes after exposure to a corpse.

Necrophiles can also be fearful of the dead, and transform their fear into a desire."

"He's an undertaker," said Reilly. "How the hell can he be fearful of the dead?"

"It does sound unlikely," said Fitz. "Maybe something else in his life happened, a traumatic event when he was young that is somehow having an effect on what is happening today. There *are* less common motives, such as unavailability of a living partner."

"I can't see that," said Reilly. "Seems he uses nightclubs to find his victims."

"But if he uses clubs to meet people," countered Gardener, "why is he having sex with dead people? It doesn't make sense."

"Could be compensation for fear of women," said Fitz. "A belief that sex with a living woman is a mortal sin. Or maybe a need to achieve a feeling of total control over a sexual partner."

"I wonder if he kills them first," said Reilly.

"Possibly," said Fitz. "In the case of the missing girls – if you find them – it may be hard to prove, but that *is* one possibility."

"Still doesn't make sense," said Gardener. "Why pick up live girls and kill them to have sex with them, if you work with the dead, and you can have all you want, trouble free?"

Fitz leaned forward. Resting his elbows on his desk, he bridged his arms and placed his chin on his fists. "That's a question for him to answer." He then leaned back in his chair, as if suddenly uncomfortable. "You have two possibilities here, gentlemen. He's either caught it more recently from someone else, who was alive..."

"Or?" asked Reilly.

"He caught it from Lucy Brown and he himself is a carrier," said Fitz. "As we know, all manner of people can carry viruses and diseases with no side effects whatsoever, while the rest of us go down like flies. The question is, does he, or doesn't he know?"

"Interesting," said Gardener. "If he knew he had it, and he continued to infect them deliberately, that has to be murder."

"Only if you can find the missing girls – where are they?" asked Fitz. "Are they even connected to him, or is it another case altogether? Maybe they are connected to him, and it's possible that he hasn't killed them deliberately."

"Meaning?" asked Gardener.

"Well," said Fitz. "Let's imagine your nightclub chap kisses a girl and takes her back to his place. If she has any underlying problems, Nipah virus could have her in a coma within twenty-four hours and dead within forty-eight. Assuming they stay the night with him, what the hell does he do when he wakes up in the morning and finds he's sleeping next to a corpse?"

"Jesus Christ," said Reilly. "This is a head spinner."

"He might know that he has the kiss of death," said Fitz, "but have psychopathic issues that permit him to continue. Which leads me to another issue."

"As if we don't have enough," said Gardener.

"The other problem you will have," said Fitz, "even if you do find the missing girls, and you do connect him to it all, will he serve a prison sentence?"

"You think a good lawyer will get him off on the grounds of mental health issues?" said Gardener. "So even if we *can* pin it on him, he won't spend time in prison."

Fitz nodded. "Not as such. He will spend his life behind bars somewhere."

"Nevertheless," said Gardener. "If what has been happening *is* down to Parkinson, he needs removing from society."

He glanced at his partner. "Come on, Sean, let's go."

Chapter Thirty-five

Viktor had worked up a major sweat, despite the underground gym in his house having top-of-the-range air conditioning. He'd spent half an hour on the treadmill. From there he managed an hour on the weights, a further session on the rowing machine, before finally hitting the crosstrainer. Now, he needed a shower.

As Viktor grabbed the towel and rubbed his hair and his face, Arthur walked in wearing his chef whites. His hands were gloved and he carried with him a tray; something he had obviously recently baked.

"You're going to like this, Viktor."

"What is it?"

"It's your favourite, with a little twist."

"Twist?"

"Yes," replied Arthur, like an excited child. "The pastry is all mine, with a layer of lemon curd and cinnamon spread across the bottom. The topping is coconut laced with rum."

Viktor glanced around. "I spend three fucking hours in here, sweating like pig, losing weight, keeping shape, and you come in with coconut fucking pie."

"All the more reason to eat a piece, you imbecile," said Arthur.

"I'm what?" asked Viktor.

"Nothing, Viktor," said Arthur. "Now sit down and eat a piece of this. You will need to replenish your energy. You can't expect a car to run without petrol, can you? How do you expect to go on all this shit?" Arthur glanced around and pointed at the machines. "On an empty stomach."

"Could be worse," said Viktor.

"How?"

"I could look like you."

Arthur grimaced. "You say the nicest things. Right, get yourself a drink, eat some of this, and I will tell you what news we have."

Viktor was all ears. "News?"

"Yes," said Arthur, turning and leaving the room.

Following a shower and a change of clothes, Viktor joined Arthur in the study. Ygor and Boris were with him. Viktor sat down and took a sip of the drink and ate a piece of pie. He knew Arthur wouldn't say a word unless he did. He'd learned over the years what kind of an oddball Arthur was. If you didn't eat his food he would sulk, tell you nothing. A piece was also handed out to Ygor and Boris, whether they wanted it or not.

"What do you have?"

"We have plenty to tell you about Alec Parkinson," said Arthur, also eating some pie. Judging by how little was left it was not his first piece.

"Tell," said Viktor.

"Today, we should take action," said Arthur. "We know what he's up to today."

"Good. Where is he?"

"At home," replied Arthur. "And we have a bit of a bonus. He's on his own and we've found out that he has a little problem."

"What problem?" Viktor asked, patiently.

"He's claustrophobic."

Viktor finished his pie, took a drink and stared at Arthur. "He's closet what?"

Arthur rolled his eyes and repeated. "He is claustrophobic."

"What the fuck is that?" asked Viktor.

"He can't stand being locked up," answered Arthur.

Viktor glanced upwards. "Serious? Maybe he'll have plenty of time to get used to it when we fucking catch him."

"No," said Arthur, leaning forward. "I mean small spaces. Being enclosed in small spaces is not good for him."

"And he's an undertaker?" asked Viktor, an idea having come to mind.

"Yes," smiled Arthur.

Viktor's grin was even bigger. "Right, let's pay him a visit and deal with this fucking germ."

"Not so fast, Viktor," said Arthur. "There is another problem."

Viktor rolled *his* eyes. "What now?"

"The girl."

"What about her?"

"How are we going to sort the matter?" Arthur asked. "What are we going to do with her? Now she's told us what she knows, are we going to let her go?"

Viktor stared daggers at Arthur, his dark eyes seemingly taking on more depth. "After the trouble she's caused me? You think I am soft? Once the undertaker man is gone, she can follow."

Viktor stood and turned to face the boys. "Everything in place with Parkinson? Old man and wife out of the picture?"

"Yes," replied Ygor. "Wife shopping for day. Father at meeting, gone all day."

"Easy, then," said Viktor. "The police aren't looking for me, they think I am out of the country. So, let's go."

He didn't wait for a reply, simply made his way to the door.

Outside, Viktor asked Ygor to bring the large van, which would be perfect for what he had in mind. Five minutes later they were leaving the premises.

* * *

Forty-five minutes later, they pulled in through the wrought-iron gates of the undertaker's residence on Otley Road in Skipton.

Viktor stepped out and glanced around. "Very nice. Very secluded, and quiet. Soon it will not be so quiet."

Ygor jumped out of the front of the vehicle, slipped around the back and opened the rear doors so that he and Boris could assist Arthur.

Viktor noticed the front door of the cottage was open. He turned to Ygor. "You are sure no one else is around?"

"You think I am stupid?" cursed Ygor.

Equally as irritated, Viktor turned on him. "No, I don't think you are stupid. I fucking *know* you are."

"Why you employ me, then?"

"Don't you think I ask myself the same question every fucking day? Now, go around the back, and take King Kong with you."

Boris laughed and pointed at Ygor with one hand, whilst he stuck a finger from the other hand to his own head and pulled a face with his tongue hanging out.

Viktor slapped Boris. "You are no better. Go round back."

"You," he said to Arthur. "Come with me."

As they were approaching the cottage, Alec Parkinson was about to leave. He spotted both men, fell backwards, and slammed the front door shut, probably hoping to lock it.

Viktor immediately grabbed the handle and pushed down, as he shoulder-charged the door. Alec had not quite managed to shut it properly. The door flew open and crashed against the wall.

Viktor caught sight of Parkinson running toward the rear of the property, as Boris and Ygor came through the back door.

At that point, thought Viktor, there was little need to rush around. He doubted Parkinson was going anywhere.

The undertaker suddenly turned and ran through the kitchen, into one corner, threw open a door, and disappeared down some steps.

"The fuck is he going?" shouted Ygor.

"Nowhere," said Viktor.

Viktor slowly followed, nevertheless still slightly wary of what he was walking into. The last thing he needed was the undertaker surprising him with a weapon.

He peered into the room with the steps, which appeared to be a basement. On the left, at the top of the stairs, he noticed a light switch, which he used.

The first thing he saw at the bottom of the stairs was what appeared to be a ton of coal, perhaps more.

He glanced at Arthur. "Why the fuck does he need all this coal?"

"Maybe he likes a nice, hearty open fire."

"Good," said Viktor. "He might be in one soon."

Viktor heard Parkinson. He was muttering to himself, and obviously trying to climb over the coal, because he heard the scraping sounds, and saw small mounds sliding around the room.

"What is he doing?"

"Probably trying to open the chute at the other end," said Arthur. "Did you see it when we came in? He has a coal chute."

He pointed to Ygor and Boris. "Get down there."

The boys descended the steps first, followed by Viktor, and Arthur. He didn't want to miss any of the man's squirming.

Parkinson quickly turned his attention from the coal chute to the two gorillas descending the steps.

"Now don't do anything stupid," he said, with his arms out in front of him.

"You started it," said Viktor.

Parkinson backed up against the wall. "I'm sure we can sort this out."

"You're right, Mr Parkinson," said Viktor. "We can, and we will."

"What do you want with me?"

Viktor noticed the sheen of sweat on Parkinson's forehead.

"To ask questions."

"I don't know anything," he replied, peering in all directions, obviously searching for an exit.

"I'll be the judge of that," said Viktor. And jury and executioner, he thought.

Parkinson's knees buckled and he struggled to remain upright.

Viktor watched Arthur walk forward, carefully. If *he* went down, no fucker would be able to lift him.

"If you'd like to step this way," said Arthur to Parkinson.

"Where are you taking me?"

Viktor grew bored and pushed past Arthur. "You ask too many fucking questions."

He grabbed Parkinson's head and banged it against the wall a couple of times. The man squealed, and whimpered and fell onto the pile of coal, disturbing it yet further. Dust rose. Arthur brought his hand to his mouth and started coughing. Parkinson's white designer shirt was almost black.

"You won't get away with this," shouted Parkinson. "There will be people here any time now."

"Shut up," said Viktor. "You people always say the same thing. Your mother is shopping and your father is at a meeting, so no one will be here soon. And it probably wouldn't matter much if they were."

Parkinson stared at Viktor with an expression of disbelief and surprise.

Viktor signalled to Boris and Ygor to stand either side of Alec, to make sure he remained upright.

"Don't hurt me," said Parkinson.

Viktor pointed at him. "Quiet! This is how it works. I ask a question. You answer. I decide next move. You understand?"

"Look–" said Parkinson.

"You understand?" shouted Viktor.

Parkinson nodded but said nothing more.

Viktor smiled. "Good. Let's start."

Chapter Thirty-six

Dennis Wilson drove his coal wagon along Otley Road, making his way to his next delivery at the funeral home. His mind was wandering to a time when life was much easier. He'd been a coalman all his life, man and boy, as they said in Yorkshire; the business having been handed down to him from his father.

Wilson was fast approaching retirement age, and as each day passed, he was growing ever wearier. But it was all he had known. Sliding out of bed in a morning was a major operation. His bones were aching, and his joints had been cracking for years. He couldn't stay awake much beyond nine o'clock in an evening, much to his wife's disappointment.

He'd been thinking of bowing out gracefully for some time. He had no one to pass the business on to. He and his wife had never been able to have children. He would have liked to see it expand into another generation. Instead, now it would be swallowed up by the other coalman in the area, who already owned three trucks.

A blue sports car suddenly came hurtling around the hairpin bend ahead, approaching him at the speed of light;

so fast in fact, that the young man nearly lost control. The driver's eyes widened to a point where Wilson thought they would fall out.

"Mad bastard," he shouted as the car passed him. "You're going to get yourself killed."

That was something he wouldn't miss. Traffic. The world was full of lunatics. Why did they always manage to take someone innocent with them? Only last week in Bradford it was a mother and her two young children, as a cokehead in a car mounted the pavement and took them through a shopfront. He had no licence, no insurance and the car didn't even have an MOT, according to the newspaper.

But he survived. Where was the justice?

Wilson indicated as he approached the large wrought-iron gate leading into the property. He waited silently as traffic in the opposite direction passed, noticing a police car in the lay-by a few yards beyond.

"Aye, you sit there," said Wilson, "enjoy your tea and your bacon sandwich, while Stirling fucking Moss is tearing up the tarmac a few miles down the road."

Traffic gone, he turned in and drove through the gates and came to an immediate stop.

"What the hell?"

A large, silver van was parked in front of the cottage. The back doors were open and the van was empty inside.

Maybe Parkinson had had a delivery of new furniture. He couldn't fault the driver for parking as close as possible. It might be white goods. They were heavier than coal.

Could be awkward, thought Wilson. They were a little close to the coal chute.

He glanced to his left, toward the main property but there was no one around. He then drove further into the estate, before slipping the vehicle into reverse and edging his way to the chute. He doubted he would be in anyone's way. There was enough room for the van to turn around when they had finished.

After stopping his vehicle, he opened the door and slowly slipped out. He'd been sat for too long, so all his muscles were now protesting. He would have to wait a minute.

Finally, he walked around the back of the vehicle before unhooking the left-hand side panel, dropping the boards, preparing to tip the first bag down the chute.

Wilson removed his flat cap and scratched his head. He could never work out why so much coal was delivered to the Parkinsons – well, to Parkinson junior to be precise. Senior didn't have half as much and his place was twice as big.

Parkinson junior must be a cold arse, unless the building was a crematorium. That might explain all the usage, he laughed.

Walking up to the empty van, he turned around, noticing the front door of the cottage was open.

He knocked and called out but no one answered. He wondered if everything was okay. He knew the place to be quiet in general, but there was always someone around.

He shouted out, asking if anyone was home. In the distance he heard voices, so he shouted again. The voices continued as if they hadn't heard him.

"Hello?" he called out. "Coal delivery."

No reply.

Wilson wondered what the hell was happening, deciding the best course of action might be to check and see if Alec *was* inside.

He checked his boots were clean and stepped into the hallway. Everything was pristine, and he figured Parkinson junior would have a fit if he found coal dust or soil or some other shit on his carpet. That's what comes of batting for the other side, thought Wilson. He'd always suspected something odd about young Parkinson, the way he farted about with his clothes and his appearance. He couldn't pass a mirror without stopping.

As he ventured further in, he was beginning to think nobody was home. But how could that be?

He popped his head around the kitchen doorframe, realizing the source of the voices was the radio.

He decided to back out. Maybe the Parkinsons were really busy. Perhaps they were up at the main property, and that silly young bastard had forgotten to close and lock his door. Not that it mattered. Crime round here must be zero.

Wilson quickly retreated, deciding to unload the coal; not that he should worry, he would be paid anyway. He preferred the human contact option, though. He wasn't so keen on Parkinson junior, but he had a lot of time for his father, Rodney. Now there was a man under the thumb. Wife wore the trousers there. Wilson laughed at that. Show him a man who said he was king of his own castle and he would show you a liar.

He leaned down and squinted into the coal chute. He really should buy some new glasses. These were fucked – or his eyes were, and he reckoned he knew which.

He peered much closer when he suddenly spotted something unusual. He removed his glasses, spat on them, before wiping them clean on his boilersuit. As he leaned in closer again, his back protested.

"What the hell is that?"

He was quite sure he could see something sticking out of the coal, something very pale, but he couldn't make out what.

He stood up quickly and his back clicked. "Oh, Jesus, not now."

He turned and made for the cottage front door, wondering if Parkinson was inside. Maybe what he saw in the coal *was* the undertaker. Perhaps he had fallen and hurt himself.

Wilson thought he had better check. He couldn't have that on his conscience.

He walked through to the kitchen, spotting an open door in the corner. That's where the coal chute would be.

The light was on in the cellar. Maybe Parkinson was down here. Perhaps he was lying there, unconscious.

Wilson took the steps slowly. The last thing he wanted was to go arse over tit.

When he finally reached the bottom however, and stared into of the mounds of disturbed coal it was very obvious something had gone on there.

Something very unsavoury. Something Wilson did not like.

He moved further in, squatted lower, and peered more closely.

"Oh my fucking God."

Wilson didn't have time to turn. In fact, he fell over into the coal in shock, emptying the contents of his stomach.

He had to allow a few minutes before he managed some composure.

When he did, he needed to leave, go back to the wagon and retrieve his phone.

He needed the police.

Chapter Thirty-seven

Reilly powered the pool car down Otley Road toward the funeral parlour. Gardener was in the passenger seat making phone calls. Eventually, Reilly slowed down and pulled into the lay-by behind the panda car.

They'd had a call earlier to say that a large silver van with tinted windows had left Viktor's house. They had been advised to follow at a safe distance.

Gardener jumped out, followed by Reilly.

As they approached the passenger window, Gardener flashed his warrant card and leaned over, asking them both their names. Both were male and tall, and had dark hair; one wore glasses. They were introduced as PCs Boasman and Robinson.

"Can you tell me what happened?" Gardener asked.

"Just like we said, sir," replied Boasman. "The large silver van left Viktor's premises about an hour ago. We kept our distance, and followed them here. They pulled into the funeral parlour."

"Did you follow them in?" asked Reilly.

"Not into the property," replied Robinson.

"Not in the car, anyway," said Boasman, glancing at his partner. "Paul here went toward the gates on foot. I stayed here. He came back after a few minutes and said there were four people."

"Who were they?" asked Gardener.

"Definitely Viktor and Arthur," said Robinson. "They had two walking tower blocks with them."

"Where did they go?" asked Reilly.

"They were milling about outside the cottage for a while," said Robinson. "I couldn't quite hear what they were saying, and I certainly didn't want them to spot me."

"Christ, no," said Reilly.

"Eventually, they all went into the cottage."

"Did you see them come out?" asked Gardener.

"No, I came back here to tell Terry." He nodded his head towards his partner.

"You didn't go back?" asked Gardener.

"No," said Robinson. "We thought it best to observe. There's only two of us."

Reilly laughed.

"Where is the van now?"

"In front of the cottage," said Robinson.

"But that's not the only vehicle in there," said Boasman.

"Why, who else is here?" asked Gardener.

"We saw a coal truck go in," said Boasman. "About ten, maybe fifteen minutes ago."

"And he hasn't come out?" asked Gardener.

"No," replied Robinson.

"Odd," said Reilly. "It doesn't take fifteen minutes to unload coal. At least, it never did down our street."

"I wonder if the coalman has walked into something nasty," said Gardener.

"If he did," said Reilly, "he's going to be a casualty now. Otherwise, he'd have come out."

Gardener turned back to the panda car. "And no one has left the property through the front gate?"

"No, sir," said Boasman.

Gardener stood up. "Call the team, Sean. I think we might want the extra back up."

The SIO waited until he had done so and together, the pair of them started toward the funeral parlour.

"What would you like us to do, sir?" asked Boasman.

"If you want to lock your car and perhaps go to the gates and just observe for now," said Gardener. "You'll soon see if we need you."

Reilly removed his bomber jacket and rolled up his shirt sleeves.

Gardener feared the worst.

As the pair of them cautiously stepped through the gates onto the courtyard, they came across the coal wagon first, blocking the entrance.

"No one's leaving this way," said Reilly, opening the driver's door and peering into the cab.

"Is he in there?" asked Gardener.

"No."

"No?"

"What does a coalman have to do with any of this?" asked Reilly.

"Probably nothing, Sean," replied Gardener. "Wrong place, wrong time, is my guess. And judging by what we can see here, he may be as you say, a casualty."

Reilly checked the back, where the sacks of coal were. "He's not in here, either."

Gardener stared at the cottage, and then around the grounds. "There is something very strange going on here, Sean."

"Something's not right," replied Reilly, staring all around the property. "Where the hell is the coalman?"

"Where is everyone from the van?" asked Gardener. "Why have they parked it here?"

Gardener peeked in through the open back doors. The van was completely empty. He stared back at Reilly, checking his watch. "You *did* call the team, didn't you?"

Reilly nodded. "And any supporting officers they can find."

"I'm not happy about being here," said Gardener. "Even with those two from the Panda car, we don't have enough people. Viktor could be mob-handed. We know there are four of them. What if the coalman is in on it, and when he brought the truck in, he had more people in the back."

"Bit overkill, isn't it?" said Reilly. "If they only want one man?"

A sudden series of shouts from the main funeral home diverted their attention. Viktor and his henchmen were outside. Arthur and Viktor appeared to be remonstrating, both waving their arms about wildly. The conversation certainly was not muted. The two henchmen with them were heading in the direction of the van.

"Oh dear," said Gardener.

"I think we're about to find out what's going down here," said Reilly. "At least it's good news."

"What is?" asked Gardener.

"There *are* only four of them."

"There shouldn't be that many," said Gardener. "According to the cleaner, the organ grinder is supposed to be in Turkey."

"I never believed that for one minute," said Reilly. "And neither did you."

Gardener nodded. "Still, have you seen the size of those two?"

"One of them is just a big lump of lard," said Reilly. "You don't think Arthur's going to be any trouble, do you? Take him down first and he's out of the game for good."

Before Reilly could add anything else, a loud shout bellowed out and the two henchmen had turned to Viktor, but were pointing at Gardener. All four then stared in their direction.

"Looks like it's all about to happen," said Gardener. "Grab those two uniforms."

Reilly didn't need to. They were already behind him.

"Fuck me," said Boasman. "Look at the size of those two."

"I told you," said Robinson.

Gardener didn't wait. He pulled his warrant card out and marched across. Reilly was behind him.

Viktor and Arthur quickly turned tail and went back into the main property. Surprisingly, the bodyguards followed.

At that point, two more squad cars pulled into the property but instead of parking near the cottage with the other vehicles, they drove straight up to the main entrance, blocking the route of the two henchmen.

Rawson, Sharp, Anderson and Thornton all jumped out.

The two big bodyguards turned and quickly came toward Gardener and Reilly.

Gardener showed his badge. "Don't do anything stupid. You're totally outnumbered."

"You think so," said one of them.

"We know so," said Reilly, approaching the two men.

One of them immediately lashed out at the Irishman, who ducked below the outstretched fist. Instead of returning to his natural height, he quickly punched the walking tower block in the solar plexus, twice to make sure. The man buckled to his knees, struggling to breathe.

Reilly turned the other. "Your turn, is it?"

The man glared at Reilly, as if he was actually considering it. Before anything else happened, Dave Rawson pulled the man's hands behind him, where Sharp put on the handcuffs.

Between them, Gardener's team apprehended both men.

"Where to, boss?" asked Anderson.

"Their own van, Bob," said Gardener. "Lock them in."

Gardener turned to Reilly. "Quite nimble for an ageing officer."

"Just protecting you, boss," said Reilly. "God alone knows what Vanessa would have said if I'd let you get injured."

"Didn't think that would bother you in the slightest."

"It wouldn't. But she'd have told Laura and that would have bothered me."

Gardener smiled and nodded. "Let's go and get the main man."

They strolled over to the large house and found Viktor and Arthur sitting quietly in the main foyer. He wasn't surprised, he figured they would not do anything whatsoever to attract any attention.

"Thought you were in Turkey," he said to Viktor.

He shrugged and raised his hands. "Best laid plans. What can I say?"

"Can we help you, officer?" said Arthur, standing.

"Sit down," said Reilly, pushing Arthur enough to help him. The chair cracked as he landed on it, but to be fair, remained upright.

"You saw that, Viktor," said Arthur. "Police violence."

"Won't do you any good relying on him," said Gardener. He then addressed Viktor. "Where is Alec Parkinson?"

As Viktor was about to speak, Arthur told him to remain silent.

Gardener leaned in a little further. "The silent treatment, and the no comment routine will not help you, either of you."

No words were spoken. Arthur was in fact, inspecting his nails.

Gardener stood up and decided to search the property. "Wait here, Sean."

Rawson and Sharp joined Gardener in the main building. He asked them to check the upstairs rooms.

Gardener checked downstairs where he found the kitchen, dining room, rest rooms – all sorts of rooms, but they were all empty.

He finally peeked into what he suspected was the chapel of rest, where he saw a closed coffin, with piped music playing.

He wasn't going to disturb that.

With everyone gathered in the hallway, he was assured that all rooms were empty.

Even the coalman was still missing. How strange, thought Gardener. He turned to Viktor. "What have you done with him?"

"Who?" asked Arthur.

"Alec Parkinson."

"Sorry, officer," said Arthur. "Never heard of him."

Gardener said to his team. "They want this the hard way."

He quickly read Viktor and Arthur their rights. "Handcuff them both, put them in the van and cart the lot of them off to the station. Sign them in and put them in separate cells."

He glanced back at Arthur and Viktor. "You will talk."

Chapter Thirty-eight

By the time Gardener and Reilly were back outside the main building, with Viktor and his men safely locked in their own van, the operational support officers had arrived, leaving enough people to see Viktor and his crew safely escorted from the premises.

That left Gardener and Reilly at the funeral home to see if they could sort out the remainder of the mess. The main question being: where were the coalman and Alec Parkinson?

As he was about to speak, Gardener's mobile chimed. He answered to find the desk sergeant, Dave Williams, on the other end.

"Dave?" asked Gardener.

"Sir, we've had a call from someone at the funeral home, you know, Parkinson's in Skipton."

Gardener glanced around, wondering how that might have been possible. He hadn't seen anyone connected to the place so far. "Go on."

"There's something very strange going on at the property," said Williams. "Seems the coalman went to make a delivery and found something very odd in the coal cellar."

"At Parkinson's?"

"Yes."

"That's exactly where we are now," said Gardener, still glancing around, wondering if that something strange was the mess he had recently cleared. But it still didn't explain where the coalman was.

"Oh, so you've seen him, then?" asked Williams.

"Who? The coalman?" asked Gardener, before adding. "No."

"Well, where is he?"

"I've no idea," replied Gardener. "We can see the coal delivery vehicle, but no coalman."

Gardener heard the desk sergeant let out a sigh. "I can't work out what's going on here."

"Did the coalman say exactly how strange his discovery was?" Glancing at Reilly, in an effort to convey something of the conversation.

"To be honest, I couldn't get much out of him," said Williams. "He was babbling, and sounded very shook up. I told him to wait at the property and we'd have someone with him as soon as possible."

"Okay, Dave," said Gardener. "We're here so we'll check it out." Before cutting the connection, he said, "You should have the team arriving shortly with some suspects. Process them, and give them the usual treatment; separate cells. We'll be back as soon as we've sorted this mess."

"What's up?" asked Reilly.

Gardener explained the conversation he'd had with Dave Williams.

"So the coalman is genuine, then?" asked Reilly, peering in every direction.

"Sounds like it," said Gardener. "So where is he?"

"He must still be alive," said Reilly. "When we arrived, Viktor's lot were over in the main building, so the coalman must be around here somewhere. Maybe he's in that cottage."

Gardener glanced to where Reilly was pointing. "What the hell is going on around here, Sean? It all started with the odd demise of Sonia Markham. We have four missing girls that might be connected, but still missing. Jodie Thomson has now gone missing. It would appear that one of our suspects, Alec Parkinson, has also gone AWOL.

And the person we've just carted away might not actually be responsible for any of it."

"I doubt that, boss," said Reilly. "Viktor's in it up to his armpits. Maybe he hasn't abducted the missing girls, or killed Sonia Markham, but the fact that he's been hanging round the clubs at the same time as all this has happened, means he's probably guilty of something. If Parkinson *has* gone missing, it may not be anything to do with Viktor."

"Maybe not," said Gardener. "Perhaps Parkinson knows a lot more than he's ever let on and he's cleared out of this place before we've had a chance to apprehend him."

"Unless Viktor got to him first, and he *has* silenced him."

"So where is he?" asked Gardener, glancing around, trying to take it all in, and possibly work out what they had done with Parkinson junior. "It's a big place, Sean, we haven't really seen all of it yet. Perhaps he is here somewhere."

"Fact is, boss," said Reilly. "We have to find out, and we have to find out today, and put it to bed. Before Briggs ends up cold casing all of it."

"It isn't good," said Gardener. "It's making us two look like proper idiots. Okay, let's start with the cottage."

"Wait a minute," said Reilly.

He pulled his mobile phone out of his trouser pocket, before glancing over at the coal truck. He called the number on the side door.

It was answered after one ring. Reilly introduced himself, and he asked the coalman where exactly he was.

"Staring at you two," replied Wilson.

Gardener glanced around and then turned in the direction of the cottage. Dennis Wilson was standing in the doorway, still very pale, and unsteady on his feet.

As they reached him, he had backed himself into the hallway and was sitting on a kitchen chair. Whatever he had seen and reported still appeared to be affecting him very badly, because Gardener could see the man was shaking.

"Would you like a drink, Mr Wilson?" asked Gardener.

"I think so," he replied. "I'd have got it myself but I couldn't trust my legs."

Reilly slipped into the kitchen and returned with a glass of tap water. He passed it over to Wilson, who took it with one hand to start with, but then used both in case he tipped it all over the carpet.

"Are you okay, Mr Wilson?" asked Gardener.

"I'm not sure," he replied, with a deep Yorkshire accent, and after finishing the water. He passed the glass to Reilly, who simply put it on the stairs.

"What's happened?" asked the Irishman.

"What hasn't happened?" said Wilson, cradling his face in his hands. "If I'd have thought today would end up like this I'd never have got out of bed."

"Have you been attacked?" asked Gardener.

"No," he replied. "Leastwise not physically."

The SIO was going to have to coax the information out of him somehow. Alec Parkinson's life may depend on it, wherever he was.

"Can you tell me exactly what happened from the moment you drove through the gates?" asked Gardener.

"And the van was empty when you arrived?" asked Gardener, after he had done so.

"Yes."

"You never saw any of the occupants?" asked Reilly.

"No."

"Have you seen Mr Parkinson?" asked Gardener.

"Which one?" asked Wilson.

"How many are there?"

"Two."

"Have you seen either?"

"No," said Wilson.

"No?" questioned Gardener.

Wilson shook his head. "Should I have done?"

"You tell us," said Reilly. "You were delivering the coal."

"But I didn't empty it, see," said Wilson.

"Why not?" asked Reilly.

"Because of what I thought I saw in the cellar."

"Which was what?" asked Reilly.

"I had no idea," said Wilson. "Eyes are not so good, these days. So I came back in, went down there. Wish I hadn't."

"So you've been into the cellar?" asked Gardener.

"Aye," said Wilson. "Didn't fucking stop, though. Not with what's in there."

Aware of something grizzly happening in the cellar, Gardener needed to move things on.

"Mr Wilson, let me just clarify something. You came to deliver coal. You haven't seen anyone on the premises, but you have seen something you don't like the look of in the cellar. Is that correct?"

"You can say that again."

"What have you seen in the cellar that made you call the station?" asked Gardener.

"I don't rightly know," replied Wilson. "Might be Parkinson, though."

"There's a *body* in the cellar?" asked Gardener.

Chapter Thirty-nine

"I think you had better stay here, Mr Wilson, whilst we investigate what has happened," said Gardener.

"Good," replied Wilson. "No fucking intention of going back down there."

"Is it that bad?" asked Reilly.

“’tis for whoever’s under that coal.”

Gardener turned to his partner. “Sean, can you call an ambulance for Mr Wilson here?”

“I don’t need one,” said Wilson, trying to stand but failing.

“I think you do,” said Gardener, helping him back in the seat, before resuming the conversation with his sergeant. “Better still, I’ll make the call. Can you nip outside and grab Robinson and Boasman, if they’re still here, and two scene suits?”

Reilly nodded and then disappeared.

Gardener had his mobile in position. He made two calls for backup, one to the station, and the other for an ambulance.

“I feel so stupid,” said Wilson.

“Not at all,” said Gardener, glancing at his watch. “You’ve had a shock. I’d like them to check you over.”

“What about the truck?”

“It’ll be okay where it is,” replied Gardener. “Leave us the keys and we’ll see it’s either moved from the gates or taken back to your house.”

Wilson put his head in his hands.

Reilly arrived back in the hall with the scene suits and Boasman and Robinson, as requested.

The SIO spoke to them. “I’d like you two to stay with him if you will, until the ambulance arrives. After that, perhaps you can guard the premises and check with us before you let anyone in?”

The officers nodded.

Gardener and Reilly slipped into the scene suits, with gloves and shoe coverings. They were about to set off when a car drove into the grounds of the funeral home and they heard a door slam.

A man suddenly appeared at the front door of the cottage. “Would someone mind telling me what’s going on here?”

“And you are?” asked Gardener.

"Rodney Parkinson."

Gardener studied the man. He was tall and thin, his face long and angular. His eyes matched his jet-black hair. He was dressed in a black business suit, with white shirt and black tie, with a pair of black brogues on his feet.

Gardener immediately displayed his warrant card, introducing himself and Reilly.

"Oh," said Rodney, obviously unaware of what to make of the intrusion. He glanced at Wilson, who still had his head in his hands. "What's wrong with him?"

"I'm afraid he's had a nasty experience," replied Gardener.

"Where?" asked Rodney.

"That's what we're about to find out, Mr Parkinson."

Rodney knelt down in front of Wilson. "Are you okay, Dennis?"

"I will be."

"What's happened?"

"Don't ask."

Rodney stood up and stared at Gardener. "Is my son around? Alec?"

"That's who we came to speak to, Mr Parkinson," said Gardener.

"What about?"

"I'm afraid that's between us and your son."

"Is it that serious?" asked Rodney. "It can't be so serious that it requires a visit from a Detective Inspector."

"Have you seen your son?" asked Reilly.

"No. I've been at a meeting all day. Haven't *you* seen him?"

"No," said Gardener.

"Have you?" Rodney asked Wilson.

"I don't know," said Wilson.

"What's that supposed to mean?"

Wilson remained seated with his head in his hands, and simply shook his head by way of an answer.

"What the hell is going on around here?" asked Rodney. "And would you please tell me why you're here?"

Gardener didn't go into detail but briefly explained what had happened to the coalman.

"I can't believe Alec isn't around," said Rodney. "His car is still in the garage."

"What I'd like to do, Mr Parkinson, with your permission, is to inspect the cellar of this cottage."

Gardener realized he was treading on thin ice because he did not have a warrant. He soon would have, if needed.

Rodney obviously wasn't stupid because it was the first thing he asked.

"No," said Gardener. "Which is why I'd like your permission."

Rodney nodded. "Because you think there is a body down there?"

"We believe there is," said Gardener.

"Is it my son?"

"We don't know, and we prefer not to stand here much longer."

Gardener knew from what Wilson had told him that it was very unlikely the body was alive, but he didn't want to tell Rodney Parkinson that.

"Look, Mr Gardener," said Rodney. "You do what you have to. I won't stand in your way. But I'd like to make a request."

"Go on," said Gardener.

"I want to come with you."

"I'm afraid you can't, Mr Parkinson," said Gardener. "A body in your cellar means it's a crime scene."

"I realize that, officer," said Rodney. "But you don't have a warrant."

"I know," said Gardener. "And I appreciate your cooperation but if it's a crime scene I need to keep the contamination to a minimum."

"It's a coal cellar," said Rodney, "with quite a lot of coal in there. I suspect it's already contaminated."

"It's okay, boss," said Reilly. "I'll get him a scene suit."

Gardener weighed the situation up and reluctantly agreed, despite it being highly unethical. "But there are conditions, Mr Parkinson. You must wear the scene suit, and when you get to the cellar, you must stay on the stairs. I am not happy about this."

"If it's my son down there, neither will I be," said Rodney. "But I'll be on hand to identify him for you."

Gardener nodded. He walked to the front door, called Boasman and Robinson and asked for another scene suit.

Once they had it and Rodney was inside it, all three headed for the kitchen and finally the cellar.

Chapter Forty

It was black – completely black. And silent.

Alec's claustrophobia had started when he was ten years old, following a trick he decided to play on his father.

Sweating profusely, and convinced he was running short of oxygen, he tried not to live through that moment again in an effort to calm his nerves – but it was seemingly impossible.

Despite being introduced early to the family business, Rodney had considered it unhealthy for his young son to see the dead bodies. Rodney's father, Frank, had done the same for him. Neither had been allowed to actually see a body until the age of thirteen.

Alec's role from the age of seven was to help in the main office, laying out brochures, tidying cupboards and shelves, and generally cleaning up. As he grew older, he was given extra duties. At ten, he had been allowed into the chapel of rest, particularly when it was a closed casket affair, where he helped with further cleaning duties.

One day, when left to his own devices because the cleaner had been needed in another part of the building, Alec noticed an open coffin. Despite knowing he was not allowed to see the body his inquisitive mind thought it couldn't hurt if no one was there to see *him*. He remembered wanting an aerial view, so he pulled up a chair, stood on it, and cautiously peered in. The coffin was empty.

Disappointed, but determined to see how things worked, he actually wondered what it would be like to lie inside. Before doing that however, he replaced the chair at the desk. Back at the coffin he removed his shoes and somehow managed to clamber in without overturning it.

It was comfortable. He shuffled around, before wondering what it would be like with the lid down.

He pulled, and it slammed shut. He was immediately taken with how dark it actually was. It also appeared to be soundproof, because he could not hear the piped music. He didn't like it. Unnerved, Alec pushed the lid upwards.

But it wouldn't move.

He tried again but to no avail.

That's when it started. His stomach swelled, he felt incredibly hot and he started to sweat, which resulted in breathing problems. Alec had punched the lid a few times but still nothing happened. He'd peed himself in fear. He'd screamed but no one came. He was in real trouble, and remained that way for four hours, until the lid suddenly opened and he saw his father's face.

By that time, the damage was done. Rodney had taken Alec into the living room of the main house, sat him in front of the fire and made him a sweet cup of tea.

Alec refused to eat or drink or talk, he simply kept shaking his head.

He was still shaking like a leaf three hours later; he was still crying, and he couldn't speak for all the tea in China.

He'd still refused to eat or drink or talk, he simply kept shaking his head.

Which was the position he was in right now: desperate to shout for help, but unable to utter a word.

Chapter Forty-one

In the kitchen, Gardener spotted the door to the cellar and headed for it. As soon as he reached it, he turned around to face Reilly and Rodney.

"I'd like you to stay here for the moment, Mr Parkinson. I'd prefer to assess the situation alone before I make any further decisions."

Rodney appeared not to like the comment but Gardener was leaving him with little choice. As he turned to leave, he nodded – almost imperceptibly – at his partner. The nod basically meant, please stay here and see he does as he's told.

Reilly took his place at the top of the cellar steps, which Gardener descended.

There was lighting on the stairs, assuring him he wouldn't miscalculate and fall. Daylight from the chute illuminated the other side of the room. The cellar was large and one thing Gardener immediately noticed was perhaps far more coal than was necessary, particularly if only one person occupied the place.

The further he descended, the more obvious it was that some kind of commotion had happened, and very recently. The mound of coal was not neatly stacked, but spread all over the floor, with large patches where he could actually see the ground – amongst other things.

Maybe Viktor and his men had cornered Alec Parkinson, thought Gardener, had caused him some serious trouble, such was the disturbance of the coal.

As Gardener reached the bottom step, he was aware of how silent everything had become. There were no longer any voices from the kitchen, nor any from the outside. He couldn't even hear wildlife – particularly birds.

Gardener stood stock-still and took everything in. Dennis Wilson was wrong. There wasn't *a* body in the basement.

Before doing anything else, he turned tail and climbed back up the stairs. When he reached the top, he walked straight past Reilly, into the hall, where he asked PC Boasman to join him in the kitchen.

Back in the kitchen, Rodney asked, "What's wrong? What's going on down there?"

"I'm sorry," he said to Rodney, before turning to Boasman. "I'd like you to stay with Mr Parkinson, and guard the entrance to the cellar."

He turned back to Rodney. "I'm afraid I can't allow you into the cellar, Mr Parkinson."

"Why not?"

"It's a crime scene."

"That wasn't part of the agreement."

"The agreement is off," replied Gardener.

"So is the inspection," said Rodney. "You have no warrant."

"I don't need one," said Gardener. "There are three bodies down there."

"Pardon?"

Gardener repeated himself.

"Three?" asked Reilly.

"Did you say three bodies, sir?" asked Boasman, his expression almost as shocked as Rodney's.

"Is one of them my son?" asked the undertaker.

"Not as far as I can see," said Gardener.

At that, Rodney Parkinson blanched and almost passed out. He suddenly reached for the table, and then a chair. As he sat down, he said. "Then where the hell is he? And who are those people down there?"

"That's what we need to find out, Mr Parkinson," replied Gardener.

"That's why we'd like to speak to him," said Reilly.

"Sean," said Gardener, nodding toward the cellar.

They descended. At the bottom of the steps, Gardener pointed to what appeared to be three separate bodies, all buried under layers of coal, each in different parts of the room. Gardener's logic came from the fact that there were three arms sticking up at different angles that were positioned too far apart to be one body.

The coal had separated enough for a leg to have poked through from one, and the right foot from another.

Gardener glanced around and spotted a shovel. He walked over, picked it up and spread the coal around in order to gain a better view.

Reilly stepped in closer and helped. In no time at all, the pair of them could see that all the bodies appeared to be female, none of which made for teatime viewing.

He glanced at his partner. "The missing girls?"

"Three of them, at least," said Reilly.

"That figures," said Gardener. "If I remember rightly, no one mentioned a mystery man who was slim with black hair the night Dawn Roberts went missing."

"That could be someone else altogether, boss," said Reilly. "She was a prostitute, she lived in a dangerous world. Might even have something to do with our foreign friend."

"True," said Gardener. "I wouldn't mind betting that these three ladies here are the ones we're looking for."

"It doesn't take a genius," said Reilly. "And judging by the state of each body, the time element fits well."

Gardener nodded, glancing around. As the coal cellar appeared to be reasonably cold and dry, the decomposed bodies were each at a different stage in the process. He supposed that, hypothetically, a body in a cool, dry cellar, covered in coal dust, which contained a lot of tar-like chemicals, could almost mummify, or at least decompose very slowly indeed.

The circumstances here were a little different.

Gardener asked Reilly if he could remember the dates of the girls going missing.

"Not really," he replied. "I think they were at three-month intervals."

"Starting twelve months ago," said Gardener.

As he glanced around, he studied the decomposition. The body that appeared to have been in the cellar the longest showed signs of advanced decomposition; some skin, mostly bones, and a bit of connective tissue. The next body still had some flesh and muscle, but was a touch juicy, to put it crudely.

The one that had been there the least amount of time was well on the way to reaching the others; the soft tissue had gone first, particularly the eyeballs: flies and maggots were present and most of the tissue was becoming liquefied, starting to ooze onto the surrounding floor. The smell was now starting to hit Gardener.

"How do you manage to get away with something like this without anyone noticing?" asked Reilly.

"You know what these people are like, Sean," replied Gardener. "We've met some pretty nasty types who will go to almost any length to hide what they have done."

"But he lives so close to his parents. You'd expect one of them to notice something."

"Well, if they have," said Gardener, "I'd lay odds it's not Rodney. His shock appears genuine."

"And we both know that a mother's love is strong enough to protect her offspring whatever they've done. But what about the smell?"

"Trouble is, they were covered in coal," said Gardener. "And from what we've seen, young Parkinson has far more coal than he needs for that very reason, I shouldn't wonder. I wish we could dig deeper."

"I know what you mean," said Reilly. "But it's a job for the boys. This place has been disturbed enough."

Gardener reached for his phone and called Williams back at the station. He explained the situation, and that he needed the SOCOs, and a PolSA team at the funeral home in Skipton, immediately. The place had to be completely closed off. The bodies needed removing, with any results as fast-tracked as humanly possible.

Once he'd finished, he said to his partner, "I don't think there's a lot more we can do, Sean. What we need now are answers, and if I have to tear this place apart brick by brick to find Alec Parkinson, I will."

"He fits the profile: slim, back hair," said Reilly. "I'm sure beard and moustache were mentioned somewhere in the witness statements."

"But where is he?"

"I'm hoping that Viktor hasn't done a number on him," said Reilly. "I want to hear what this guy has to say for himself."

"That makes two of us," said Gardener.

They took the stairs back up to the kitchen. Rodney was still sitting at the table, his expression pale, but he had tea in front of him. PC Boasman was standing near the window.

Gardener took a seat.

"Is my son down there?" asked Rodney.

"No," said Gardener.

"No? Well, who is?"

"We don't know," replied Reilly, also taking a seat. "We know there are three female bodies down there that may well fit the description of three girls that have been missing for quite some time."

"What are you trying to say?" asked Rodney.

"Have you any idea where your son is, Mr Parkinson?" asked Gardener.

"If I knew, do you think I'd be sitting here?" replied Rodney. "Whatever's gone on down there, you're not the only ones who would like an explanation."

"Do you have your mobile on you?" asked Gardener.

Rodney checked. He did. Gardener asked him to call Alec. The phone rang out but went to voicemail.

"Where was he supposed to be this afternoon?" asked Gardener.

"Here," replied Rodney. "All afternoon."

"Has your son been okay over the last few months?" asked Gardener. "Has he been acting strangely, or worried about anything?"

"I'm not aware of him having been worried about anything," said Rodney. "But if I'm being truthful, I do think he's been acting weirdly. But I have no idea why."

"Weird in what way?" asked Reilly.

"He's been very quiet, withdrawn," said Rodney. "I know he's an undertaker, and he's never been the life and soul of the party, but of late, he does appear to have been distracted."

"Would you have any idea why?" asked Gardener. "Does he have any financial problems?"

"I doubt it," said Rodney. "He works for the family business. He lives here rent free."

"Nothing else bothering him," said Reilly. "No women problems?"

Rodney put his head in his hands. "To be honest I've never really seen him with a woman."

"Any men problems?" asked Gardener.

Rodney stared daggers at Gardener. "That's a bit personal, officer."

"Not particularly," said Gardener. "No offence was meant, but we don't know your son's sexual preferences."

Rodney nodded. "To answer the question, even though I haven't seen him in a relationship, I don't think he's gay. I just don't think he's interested."

That's not how Gardener would have put it, not with three female bodies in a serious state of decomposition in the cellar.

"And though I can't see that he would be mixed up in murders," said Rodney. "I really can't think of any other explanation. I mean, how else do you end up with three bodies in your coal cellar? It doesn't make sense."

Gardener could see that Rodney was torturing himself.

"His mother is not going to like this. How long have they been there, would you say?"

"We will need forensics for that, Mr Parkinson," said Gardener. "However, at a guess I'd say the oldest might be around twelve months."

"Surely not," said Rodney, putting his head in his hands. "What the hell is going on here?"

"Have you never noticed anything?" asked Reilly. "No excess coal deliveries, no odd smells?"

Rodney shook his head. "My wife and I don't really spend a lot of time over here. He has most of his meals with us in the big house. My wife will sometimes cook a meal and bring it over and slip it into his fridge. But by and large, we leave him to get on with things. As for the coal, I can't say we have, we simply pay the bill when it comes in."

"Does your son go to nightclubs at all?" asked Gardener.

"Quite often," said Rodney. "But only on a Saturday night."

"Any in particular that you know about?"

"He's usually in Leeds," said Rodney. "I have heard him mention Wakefield."

"And you're sure you have no idea where he is at the moment?" asked Reilly.

Rodney shook his head. "I really can't imagine."

"You mentioned the big house a few moments back," said Gardener. "I think we ought to go and have a close look around."

"Yes, of course," said Rodney, standing. "Do I need to keep the scene suit on?"

Gardener nodded. "It won't harm anything."

All three men stood and left the kitchen, with Boasman following closely behind. In the hall, Dennis Wilson was missing. Robinson said an ambulance had picked him up.

As all five men trooped outside, Gardener asked Robinson and Boasman to guard the gate at the front, for when the SOCOs and the PolSA team arrived.

Rodney pointed out that Alec's car was parked in the garage, so he had to be around somewhere.

Gardener would like to think so as well, but Rodney was not aware that Viktor had visited his son.

All three men entered the house, and Gardener mentioned that they *had* previously made a brief search of the premises but they had not found Alec at all.

"You've already searched here?" questioned Rodney. "But you saw nothing of him?"

"No," said Reilly.

Rodney checked all of the downstairs rooms before finally glancing into the chapel of rest.

He was about to shut the door, when he said. "Wait a minute."

"Something wrong?" asked Gardener.

"The coffin lid is closed."

Gardener remembered seeing that. "Shouldn't it be?"

"It wasn't when I left here," said Rodney. "It's possible that my son might be trapped inside. But how the hell has he ended up in there? He's claustrophobic for God's sake. Being trapped in there could kill him."

Gardener went over and lifted the lid. Alec Parkinson was laid straight as an arrow, with his arms folded across his chest. His clothing was covered in coal dust suggesting he had been trapped or assaulted in his own cellar, likely by Viktor. He had soiled himself.

His skin was ghostly white, his eyes closed. His face was tear-stained, which when mixed with the coal dust resembled streaks of mascara. Alec was breathing heavily despite his lips being tightly shut.

"Mr Parkinson," said Gardener to Alec. "Are you okay?"

"He won't answer," said Rodney. "He could be like this for days."

Gardener glanced at Reilly. "Sean, give me a hand, please."

Together they lifted him out of the coffin, and all the while, Alec Parkinson was as stiff as a board. He did not bend, not once. It was like handling a tailor's dummy. Even when they had him out, they had to lay him on the floor, because his body was so tense, he couldn't possibly have taken a seat.

Rodney bent down and stroked his son's forehead. "You're going to be fine, Alec. Don't worry."

Gardener asked Rodney to step outside into the hall for a word.

"I realize everything he's gone through, but we're going to have to take him to the station for questioning."

"He needs a doctor, officer."

"He will see one," said Gardener. "At the station."

"He might need a hospital."

"If the police doctor deems it so, he will be taken, but he'll be under police guard. With all the information we have in our possession, and everything I have so far seen, I am going to have to charge and question him about the bodies in the cellar."

Chapter Forty-two

Almost thirty hours had passed since Gardener had read Alec Parkinson his rights. Whether or not he had been able to understand was another matter. Rodney had not objected.

Upon arrival at the police station, the undertaker had been made comfortable. He'd been seen by a doctor, who had found nothing physically wrong with Alec. Before he would pronounce him fit for interview however, he wanted to examine him again the following day.

During that time, Gardener had moved heaven and earth to fast-track the dental records of the four missing girls on file. It had proved impossible for Dawn Roberts, because there was no one that he could talk to, nor did he have enough information to proceed. Relatives of the other three were more than happy to give permission, and that was all he had needed.

He now knew that the bodies he had found in the cellar of the funeral home cottage belonged to Katherine Field, Amelia Simms and Diane Drayton.

Three hours previous, the doctor had said that Parkinson was talking normally, and was happy to speak with the detectives when ready.

Gardener and Reilly met outside the cell, both wearing face shields in view of the fact that Parkinson may be a carrier of the Nipah virus. They quickly discussed what they needed to do, and noted the fact that Parkinson had so far waived his rights to a solicitor – duty or otherwise – but was free to request one whenever he wanted.

They opened the door and stepped inside. Alec Parkinson was dressed in police-issue custody clothes. In front of him, on the table, stood an empty cup with the remains of cold tea.

Gardener took a seat and asked Parkinson if he was okay. The young man nodded. He then asked if the undertaker would like another drink, to which he also nodded, he would.

Once Reilly had returned with all the drinks, Gardener once again read him his rights and started the recording facility. He informed Parkinson that he knew about the claustrophobia and the root cause of it, from Rodney.

"How did you end up inside the coffin, Mr Parkinson?" asked Gardener.

"It was that bloody maniac, Viktor," replied Alec. "I hope you have him and his thugs locked up. That man is dangerous. He shouldn't be allowed out."

"Why did he do it?" asked Reilly.

Alec raised his hands in defeat. "I have no idea."

"You must have some idea," persisted Reilly.

"No," protested Alec. "He's a drug dealer. He's unpredictable. They do strange things."

"So, you're telling me that he ended up at your house," continued Gardener, "and he placed you inside a coffin and you have no idea why?"

"No."

"Had you met him before?" asked Gardener.

"Not really."

"What does that mean?" asked Reilly.

"That I've seen him around," replied Parkinson. "He's not the kind of person I would normally associate with."

Gardener had to give him credit for sticking to his story, but it wouldn't help him in the end.

"What did he want?" asked Reilly. "He must have said he was there for a reason. He came mob-handed."

"How long are you going to keep me here?"

"We would appreciate it if you answered *our* questions," said Gardener. "Honestly, if you can. That way we'll all be out of here much quicker. Now, I'll ask you again, why did Viktor call on you?"

Parkinson must have listened to Gardener, and suddenly relented. "He had it in his head that I had blamed him for that girl who died in the nightclub a few weeks ago."

"And why would he think that?"

"I've no idea. Maybe someone told him that. You'll have to ask him."

Now Gardener had him talking, he was not to be deterred. "Whilst it *is* possible that Viktor may have something to do with the death of Sonia Markham, our investigation has found no evidence to back that theory up."

Parkinson relaxed slightly, his shoulder dropping a little. "You won't find any evidence, will you? He's a slippery character."

"He's not the only one," said Reilly.

"Meaning?"

"Do the names Katherine Field, or Amelia Simms mean anything to you?" asked Gardener.

He did not mention Diane Drayton because they had already questioned the undertaker previously about her and he'd admitted to remembering her.

"No," said Parkinson. "Should they?"

"Maybe," said Reilly.

"How?"

"When we spoke to you last, we asked you if you frequented nightclubs," said Gardener. "You never said either way, you evaded the question by asking another. You said, 'I'm an undertaker, what would I be doing in the nightclubs?' Do you remember saying that?"

"I remember."

"Your dad seems to think different," said Reilly.

"What's he been saying?" Parkinson tensed up again.

"That you *do* go, mostly on a Saturday night," said the Irishman.

"Look." Parkinson put his hands out in front of him, a gesture that was supposed to say that he might be levelling with them. "I've been once or twice but I don't make a habit of it."

"Once or twice?" asked Reilly.

"Yes, once or twice."

"Are you sure?" pressed Gardener.

"What is this," asked Parkinson. "*The Chase*?"

If it was, thought Gardener, you were never going to beat the chasers. "And you definitely do not know the names Katherine Field, or Amelia Simms?"

"I've told you once already," said Parkinson, growing agitated. "I don't know them. Why do you keep asking?"

"Can you explain why you have three bodies in your coal cellar?"

"What?"

"Bodies," said Reilly. "You have three in your cellar. Why?"

An elongated silence in the room elevated the tension, but Gardener had no intention of breaking it.

Finally, a very pale Parkinson spoke. "You've been in the cellar?"

"We have," said Gardener. "So, if there is anything you'd like to tell us, I would suggest that now is a very good time."

Alec remained silent, obviously considering his options. But a nervous tic in his left eye started to give the game away. His tension was rising.

"Mr Parkinson," said Gardener. "We are in possession of an awful lot of information, and we are trying to help you when we suggest that if you know anything that could help us with our investigation, that you tell us now. It might be better for you in the long run."

The undertaker still remained tight-lipped.

Reilly leaned forward. "We're not here to trick you, Alec, old son, but as my boss says, we have a serious amount of information that implicates you in some unsavoury actions, not to mention three dead bodies in your cellar. I really think you should make things easier for yourself and be honest with us, let us clear up this matter."

Finally, after what seemed forever, Alec Parkinson nodded, and asked for a solicitor.

Chapter Forty-three

Three more hours passed before a solicitor turned up. He then spent an hour in the interview room with Alec, before the detectives were allowed back in.

When everyone was seated, Evill said, "I have spoken at length with my client, detectives, and I have advised him to cooperate in every way possible."

At that, Alec Parkinson broke down. He started by confirming how well he knew Lucy Brown, that he had in fact had sex with her, which was how he caught the Nipah virus.

Of the three missing girls, the first two to go missing were down to Alec. Katherine Field spent the night with him despite him not being able to do the business. The next morning, he found her dead in his bed. He went into an instant panic, and decided his only course of action was to drag her down into the cellar, where he buried her beneath the mound of coal, whilst trying to work out what to do – which was eventually nothing.

Amelia Simms was also with Alec, and the circumstances of her demise were similar. He figured then that it must have something to do with him – though he had no idea what.

He did in fact lie when he told them that he drove in the opposite direction to Diane Drayton's house; he had offered her a lift. She didn't actually want anything to do with him in the car. She had said she was happily married and requested more than once that he leave her alone and stop the car and allow her out. Frustrated and fearing he had nothing to lose, he attacked her.

When, for some reason, she lost consciousness he forced her into the boot of the car and drove home. She was still out cold when he opened the boot, and he decided to shut and lock her in a coffin, where he left her for three days. That had only been possible because his parents were on holiday for the week. He then emptied the coffin and buried her under the coal with the others.

Gardener was completely disgusted by the man and his actions, deciding that everything he had done, he had done knowingly. He felt it was time to go in for the kill, tapping Reilly's foot under the table.

"You said you had sex with Lucy Brown, was that before or after she had died?" asked Gardener.

Evill glanced at his client, and then back at Gardener.

"Let's hope it was before," said Reilly. "Because if it was after, it could only mean one thing."

"It wasn't before, was it, Mr Parkinson?" said Gardener, turning the screw. "Lucy Brown had been on the placement for a month, returned home and was picked up at the airport by her father and went straight home and died there. It's not possible you could have had sex with her before she had died."

"Why did you do it?" asked Reilly.

Alec took an age to answer, glancing at his brief a couple of times, who offered no advice.

"I'm impotent," Alec finally replied. "I'm afraid I cannot perform with living girls."

"What about the girls whose bodies we found in the cellar?" asked Gardener.

"Oh, no," said Parkinson. "They *were* alive when we tried."

"So, you could have sex with living girls," pushed Reilly.

Alec dropped his head in shame. "No. We only ever kissed, but they stayed the night. They were dead the next morning."

"All of them?" asked Reilly.

"Yes." Alec wept. "I didn't know what to do. I could have gone to prison for their murders, but I didn't murder them."

"You didn't do them any favours, though, did you?" said Reilly. "You should have reported it, Alec, old son."

"You'd have locked me up."

"I'm not sure what we'd have done," said Reilly. "But if you had come clean, reported it, I doubt you'd have been tried for murder with a good brief."

"It's you, isn't it?" asked Gardener.

"What's me?" asked Parkinson.

"You're the carrier," replied Gardener. "You had sex with Lucy Browne, caught the virus from her, but you never suffered with it. You never had any symptoms. Maybe, at first, you didn't know you were a carrier, but didn't it strike you as odd that you spend one night with these girls and each of them died in your company?"

Alec could only nod.

"When exactly did you suspect?" asked Gardener.

"Suspect what?" asked Alec.

"You must have known something was wrong? When did you suspect you were a carrier?" asked Reilly. "How did you find out?"

"I had a test."

"You had a test?" repeated Gardener. "If you had a test and it came back positive, surely your doctor must have given you advice, or medication, or at the very least reported the fact?"

"I didn't have it done at the doctors. I went out of town to a private clinic, gave false details, so they couldn't trace me."

"Which makes it murder," said Gardener. "At what point did you have the test? How many girls had died?"

"Two of them."

"So, if you're not responsible for the murder of girls one and two," said Reilly. "You're definitely responsible for three and four."

"Four," repeated Alec. "I only spent time with three of them. Technically I only killed the third."

"You're forgetting where all of this started for us, my old son," said Reilly.

"You're also responsible for the death of Sonia Markham."

Gardener suspected it could be five, if they could find the body of Dawn Roberts. Without it, they would have to keep digging; but for now, they had enough to send Alec Parkinson down for quite some time.

"Do you know someone called Jodie Thomson?" asked Gardener.

"No," replied Parkinson.

Gardener produced a photo from a folder.

"Oh, yes," said Parkinson. "I do recognize her. I just didn't know her name. She came to the funeral parlour recently, to talk about the arrangements for her friend's funeral. Why, has she gone missing?"

Gardener nodded.

"Look," said Parkinson. "I know I've lied to you about all the other girls, but I'm not lying when I say I have no idea where *she* is. Honestly, I don't. She is nothing to do with me. I have not picked her up, kissed her, or slept with her."

Gardener was very tempted to believe him, in light of the fact that Jodie Thomson had been snooping around and asking about Viktor.

He also asked the undertaker about a girl called Dawn Roberts.

"Same again," said Parkinson. "I definitely don't know anyone called Dawn Roberts."

Gardener produced another photo.

"No." Alec shook his head. "I've never seen her."

Gardener also believed that. The circumstances in which the prostitute disappeared were different to the other girls. That was another question and answer session with Viktor, and it could well end up being a cold case for many years to come.

After quite some time, Parkinson spoke. "What's going to happen to me?"

The SIO rose from the table. "That's not for us to decide, Mr Parkinson. That, I'm afraid, will be down to the Crown Prosecution Service."

Gardener glanced at Evill, and then back at Parkinson. "But I suggest you get yourself a very good brief."

Gardener and Reilly left the room. Outside, Gardener turned to Reilly. "I might have suggested Arthur Pierrepoint, but I think he's going to be tied up for quite some time, don't you, Sean?"

"Only if we do as well with Viktor as we have with *him* in there."

Chapter Forty-four

That however was not the case. Gardener and Reilly spent an hour with both Viktor and Arthur. They were questioned about why they had gone to the undertaker's property, why they had placed him in a coffin, and what they had eventually intended to do with him.

Both had remained totally silent.

They went on to question them about Dawn Roberts and Jodie Thomson. Once again, neither of them admitted to anything.

It was a difficult situation for Gardener. There wasn't a great deal on which he could hold either of them much longer. Alec Parkinson had already admitted responsibility for Sonia Markham's death, and those of the three missing girls.

They did not have a body for Dawn Roberts, and very little in the way of evidence to suggest that Viktor had been tied up in her abduction, or possible murder. They had no idea where Jodie Thomson had gone. Despite feeling that Viktor was involved, nothing could be proved.

The only thing he could pin on Viktor was assault. For that, he could not hold either him or Arthur much longer.

Gardener felt he needed to press very heavily concerning the whereabouts of Jodie Thomson. Of all the people he needed to find, it was her. She had only been missing a few days, and there was a very good chance she was still alive.

He checked his watch. It was approaching midnight and he wasn't sure there was much more he could do. When he and Reilly dropped into the incident room, they found DCI Briggs staring at the whiteboards.

"How did you get on?" he asked.

Gardener updated him, and then asked if there had been any news on Jodie Thomson in his absence.

Briggs said there hadn't. She was still missing.

"I can only think of one place she might be," said Gardener.

"Where?" asked Briggs.

"Viktor's house," replied Reilly. "There's a lot more to that place. If you wanted to hide someone, it would be big enough."

"And she had spent a considerable amount of time around the town asking about Viktor," said Gardener. "Maybe he found out, and perhaps went after her."

Briggs was obviously thinking about it. "Then you have only one option open to you."

"Search Viktor's property," said Gardener.

"That's all you've got, Stewart," replied Briggs. "Question is, do you want to do it tonight?"

"We have to," said Gardener. "Her life could be in danger. If she's been locked up in that place since Viktor decided to visit Parkinson, then she's been alone for at least forty-eight hours, maybe more."

"Christ," said Briggs. "They're going to love me for this."

* * *

Despite the urgency of the situation, night had rolled on into very early morning before Gardener, warrant in hand, was standing on the front doorstep of Viktor's house in Roundhay.

He banged loudly on the door, unaware of who, if anyone, might be in the place.

The door suddenly opened before he could bang again. The lady was perhaps mid-forties, with her blonde hair tied up in a ponytail. She was very slim, wore a blue top and tight dark pants and trainers.

"Can I help?"

Gardener introduced them both before producing the necessary paperwork to search the property.

"Search it?" asked the cleaner. "I don't think Mr Viktor would like that."

"We're not too worried what he thinks," said Reilly.

"Well, what are you looking for?" asked the cleaner.

"Is there anyone else here?" asked Gardener. "Apart from you?"

"There are three of us altogether."

"Can you go and get them, please?"

The cleaner's expression suggested she had another question but thought better of it. Within minutes they were all standing outside on the steps leading to the front door. The other two girls were not English.

"Do you know if there are any guests staying here?" Gardener asked.

"I don't think so," said the cleaner.

However, Gardener caught an expression from one of the Asian girls that said otherwise.

He asked her the same question.

"I not know."

"But?" asked Reilly.

"I think I hear something when I clean lower levels. Maybe just radio."

Lower levels, thought Gardener. "Can you show me, please?"

The girl nodded. She took them through the house, into the study, and to a door that hid a lift. She rode down with them and suggested there were a number of rooms either side of the hall.

Gardener asked which one she thought she had heard something from. The girl took them to the door. Gardener tried the handle but it was locked.

At that point, a voice from the other side shouted.

"Hello?"

Gardener thought he recognized the voice. "Is that you Ms Thomson?"

"Yes. Who is that?"

He told her who he was, before asking the Asian girl if she had a key. She didn't, but she knew where a spare set was kept. She left, only to return a minute later, when she let Gardener and Reilly into the room.

The relief on Jodie Thomson's face told Gardener everything he needed to know: that she was frightened, almost certainly being kept against her will, and had no idea what was going to happen to her.

She pretty much collapsed onto her bed and wept.

Finally, she said. "I thought he was going to kill me."

"Has he hurt you?" asked Gardener.

"To be honest, no," said Jodie. "Look around you, it's hardly a prison cell. It's warm and comfortable. He's fed me. He hasn't hurt me at all, but I didn't think I was going to leave here."

She wept again.

"It's okay, Ms Thomson," said Gardener. "We have you now and we can promise that nothing is going to happen to you."

"Can I go home?"

"Eventually," said Gardener. "We'll need to take you to the station first, check you over, take a statement. We'll let your parents know where you are."

She put her head in her hands. "Oh, thank God."

Gardener glanced around. He'd seen people kept against their will in far worse places. He was struggling to weigh up Viktor. On the one hand he was very dangerous, cared very little for people. Yet here he was, keeping someone against their will in the lap of luxury.

Eventually, Jodie glanced up at Gardener. "I was wrong."

"About what?" he asked.

"Viktor didn't kill my sister, Pippa. He couldn't have done."

"What makes you say that, Jodie, love?" asked Reilly.

"Because of the holiday snaps that he showed me on his phone," she replied. "He wasn't even in the country. He was in Latvia with family."

"Doesn't mean he didn't have anything to do with it," said Reilly. "He may have sold the drugs to someone who did eventually kill her."

"We can, at the very least, charge him for kidnapping," said Gardener.

"Actually," said Jodie. "If you push hard enough, you might be able to get him for murder."

"Murder?" repeated Reilly.

"How?" asked Gardener.

"I saw one photo too many," said Jodie. "It was a girl. I asked him who she was, and he said she was just a local girl, and that I wouldn't know her."

"Did you?" asked Reilly.

"Yes," said Jodie. "It's that girl you put a press release out for, Dawn something or other."

"Roberts?" asked Gardener.

"Yes, that's her," said Jodie. "He has a photo of her on his phone. It's bound to be dated, like the holiday snaps. Why would he have her on his phone if he didn't know her?"

"That's a good question, Ms Thomson," said Gardener. "One that we will find out the answer to."

Gardener took Jodie Thomson back upstairs and put her in the pool car. He asked the cleaners to leave everything, go home, or report back to their employers, so he could secure the house. He then called the station and asked for SOCOs and a PolSA team.

"Case closed?" asked Reilly.

"I hope so, Sean," replied Gardener.

"I hope we don't have another like this one."

"That makes two of us," said Gardener. "Let's get to the station, sort it out and, hopefully give three families some closure."

"If Dawn Roberts has someone, and we can pin her disappearance on Viktor, we could make it four."

Gardener smiled. He really hoped so.

Epilogue

Later in the day, Briggs found Gardener in his office, tying up paperwork. He took a seat opposite, and placed a cup of tea in front of him.

"Well done, Stewart," said Briggs. "Good result all round."

"I don't mind admitting that there were times when I thought it was going against me."

"I never doubted you."

"Serious?" asked Gardener, taking a sip of his tea.

"You're a great detective with a great team," said Briggs. "I know it must have sounded like I was uncertain, but I knew you were capable, and I was trying to get the best out of you."

"Looks like it worked."

"You've had a lot of good results because you're dedicated and you care. You were passionate about this case and I decided to let you run with it."

Gardener nodded.

"Pleased I did," said Briggs. He stood up and made to leave but turned and smiled before reaching the door. "This conversation never happened. If the Irishman hears about all this praise, he'll take advantage."

Gardener laughed.

"Now go home and get some rest," added Briggs, before leaving.

Acknowledgments

All authors owe a debt of acknowledgment to someone, for a whole variety of reasons. No author works on their own. And for those two particular reasons, I feel it's only fair for me to thank one or two people for their help with IMPROPER.

Firstly, my publishers, The Books folks, if for no other reason, than their eternal patience in working with a dinosaur who does not understand technology in the least.

My editors, Shirley Khan and Clova Perez-Corral, also deserve praise for knocking the book into shape.

Darrin Knight, my real-life Gardener and Reilly all rolled into one; a man who has threatened untold tortures on me for many years, but whose help I could not do without. And Bob Armitage, whose chemical knowledge has often been tested to the limit in nearly every Northern Crimes book.

And finally, to my friend Lucy, without whose input this book would never have seen the light of day. It was Lucy who first gave me the idea for IMPROPER.

If you enjoyed this book, please let others know by leaving a quick review on Amazon. Also, if you spot anything untoward in the paperback, get in touch. We strive for the best quality and appreciate reader feedback.

editor@thebookfolks.com

www.thebookfolks.com

ALSO AVAILABLE

If you enjoyed IMPALED, the twelfth book, check out the others in the series:

IMPURITY – *Book 1*

Someone is out for revenge. A grotto worker is murdered in the lead up to Christmas. He won't be the first. Can DI Gardener stop the killer, or is he saving his biggest gift till last?

IMPERFECTION – *Book 2*

When theatre-goers are treated to the gruesome spectacle of an actor's lifeless body hanging on the stage, DI Stewart Gardener is called in to investigate. Is the killer still in the audience? A lockdown is set in motion but it is soon apparent that the murderer is able to come and go unnoticed. Identifying and capturing the culprit will mean establishing the motive for their crimes, but perhaps not before more victims meet their fate.

IMPLANT – *Book 3*

A small Yorkshire town is beset by a series of cruel murders. The victims are tortured in bizarre ways. The killer leaves a message with each crime – a playing card from an obscure board game. DI Gardener launches a manhunt but it will only be by figuring out the murderer's motive that they can bring him to justice.

IMPRESSION – *Book 4*

Police are stumped by the case of a missing five-year-old girl until her photograph turns up under the body of a murdered woman. It is the first lead they have and is quickly followed by the discovery of another body connected to the case. Can DI Stewart Gardener find the connection between the individuals before the abducted child becomes another statistic?

IMPOSITION – *Book 5*

When a woman's battered body is reported to police by her husband, it looks like a bungled robbery. But the investigation begins to turn up disturbing links with past crimes. They are dealing with a killer who is expert at concealing his identity. Will they get to him before a vigilante set on revenge?

IMPOSTURE – *Book 6*

When a hit and run claims the lives of two people, DI Gardener begins to realize it was not a random incident. But when he begins to track down the elusive suspects he discovers that a vigilante is getting to them first. Can the detective work out the mystery before more lives are lost?

IMPASSIVE – *Book 7*

A publisher racked with debts is found strung up in a ruined Yorkshire abbey. Has a disgruntled author taken their revenge? DI Stewart Gardener is on the case but maybe a hypnotist has the key to the puzzle. Can the cop muster his team to work some magic and catch a cunning killer?

IMPIOUS – *Book 8*

It could be detectives Gardener and Reilly's most disturbing case yet when a body with head, limbs and torso assembled from different victims is discovered. Alongside this grotesque being is a cryptic message and a chess piece. A killer wants to take the cops on a journey. And force their hand.

IMPLICATION – *Book 9*

When a body is found in a burned-out car, DI Stewart Gardener quickly establishes that a murder has been concealed. But with a missing person case and a spate of robberies occupying the force, he will struggle to identify the victim. When the investigations overlap, he'll have to work out which of the suspects is implicated in which crime.

IMPUNITY – *Book 10*

After a young woman passes out and dies, the medical examiner makes a grim discovery. Someone had surgically removed her kidneys. Detective Stewart Gardener must find a killer evil enough to think of such a cruel act, let alone have the gall to carry it out. It looks like revenge is a motive, but what had the victim, by all accounts a kind and friendly girl, done to anyone?

IMPALED – *Book 11*

When Gardener is called to investigate a crime, he has no idea of the terrible scene that awaits him. The corpse of a man has been found with nails driven into his chest and no hands. There are no witnesses to the crime, just reports of a strangely dressed man seen nearby. Gardener feels a serial killer is at work, and the clock is ticking.

All FREE with Kindle Unlimited and available in paperback!

Other titles of interest

THAT CARE FORGOT by James Warren

Junior attorney Rebecca Holt isn't too happy when given the pro bono case of a convicted murderer. Yet Nick Malone isn't really interested in his parole hearing, rather he is obsessed with a serial killer who terrorised New Orleans in the 1990s. When Malone reveals his secrets, Rebecca is faced with a life-changing decision.

MY TWISTED COUSIN by Shane Spyre

Teenager Harper hates her younger cousin Audrey, who is always getting into trouble. So when she is sent to stay with her, she decides to make the visit as difficult as possible. She goads Audrey, winding her up into a frenzy. But Harper has underestimated the effect of her actions, and as matters escalate, she'll be lucky to escape alive.

All FREE with Kindle Unlimited and available in paperback!

www.thebookfolks.com

Made in the USA
Coppell, TX
26 March 2025

47560102R00148